a clean slate

LAURA CALDWELL

graduated from University of Iowa, before getting her law degree from Loyola University Chicago School of Law. Laura was a trial lawyer for many years, specializing in medical negligence defense and entertainment law. She is widely published in the legal field, as well as in numerous mainstream publications. *Burning the Map,* her first novel, was published by Red Dress Ink and chosen by Barnes & Noble.com as one of "The Best of 2002."

Laura is currently a writer and contributing editor at *Lake Magazine,* as well as an Adjunct Professor of legal writing at Loyola University Chicago School of Law. Please visit her online at www.lauracaldwell.com.

a clean slate

laura caldwell

**RED
DRESS
INK**™

First edition November 2003

A CLEAN SLATE

A Red Dress Ink novel

ISBN 0-373-25038-X

Visit Red Dress Ink at www.reddressink.com

Printed in U.S.A.

All my admiration and appreciation to the following people: my stellar editor, Margaret Marbury, Maureen Walters at Curtis Brown, Ltd., everyone at Red Dress Ink (especially Laura Morris, Tania Charzewski, Craig Swinwood, Margie Miller, Maureen Stead and Don Lucey), Beth Kaveny, Suzanne Burchill, Kelly Harden, Ginger Heyman, Trisha Woodson, Ted McNabola, Joan Posch, Rochelle Wasserberger, Hilarie Pozesky, Alisa Speigel, Katie Caldwell Kuhn, Margaret Caldwell, William Caldwell, Karen Billups, Stacey Billups, Kelly Caldwell, Dr. Stuart Rice, Kim Wilkins, Joe Ford, Joel Odish, Anthony Parmalee (photographer extraordinaire) and Greg Brown and Roberto Puig of BMG Model Management.

Lastly, and once again most importantly, thanks, love and overwhelming gratitude to Jason Billups.

"Life isn't about finding yourself; life is about creating yourself."

—George Bernard Shaw

1

Have you ever had a moment when you've known—I mean, logically known in your head—that you're a fantastically lucky person, that you're truly fortunate to have an education, to live in a nice place in a great city, to have friends who care about you and all that, but you just can't get yourself to actually feel it?

Well, I was having one of those moments on the day it all started. I stood in the dry cleaners, where the temperature was about a hundred eighty degrees from the pressing and steaming machines.

"Sorry, sorry. No clothes for you," the tiny Asian woman said as she came back to the cracked linoleum counter for the third time.

I clicked my nails on the counter and expelled a massive breath of hot air, trying to maintain rational thought. "Can you please look one more time? I brought in a whole bag of clothes last week." I tried not to think of my favorite black pants—my skinny pants—which had been in that bag.

"You have ticket?" The lady waved a pile of pink slips.

"No," I told her. I never saved those pesky things. Never had to before.

She shrugged. "I look again." Wiping sweat from her eyebrows, she turned away. As she disappeared into a sea of hanging, plastic-covered clothes, I tried to guess her size. Was it possible that she had stolen my black pants and was wearing them on the weekends?

I felt one of my temper tantrums coming on, but I forced it down. I am lucky to be alive, I told myself as I leaned on the counter, fanning my face. I am lucky because I am now losing weight at an average of a pound a minute. I am lucky because I have a great town house and a nice boyfriend who is soon to be my fiancé, and a decent job and lovely friends. I've really got the world by the tail.

The problem was this—I wasn't buying a word of it. My nice boyfriend soon-to-be-fiancé, Ben, was at my great town house, true, but he wouldn't be so nice when he learned that his favorite French-blue shirt had been destroyed by the dry cleaners from hell. And the decent job I had—as a research analyst at an investment bank called Bartley Brothers—was starting to look like a ticket straight to nowhere-ville. I'd been toiling for years, digging up information on retail stocks so that my boss could pass on my recommendations and then take all the credit when we made money, or blame me when we lost it. After almost eight years of promises that I would soon be considered for partnership, it still hadn't happened. Finally, my best friend, Laney, my sanity advisor, was off at some marketing conference (read: company boondoggle) in Palm Beach.

"Sorry," the dry cleaner said, emerging from the plastic sea, looking even more red-faced and sweaty. "We have nothing for you." She gave another helpless shrug.

"Can you *please* keep looking, and I'll stop back later in the day?"

"Okay, okay."

I stomped out of the sweltering store, a crisp Chicago breeze hitting me blessedly in the face. As an El train clamored to a halt on the tracks over my head, I trudged up Armitage Avenue, muttering obscenities about my missing clothes and the incompetence of the dry cleaners. The street was full of couples doing Saturday morning errands hand-in-hand, along with the post-college baseball-hat crowd searching for hangover grub.

I took a couple of deep breaths, but they brought no relief from my cranky mood. Ben rarely, if ever, held my hand and did errands with me on the weekends. Saturday mornings were his time to run with his marathon group or train for one of the other races he was constantly entering. It didn't bother me...not really. Because Ben worshipped at the Church of Holy Workouts he had an amazing body, something that benefited me as well as him. Yes, sex was fine. More than fine, actually. But if I were forced to lodge one complaint about Ben, it would be this—we no longer had any of those couple-y, sappy-eyed rendezvous, such as candlelit dinners or surprise weekends at a log cabin. Romantic interludes just weren't his thing these days, or at least that's what he told me, what I told myself to make myself feel better when I saw other couples having picnics in Lincoln Park and horse-drawn carriage rides down Michigan Avenue.

Ben was sweet and funny and wonderful in his own way, though. He would cheer me up by singing show tunes in a falsetto voice, and when it was time to carbo-load for his next race, he'd cook huge pasta dinners for the two of us. And last January when my sister, Dee, died, Ben was amazing—an absolute rock. I couldn't have gotten through it without him.

At Bissell Street, I took a left and walked along the sidewalk, crunching over a golden bed of fallen leaves, moving past the rusty autumn trees and stone three-flats until I hit the stretch of brick town houses, one of which was mine (something I was inordinately proud of). I'd saved all my paychecks from Bartley Brothers, and this place was the first home I'd ever owned, the place Dee used to love to stay when she came to visit, the place where Ben and I would live when we were married. The sun was peeking through the red curtain of trees, making an X-like pattern on the town homes. Normally, I would have loved to take photos of that—I liked the way the rays made crosshairs on the brick—but I was too annoyed by the dry cleaning debacle to think about getting my Nikon.

Before I went inside, I stopped at the bank of oblong silver mailboxes in the little courtyard located right behind the town houses. I stuck the key in the third one, my box, and tried to turn it to the right as I always did, but it wouldn't budge.

I screwed my face up tight and tried again. Maybe the eager-bunny mailman had stuffed a stack of magazines in there, jamming the lock. I tried over and over, but the key wouldn't turn.

I took it out and jiggled it in my hand, as if that would help. I was looking back at the box, lifting the key to try again, when I noticed what was wrong. The tiny black plate with white letters affixed to the box, the plate that should have said my name, KELLY MCGRAW, instead read BETH & BOB MANINSKY.

What the hell? I moved down the row of boxes, peering closely, reading each one: LILY CHANG, SIMON TURNER, MILLER/SAMSON, and on and on, but no KELLY MCGRAW.

I repeated the process two more times, then stood still, swiveling my head, looking at the trim bushes that were beginning to turn red at the edges and the brick walls of the surrounding town houses. Was there another bank of mailboxes somewhere? No, that couldn't be right. This was the only set, the same place I'd been getting my mail for almost a year.

And then I figured out what it was. The damned management company. The company to whom I paid two hundred dollars a month so that they could refuse to repaint the garage door or fish a spoon out of my clogged sink. They'd screwed up once more.

Muttering again, I strode around the side of the town houses and up the front stairs to my place. The door was tall and painted green to match the trim on the bay windows. I tried the doorknob, but it was locked. Ben must have headed out for a run already. Just as well. I could prolong telling him that he'd probably never see his French-blue shirt again.

I put the key in the lock, or at least I tried, but it didn't insert smoothly. Finally, I got it in and attempted to turn it. Déjà fucking vu. This lock wasn't working, either. I wrestled with the key, grasping it with both hands and trying to force it to the left, as the wind whipped my hair in front of my face so I couldn't see. *Deep cleansing breaths,* I told myself in a low soothing tone, just like the woman in my meditation tapes would say it. *Inhale in, exhale out.* I did this a few times, batting my hair out of my eyes, then tried the key again. No luck.

My deep-cleansing-breaths mantra turned to thoughts of violence. I would have to physically harm everyone in the management company now. This was ridiculous.

On the off chance that Ben was still home, I rang the doorbell. *Ding, ding, ding*—I could hear it going off inside. If he was home, doing his prerun stretches, he would be annoyed, but I didn't care.

Ding, ding, ding, ding—I tried one more time, and then, thank God, I heard footsteps inside pounding down the stairs.

As the door swung open, I was already in midrant. "The dry cleaners lost our stuff, can you believe it? They say they'll look some more, but it's as good as gone. Your blue shirt was in that load, and my favorite black pants—and then the mailbox was messed up and…"

My body froze, along with my tirade, as I realized that Ben hadn't opened the door. It was someone else. Someone I'd never seen, some *woman.*

She had short blond hair cropped close to her head. In fact, she looked a little like the pictures of Ben's high school girlfriend, Toni, the woman he said he'd always love. And then the truth of the situation hit me. Ben was cheating on me, right here in my own house, getting his groove on with some girl who looked like Toni, when I'd only been gone an hour or so. Unbelievable. This wasn't happening. Now I would have to kill Ben along with the management people. A thousand thoughts flew through my brain like birds let out of a cage. I couldn't hold on to just one.

"Hi, can I help you?" the Toni look-alike said, a sweet smile grazing her face.

"Can I help *you?*" I crossed my arms over my chest, then, thinking better of it, dropped them and pushed past her inside.

"Hey!"

The first thing I noticed was that my high mosaic table, the one made of tiny pieces of broken glass, the one I'd bought at an art fair, wasn't there. Instead, in its place, there was a heavy wooden coat tree, its arms jutting out, holding a woman's pink trench coat and a tiny kid's sweatshirt.

"What's going on here?" The woman's voice was low and cautious, the kind of voice cops use with loose criminals on TV.

I wanted to make a smart comment, ask her the same thing, but a flock of doubts flew around in my head along with the other birds. "This is my house," I said, but I heard my voice waver.

I spun around to check something, and sure enough, there it was, next to the coat tree. The dent in the drywall where Ben's skis had fallen against it last year. This was my place, so what was the Toni look-alike doing here? And what was with that coat tree?

"No," she said. "This is my house. My husband and I bought it a few months ago."

I bit my lip and looked at her, confused. "Is Ben here?"

"There's no Ben who lives here. What's your name?" She took a step closer to me, as if she was afraid I'd move farther into the house.

I peeked my head around the corner and into the study, expecting to see the big, scarred desk that my mom had given me when she moved to L.A., but in its place was a playpen with yellow mesh sides and a jumble of brightly colored toys.

"Kelly McGraw," I said, yet even that came out a little unsure.

The woman gave me the sweet smile again. "Oh, *you're* Kelly McGraw! I'm Beth Maninsky. We never did meet you at the closing." She held out her hand.

"Closing?"

"Sure. We bought this house from you, but you gave your lawyer power of attorney, so we never officially got to meet you when we closed on the house. We love it, though. Did you stop by for old times' sake?" She tried the smile again, but when I didn't shake her hand, the grin faltered, and now she was looking as perplexed as I felt.

"Closing?" I said again. "I sold this house?"

She nodded, gazing at me warily.

From somewhere above, I heard the cry of a baby, short at first, then a full-on wail. Beth Maninsky's eyes shot to the ceiling as if she could see through it.

"A baby?" I couldn't seem to form a full sentence.

"Scottie. I should get him. Now can I help you with anything?"

I just stood there. What was happening?

"Kelly? Are you all right?"

Beth Maninsky looked almost scared now, so I just nodded and moved to the door, then out to the stoop. I stood there looking at the house, *my* house.

Beth Maninsky stood in the doorway, fairly blocking it with her body. "Can I call someone for you?" There was warmth in her voice.

It took me a second to answer. "No. I'll go to my boyfriend's place."

"Okay." The wail of the baby got louder behind her. She glanced in the house, then back at me. "You sure you're okay?"

"When you…" I paused, barely able to say the words that didn't seem true "…bought this house. Did you learn why I…sold it?"

"Our Realtor told us that you thought it was too big for one person."

"Right." I nodded as if I could convince myself that this was really happening, that someone named Beth Maninsky, who looked like Toni, owned my house.

"Nice to meet you," Beth Maninsky said.

My front door closed, and I heard the lock click inside.

2

As I walked along Bissell Street again, the fall wind felt brittle instead of crisp and the city seemed cool and gray instead of filled with warm autumn tones. I didn't notice the light on the buildings anymore or think about the photos I could take. Instead, I concentrated on figuring out what had happened. There had to be an explanation. I knew that. I hadn't gone to college or worked in the straight-lines, think-inside-the-box world of finance for nothing. There was always a reason for things.

So I hoofed it all the way up to Ben's place in Wrigleyville, entertaining several possibilities. One—this Beth Maninsky was a covert operative for the CIA who'd taken over my town house in order to set up an elaborate cover. Crazy, outlandish, I know, but I'm fond of spy novels, and it was the first potential that came to mind. Two—Beth Maninsky really was Ben's high school girlfriend,

Toni, who was still crazed about him and had somehow arranged to take my place in his life. This also seemed a little outrageous, since I'd only set out for the dry cleaners that morning. She would have needed to work pretty damn fast.

But was that actually true? Had I really left for the dry cleaners just a few hours ago? Suddenly I wasn't sure. I stuck my hands in the pockets of my leather jacket and put my head down, concentrating on each step, each seam in the pavement. My sense of timing still seemed off. I couldn't remember waking up that morning or going to my mother ship, Starbucks, for a Venti Nonfat White Chocolate Mocha, my usual Saturday-morning treat. Still, that kind of memory trick happened, didn't it? It was like driving home on your normal route and suddenly discovering you're in your driveway and yet you can't recall the drive itself.

Something niggled in my brain—a third possibility. I really had sold my town house and I really couldn't remember it. I felt even colder with the thought, and I turned my collar up against the wind. *Ridiculous,* I said silently. *Preposterous.*

Luckily, I didn't have to argue with myself much longer because I'd reached Ben's building, a squat, multi-unit place that made up for its lack of character with cheap rent and a great location, only a few blocks from Wrigley Field. I peered at the vertical list of names next to the buzzers, and, thank God, there it was. BENJAMIN THOMAS, fifth from the top, right where he should have been. I hit the buzzer.

A shot of static came over the intercom. "Who is it?" said a woman's cheery voice.

"Sorry. Wrong buzzer." *Please, please, please let it have been the wrong one.*

I peered at the list again, and with exaggerated slowness, I put my finger on the brown button next to Ben's name and pressed.

Same staticky burst. Same woman's voice—not as cheery this time—saying the same words.

I froze. Something was wrong. Really, really wrong. But somehow my eternal optimism (or maybe my eternal stupidity) kept insisting there was a logical reason for all of this—something I would laugh about later.

I couldn't laugh now, though, couldn't even manage a smile, just a simple question laden with trepidation. "Is Ben home?"

"Kelly?" the woman said, clearly irritated.

"Yes?"

"Jesus. Not again." A fizz of static, and then the intercom went silent.

I stood chewing on my bottom lip once more, debating what to do—piss off this woman in Ben's apartment by hitting the buzzer again or break in and kick her ass. After about fifteen seconds, someone appeared behind the glass door. I squinted and made out Ben's small, lean frame, his rock-hard legs in blue jogging shorts. Raising my hand, I gave a half wave, then let it fall.

Ben opened the door, but he didn't invite me in or even come out on the front stoop with me. He just sighed, holding the door open with one arm, shoving his other hand through his damp brown hair. He'd obviously just come back from running. He had that pink flush to his cheeks.

"Kell, you've got to cut this out."

I tried to get my mind around his statement. I forced myself not to rush inside and hug him. "What do you mean?"

"You know what I mean. Stopping by like this, calling at all hours. She wants me to get a restraining order."

"Who?"

A chest-heaving exhalation. "We've had this conversation. Don't make me go through it again. I love you. I always will."

Just like you'll always love Toni, I thought.

"But I'm with Therese now," he continued, "and you have to accept that."

I put my head in my hands and rubbed at my temples. Another possibility came to mind—this was all an elaborate hoax. Laney would jump out from behind Ben at any minute and scream, "We got you!" The problem was Laney would never be that cruel, nor would Ben. He may not have been the most romantic guy, but he was always kind.

"C'mere, Kell." Ben stepped out and let the door close behind him. He grabbed me in a hug, just as I hoped he would. I could smell the clean, outdoor scent of his sweat and feel the muscles of his back beneath the long-sleeved T-shirt.

"I don't know what's going on. I don't understand anything." I squeezed him tight, hoping that this gesture would make it all go away, this whole horrible day, but too soon the embrace was over. He let me go, and I felt the cool air swirl around me again.

"I know it's been rough, but you'll get through this. You always do." He pushed his hair off his face and gave me a smile I recognized—the one he saved for his grandmother or the restaurant managers he would cajole into giving us a table.

I opened my mouth to tell him what had happened this morning, how I suddenly couldn't make sense of anything in my life, but he gave me that patronizing grin again.

"You're tough." He punched me lightly on the arm like we were buddies, like we hadn't been lovers for four years, like we weren't supposed to be engaged soon.

"Ben," I said, trying to ignore his patent condescension, "something's going on that I don't understand. I don't remember all sorts of things. I don't remember us breaking up. I—"

"Kell, I just can't do this again. I can't rehash the whole thing over and over, okay?" He cupped my cheek for a second, the way you would a child who had food on his face.

I pulled my head away. "No, you don't get it."

"I do. I get that you're going to make it through this. You're going to be okay." He spoke these last words in a soft, hang-in-there-kid kind of way that infuriated me.

I glanced down at a spot on the sidewalk that looked strangely like old blood, then back up at his pitying eyes. "You're absolutely right. I'm going to be fine. Fantastic even."

"There you go," Ben said in what was probably the smuggest tone I'd ever heard. "That's the ticket."

Yeah, that's the ticket all right, I thought. The ticket out of here. I didn't have a clue what was going on, but I wouldn't give him the satisfaction of seeing me fall apart.

"I'll see you around." I tried to sound flip, like I didn't care, but I could feel the tears welling in my eyes. "See you," I said again, then turned away.

As I walked up the street, my head down, my hands in my pockets, I could hear Ben buzzing his apartment, and the woman's voice say over the intercom, "Ben, is that you?"

"It's me, hon. Let me up."

I stopped at Chuck's, the first bar I found. Inside, it was dark, with at least five different football games blaring from at least ten different TVs. The tables were full of people cheering and screaming, baskets of fries and pitchers of beer in front of them. I slipped onto a stool at the bar.

"What can I get you?" the bartender asked me. He leaned forward and dried a spot of water on the wood with a quick flick of his towel.

"Beer."

"Okay. Well, we have twenty-three different labels, so what kind do you want?"

"Doesn't matter." I usually drank margaritas, but it seemed too festive a drink.

The bartender stood there for a long minute, staring at me, before he moved toward a silver tapper and picked up a glass.

What was happening to me? What had happened to my town house, to my relationship with Ben? I wished desperately that I could rewind the day back to that moment at the dry cleaners when I was being pissy about losing a pair of black pants and the fact that my job wasn't so great. If I could just go back, I would *truly* realize how lucky I was right at that moment. I would appreciate it somehow.

But my mind kept skidding away from the dry cleaners and rushing through the rest of the day. Why hadn't I known that my place had been sold, that Ben and I had broken up?

The bartender pushed a glass of amber beer in front of me without a word. I took a sip, and I made myself review what I *did* know about myself. Name: Kelly McGraw. That was correct, wasn't it? Beth Maninsky seemed to know that Kelly McGraw used to live in her house, and Ben had called me Kell, so that had to be right.

What else? Parents: Sylvie and Ken McGraw, who'd had me while they were married for a very brief period and living in Fort Myers, Florida. My father was a complete shit who took off a year after my birth, and my mom reverted to her maiden name, Sylvie Custer, even though she hated it. It was too close to custard, she always said, and made her sound like some sort of pudding.

Childhood: my mom worked her way from being a secretary at a TV station to a production assistant there, and a few years after that, she married Danny Rosati, a local crime boss who was the subject of an exposé she'd helped put together. Danny wasn't much of a dad to me. He always treated me more like a pet, patting me on the head and giving me treats when I was good. He did give me my first camera, though, and for that I'd always be grateful. My mom gave birth to my half-sister when I was six. She was named Delores after Danny's mom, but except for Danny, everyone called her Dee. Dee was always a frail kid, but she had the greatest toothy smile and the loudest laugh you'd ever heard.

After my mom divorced Danny, we moved to Atlanta so she could work for a better TV station, and we stayed there until after my freshman year in high school, when we moved to Chicago. I joined the yearbook staff at my new school because at least I could take pictures, even if they were of people I didn't know—and that was where I met Laney. We'd been best friends ever since. We went to different colleges but visited each other constantly and shot up our phone bills. After we graduated, we got an apartment together in Lakeview and shared it until a few years ago.

Laney is the most energetic person I've ever met. Sometimes she'll call me at eight in the morning, before she leaves for her account exec job at a marketing firm, and she'll tell me that she's already done her laundry, given herself a leg wax and taken a kick-boxing class at the gym. Laney was *the* person, other than Ben, who'd saved me when Dee died last year in a car accident. My mom and I couldn't comfort each other; we reminded each other too much of Dee. My mom left Chicago—fled really—for L.A. last April to take a job with an entertainment news show, and Laney and Ben became my only family in town.

What happened after April? I tried to think about stocks I'd researched at work, weekend trips I'd taken, street fairs I'd gone to over the summer. Nothing. I couldn't remember anything from May up to now, the beginning of October, a span of five or so months.

I took a gulp of my beer, hoping it would help, maybe induce some kind of alcoholic flashback. Nothing again. I had to talk to someone about this. Ben was out. Laney was my only support now, and she was in Palm Beach. Or was she?

I sat up straighter on the stool and pushed my beer away, trying to concentrate. Laney had gone to a marketing conference in Palm Beach for a week. But was that *this* week? I'd been wrong about so many things today.

I threw five dollars on the bar and took off for the pay phone. As I pushed my way toward the rest rooms, I noticed that everyone else in the place seemed to be having a fantastic time. People were slapping high fives when touchdowns were scored, pouring beer for their friends, throwing their heads back and laughing at stories from the night before. I'd had days like this, spent watching football and drinking in a smoky bar when it was bright daylight outside. Those times had always seemed simple, uncomplicated, and yet while they were happening I'd be drifting off about whether I'd make partner, whether I should ask Ben to move in with me. Once again, I wished I could hit Rewind and just enjoy that time, instead of letting my mind take me somewhere else.

Luckily, there was a pay phone in the women's bathroom, so the noise was dimmed. I dialed Laney's number, thinking that even if her voice mail answered I could talk and talk, and she would pick it up eventually. Sometimes, when we got busy, Laney and I communicated solely by voice mail. We knew each other so well that we didn't have to be on the phone to feel like we were talking to each other.

I was starting to think of how I would phrase it, this strange, scary day, when I heard the chipper tones of Laney's hello.

"Oh, God, you're home." I was so relieved that I actually leaned my head on the dirty phone box. "You're not in Palm Beach."

"Palm Beach? That was months ago."

A chilly feeling passed through me. "Lane, something's wrong."

"I know, sweetie. Now hold on for a second, so I can sit down." I heard Laney closing her refrigerator and, a moment later, her slight exhalation as she sat on the couch. "Okay. Shoot."

How did she know something was wrong with me? "Well, uh, for starters, apparently Ben and I aren't dating anymore."

"Apparently? Honey, he dumped you months ago, and

you've *got* to move on. Really. He's just not worth this moping around."

"Months ago?" My voice came out tiny and scared.

"On your fucking birthday, remember?"

A group of women came into the bathroom, giggling and shoving past me.

I ducked my head and cupped my hand around the receiver. "That's just it. I can't remember."

"Where are you?"

"Chuck's."

"The bar by Ben's place?" Her voice went a little high. "You didn't go to his apartment again, did you? Kell, you've got to—"

"Laney, listen to me. I don't remember." I enunciated my words. "I don't remember selling my town house. I don't remember Ben breaking up with me. I can't seem to remember anything about the last five months."

A small silence. "Are you kidding?"

"Why would I kid about that?" My voice got loud and one of the women swung around, raising her perfectly arched eyebrows at me. I ducked my head again. "I need your help. I don't know what's going on."

"Whoa. Okay, look, I'll jump in my car and be there in ten minutes. Wait for me outside."

Laney's light blue, beat-up Mustang convertible screeched to a stop in front of Chuck's. Before I could take two steps, she'd jumped out and was running around the side of the car. Her dark brown hair was in its usual perfectly messed style with a swoop of bangs over one eye. She wore a black miniskirt, black knee-high boots and a fuzzy orange cashmere sweater.

She gave me a quick hug, then pulled back and held me at arm's length. "You okay?"

"Not really," I said, but then I couldn't help smiling.

Laney did that to me. Just being around her made me feel better.

"What are you grinning at, girl? You've totally freaked me out. Get in the car." She gave me a pat on the ass and opened the passenger door.

"So what's going on here?" she said when she'd taken the driver's seat.

"I was hoping you could tell me."

"First things first." She lifted a cardboard coffee carrier, two white cups from Starbucks tucked inside, steam seeping from the openings in the top. "You sounded like you hadn't gotten your fix yet."

"Oh!" I said. "White chocolate mocha?"

She nodded.

"Nonfat?"

"Of course."

"I *love* you." I took a sip, the warm, creamy concoction sweet on my tongue.

I know that lots of people hate Starbucks. They complain that these little green-and-white stores are the devil's work, the corporatization of the coffee world, but I just don't care. I've tried the others, the mom-and-pop coffee shops, the trendy little tea places, and nobody—and I mean *nobody*—makes anything close to my white chocolate mocha. It's comfort in a cup.

Laney squeezed my hand, then put the car in gear and pulled away from the curb. "All right, tell me what happened today."

I went through the whole thing—the dry cleaners, my town house, Beth Maninsky, and finally my talk with Ben. As I spoke I stared at the hula girl that was stuck to Laney's dashboard, the one that made swivels of her hips each time the car bumped or turned. For some reason, the movement of the girl's tiny hips soothed me. Laney had owned the hula girl since high school, and it had been on the dash of every car she'd had since. It was a permanent fixture, something I could recognize.

"Kell, I don't get this," Laney said. "Your memory was fine last week."

"Was it?"

"Yeah."

Silence filled the car.

"Jesus," Laney said. "Are you telling me that you really can't remember anything about the last five months?"

"Nada."

She stared intently at the road. "What do you remember about your birthday?"

May 3. May 3. May 3. I chanted the date in my head as if it might conjure up some images, but I could only remember my thoughts about my birthday in the weeks leading up to it. I'd been expecting Ben to propose on that date. I'd told him in February, a few weeks after Dee died, that I wanted to get married, that I wanted to be engaged by my birthday, and Ben had indicated he wanted the same thing. So as that day drew near, I made sure to have my nails done to perfection. I'd shaved and plucked nearly every stray hair on my body. I'd even bought a new black dress to wear to dinner. But the actual day of my birthday? I couldn't recall a thing, and I told Laney as much.

"Oh, boy." She sighed.

"What? What happened?"

She gave me a sidelong glance. "Maybe we shouldn't go there just yet. You should sleep, you know, then see how you feel."

"Other than scared shitless, I feel fine. *Tell* me."

"I don't know…"

"Laney!"

"Are you sure?" she said. "Do you really want to hear it?"

"Of course."

"Okay, well, I told you Ben dumped you that night."

I felt my mouth form a tight line. "Yes, so you said."

"He's a complete shit. Absolutely no sense of timing. But that's not the only thing that happened."

"What," I said, "is the other thing that happened?"

Laney stopped at a light and gave me a look. "I hate to be the one to tell you this."

My stomach twisted. "Just get it out."

"Bartley Brothers laid you off." She squeezed my hand. Someone honked behind us, and Laney gave the driver the finger before pulling into the intersection.

"You've got to be kidding me," I said. "Tell me that you are kidding."

Laney shook her head. "Sorry, hon."

"They *fired* me?"

"No, no. You got laid off. Major difference."

"How so?"

"They gave you nine months' severance pay."

My mouth snapped shut for a moment. I didn't know what to think about that. On one hand, I'd worked my ass off at that place, praying that it would pay off one day, that I'd be a partner eventually. To have that all washed down the toilet was maddening. But on the flip side, I'd been bordering on miserable there for the last few years, and I'd always secretly wanted to be one of those people who got axed with a golden parachute.

Then the effect of what Laney was saying hit me. "Are you telling me that I got laid off on my thirtieth birthday?"

"'Fraid so, sweetie."

"*And* Ben broke up with me?"

"Pretty much."

A few seconds went by. The hula girl's hips swirled and swayed as Laney turned a corner. "That," I said finally, "has got to be the worst goddamned birthday on the planet."

The car was quiet for a minute, but pretty soon, a short,

reluctant chuckle came out of my mouth. "It would almost be funny if it wasn't so sad," I said.

"Right. Under different circumstances."

Another half chuckle, a sort of shocked cough, escaped me, and Laney followed with one of her own. And then I couldn't help it—I did it again. A few seconds later we were both giggling, slowly and stupidly at first, until the sound caught a rhythm that rolled and grew louder, and soon our laughter filled the car. It felt like the first time I'd laughed in forever.

I was wiping my eyes, trying to get myself under control, when I noticed that Laney had stopped in a circular drive of one of the Lake Shore Drive high-rises near Addison.

"What's going on?" I said. "What are we doing here?"

Laney pursed her mouth and gave a quick whistle, the way she did when she was nervous. "You don't remember this, either?"

I glanced out the window at the building—tall, made of huge gray blocks, a plate-glass window in front of a large marble lobby. As far as I knew I'd never been in the place.

I looked back at Laney. "What's to remember?"

"You live here."

3

I walked into the lobby and took in the details, hoping for something that would trigger my memory, some plant or chair or *something* that said, *Yes, I live in this building.* But the gray marble floor seemed as unfamiliar as the front desk and the man sitting behind it, so when he stood and said, "Afternoon, Miss McGraw," I almost choked.

Laney put her hand on my arm and steered me to the left. "How are you, Mike?" she called over her shoulder as we walked.

"Fine, Laney. Have a good one."

"How does he know me?" I whispered.

"I told you," Laney said, keeping her voice low, "you live here."

"Then how does he know you?"

"Because I'm a fabulous friend, and since you won't go

out anymore, I visit you all the time. I know that guy better than you do."

We'd reached the end of the marble hallway. Laney turned me to the right and walked me through double doors into a sitting room. At the end of the room was a set of elevators, where Laney was directing us.

"What do you mean, I won't go out?" I said.

Laney made that nervous whistle again. "Well, aside from your frequent trips to Ben's place, you rarely leave the house, so I bring you food, and we hang out and talk."

I squeezed my eyes shut for a moment and tried to conjure an image of an apartment, Laney and I sitting on a couch talking, maybe giggling, but my mind was a blank.

"What do we talk about?"

We'd reached the elevators. Laney hit the button for the twelfth floor. "You know—Dee, your mom, Bartley Brothers. We talked about Ben a lot, of course. You kept saying that now that he'd broken up with you, you were never going to have your first kid before you were thirty-five. And you talked about how much you loved your town house."

"I did love that place. So why did I sell it?"

"That's what I've been asking you. You made a chunk of cash on it, but you weren't really hurting for money. You just kept saying that if you weren't going to live there with Ben, you weren't going to live there at all."

I scoffed. "That's ridiculous."

Laney stared at me for a second. "Exactly. You really don't remember any of this, do you?"

I shook my head. "So what about you?" I said. "What's been going on with you? I can't remember that, either."

"Well, we haven't talked about that much."

"Why?" And then I realized. "Oh, I'm such a horrible friend! I'm so sorry. You've been coming over here, listening to my woes, and we haven't spent any time on you, is that it?"

Laney shrugged. "You needed me."

"Well, of course, but that's not an excuse."

"Sure it is. Seriously, it was nice to be needed. It's no big deal that we didn't talk about me that much."

"It is a big deal." I followed her out of the elevator. "I'm really sorry."

"You'd do the same for me."

"Still—"

Laney put her hand on my shoulder and stared into my eyes. "You've been bad, Kell. I mean really, really depressed. It's been a little scary, if you want to know the truth."

Just those words felt scary to me. Generally, I can handle the crap that life dishes out. I'd seen my mom go through a million brief relationships and fall apart with each one, so I'd found my own way to hold it together. Even after Dee died, when I was the saddest and angriest I'd been in my whole life, I was still able to work, to go out with Laney for margaritas and talk about it. I was able to keep going.

Laney gave me a reassuring smile. "Do you have your key?"

I stuck my hands in my pockets and pulled out a few bills, a lip balm and a small key ring. Hanging from the ring were three keys, along with the little sombrero key chain that I got during a trip to Tijuana, and the silver pendant with the Bartley Brothers logo that the bank had given as a Christmas present last year. I made myself focus on the keys. One was my mailbox key—or rather, what I'd *thought* was my mailbox key this morning. The second was a small one for my gym locker, and then there was a third. It was a gold key with a fat, square head, and it seemed like it was glinting malevolently at me under the fluorescent lights of the hallway.

Laney pointed at it. "That's the one."

* * *

"Oh my God," I said.

The place was a disaster. I don't mean the structure of the apartment itself. The white walls were unmarred, and there was a large bedroom, an equally large living room with a street view, and a European-style kitchen with new appliances. But there was stuff everywhere, as if a tropical storm had blown through the place. My clothes were strewn over the bed, the couch, the dresser. Wads of Kleenex overflowed from the wastebaskets, and old mugs with crusty tea bags sat on the nightstand and coffee table. A ton of pictures I'd taken of Ben were on my dresser, as if it was a shrine to him.

"Christ," I said. "It's a train wreck."

Laney nodded but stayed quiet.

I looked down at my feet and saw my favorite smoke-gray sweater crumpled next to the couch. "How could I do this to cashmere?" I said, picking it up.

I recognized most of the other stuff, too—my furniture, my clothes, my sage-green duvet on the bed and framed photos that I'd taken of Laney, my mom and Dee. But nothing else about the apartment seemed like mine.

"I must have been really down," I said as we stood in the middle of the living room, surveying the damage.

It's a known fact to Laney and me that whenever I feel crazy or out of control, my cleaning skills completely leave me. You can always tell the state of my life by the state of my apartment. I'd just never seen any of my places that bad before.

"That's an understatement," Laney said simply.

We walked through the place again, and this time I tried to take in more than the filth. I noticed a new phone in the kitchen, a white model that matched the appliances, with a plastic-covered panel that listed the names of people who were on speed dial. I'd written only three names there—Ben, Laney, Ellen.

"Who's Ellen?" I asked.

Laney took a seat on one of the stools that looked into the kitchen. "Ellen Geiger."

I blinked a few times. "Why is Ellen Geiger on my speed dial?"

Ellen Geiger was a psychiatrist I saw briefly after Dee died. I thought she was nice enough, a good person to talk to, and she had helped me sort out a few things. But I remember I felt I was coming out of my mourning, that I could deal with the pain and anger on my own, so after a while I just stopped going.

"You keep Ellen Geiger in business," Laney said.

Too frightened to ask what she meant, I went about opening the cabinets. My nice set of pots and pans looked dusty and unused, my refrigerator and freezer nearly empty except for a loaf of bread that was starting to green around the edges and a tub of chocolate chip ice cream with severe freezer burn. I opened the cabinet next to the fridge, and there, in front of an old bag of pretzels and a few cans of tuna, were four brown plastic bottles. Prescription bottles. I picked up the first three, reading the medications noted on the white labels—Wellbutrin, Prozac, another Wellbutrin.

I looked at Laney. "Antidepressants?"

She nodded. "You've been trying a few of them."

"And?"

"They don't work so well."

I turned back to the cupboard and looked at the fourth one. The label stated that it was for pain, and it bore bold orange warnings about taking it only with food. It had been prescribed by Dr. Markup, the general practitioner whom both Laney and I had seen for years.

"Pain relievers?" I asked Laney.

"You've been getting these nasty headaches. Migraines, I guess."

This was all so confusing—this apartment that didn't

seem like mine, the depression and headaches I didn't re-member. I felt completely removed from the life I'd sup-posedly been leading. Maybe if I heard more about it... Maybe I *needed* to hear more.

I sat on the counter facing Laney. "Okay, tell me."

"I did. You've been down."

"No, I mean give me the whole chronology—how it went, when it started, you know."

She grimaced and shifted on the stool. "Well, there's no doubt that it started on your birthday. You were all giddy that morning. You called me from work to say that you were looking good, feeling good and ready for your dinner with Ben. Then an hour later, you called again from your cell phone, and I could barely understand a word you were saying."

"I was crying?" I tried to jump-start some memory.

"No, you were *raging*. You know how you get sometimes?"

I nodded. It wasn't something I was proud of, but I had an occasional flaring temper that I had no control over, which is why I'd wanted to strangle the dry cleaner this morning and the reason, a few hours ago, I'd been plotting ways to terminate everyone in my management company. *Ex*-management company, I reminded myself.

"You told me that they'd laid you off," Laney continued. "Budget cuts or something. They tried to give you six months' severance, you railroaded them into nine and that was it. They said you could stay on for a month or so. They were going to assign you a desk and a cubicle so you could look for a new job."

"That's insulting!"

"Exactly. You couldn't believe that this place that should have been making you partner was offering to put you in a cube so you could try and start over somewhere else. You told them to go to hell and just walked out."

"And so I wasn't depressed yet?"

"Oh no." Laney chuckled. "Just pissed off."

"Okay, so then what?"

"Well, naturally you went shopping."

I nodded. It made absolute sense to me. I was required to shop as part of my job because I was a retail analyst for Bartley Brothers, and it was my duty to keep up on trends, but I also used retail therapy as a pick-me-up. Laney did, too. It always did the heart good to spend money you shouldn't on something that made you look or feel fantastic.

"So you bought these great shoes to go with the black dress you were wearing for dinner," Laney said.

I was tempted to interrupt and ask for details about the fabric and the heel, but decided it probably wasn't the time.

"Anyway," Laney continued, "you were actually fine by the time Ben came to pick you up. He took you to the Everest Room. He told you how sorry he was that you got laid off, how ludicrous it was for them to let you go. You were sure he was going to propose. You said besides being fired you were having a great day. Everything felt perfect—the candles, the champagne—and so when he said he needed to talk about something, you thought that was it. But instead, he started this spiel about how he thought he'd be ready, he *wanted* to be ready to marry you, but he wasn't. He gave you that bullshit line about how it wasn't you, it was him."

I crossed my arms and leaned back against the cabinet. "Please tell me I dumped the champagne bucket over his head." If there ever was a legitimate time for one of my temper tantrums, that night sounded like it.

"I wish," Laney said. "You just told him to leave, and once he was gone, you realized that you had to pay the bill."

I tried to laugh, I really did, but Laney's words sounded like a bad joke. A pathetic woman who'd given her man an ultimatum to marry her or else, sitting there with her "or else"—a full bottle of champagne and the bill. So instead of a laugh, my voice came out a groan, and then I couldn't help it, I let the tears come.

"Honey." Laney jumped up from the stool and came around the bar to hug me. "It's okay."

"I'm sorry," I mumbled through my tears and Laney's fuzzy sweater. "You've done this already, haven't you?"

"Doesn't matter." She stroked my hair. "Let it out."

How could Ben, the man I thought I wanted to marry, be so thoughtless? We'd been together for four years, forever it seemed. We were meant for each other. How could he just end it all when he'd given me the impression that he wanted the same thing I did?

As I sniffled and cried some more into Laney's sweater, I started to wonder about Ben's desires, what he had really wanted. It wasn't that I didn't remember the talks we'd had about marriage. Those had happened in February and March after Dee died, a time I recalled clearly. But maybe he hadn't really wanted a life together. Maybe he simply hadn't disagreed with me when I said I did.

"And so that was it?" I said to Laney, using a paper towel to wipe my eyes. "That's when I got so depressed?"

"Yes and no." Laney picked up a stray pen, staring at it as if she was thinking hard. "You were down, don't get me wrong. You'd taken two big blows in one day, and only five months or so after Dee died. You were crying a lot and acting a little weird, but something else happened a few weeks later."

"What?"

She started tapping the pen. "I don't know. You wouldn't tell me. But you went from an I-need-to-sit-around-in-my-pajamas-for-a-few-weeks kind of mood to an I'm-taking-drugs-and-seeing-a-therapist-and-stalking-Ben kind of mood."

I jumped down from the counter. "I was *stalking* Ben?"

"Well, that's his word. I'd just say that you were trying a little too hard to get him back. You would often wait for him outside work and, a couple of times, you went inside his apartment and waited there."

"Jesus, that's humiliating."

"It was so unlike you. You sold the town house next, which I couldn't believe, and then you rented this place. There's nothing much to tell after that. You've pretty much been holed up here for months. I can't believe you don't remember this."

"None of it. But you know what?" I started to clean up the kitchen, using a sponge to scrub a sticky, chocolatey-looking circle off the countertop. "I don't want to remember. I feel like my old self, and why would I want to go back to that nastiness you're telling me about?"

Laney stood up and started helping me. "I don't want you to go back, either, but you should visit Ellen or Dr. Markup or *somebody.*"

"Dr. Markup? C'mon." Dr. Markup is good for the basics like flu shots and such, but otherwise he's a human prescription and referral machine. "You've got jaw pain? Here's some codeine and the number of an oral surgeon. Something in your eye? Use these drops and go see my optometrist friend. Sore throat? Let me give you the name of an ear, nose and throat guy."

"Well, it can't be good for you not to remember," Laney said.

"Maybe it is good, though. Maybe it's my mind not wanting to be in that place anymore, wanting to get on with it."

"Maybe," Laney said, although she didn't sound convinced.

"Look, I don't remember what you're talking about, being depressed and moping around this place, but I don't want to. I'm hurt and pissed off as hell about Ben." I took a deep breath and tried to shake him out of my mind. "And I miss my town house. Other than that, I feel okay—great even." I was relieved to find that I was speaking the truth.

As I was talking, I opened what looked to be a hall

closet just outside the kitchen to see what lurked in there, but before I could concentrate on the contents I noticed a full-length mirror hanging inside one of the doors. I turned to face the mirror, and I could feel my mouth dropping open.

"What is it?" Laney said from the kitchen.

I couldn't talk. I was too busy looking at myself—a drawn, unhealthy-looking, unfashionably dressed self that I barely recognized. My light brown hair, which I normally wore straight to my shoulders, was dingy and frizzy, with enough split ends to conduct electricity. My face was pale, almost gray, my cheeks sunken in, my mossy-green eyes red around the rims. I had on the leather jacket I'd bought last winter, which was a still-cute blazer style, but the jeans I wore were baggy and at least ten years old. My sweater was olive-green and shapeless—one of Ben's. And the pièce de résistance were the shoes. Lumpy, brown suede walking shoes that I'd bought for a hiking trip Ben and I took years ago. Comfy, sure, but I'd never worn them around town.

Laney had moved behind me and was looking over my shoulder in the mirror.

"When was the last time I went shopping?" I asked her.

"Fucking ages."

I kept staring at the ugly shoes, the hideous sweater, the god-awful jeans. "I wouldn't even know what to shop for anymore. I wouldn't know where to start."

"We might need a professional," Laney said.

"What do you mean?"

"Do you remember the personal shopper at Saks? The one who helped me on the Herpes Project?"

A year ago, Laney had been in charge of a statewide herpes campaign targeted at the twenty-something bar crowd. They'd turned to a personal shopper at Saks to outfit the people featured in the ads, and, as a result, the men and women who were supposedly plagued with genital sores looked gorgeous and hip. It was enough to make you think herpes wasn't so bad, after all.

I nodded, unable to take my eyes away from my image in the mirror.

"She was pretty damn good," Laney said. "She'll size you up and then bring in a million things, and you just keep trying them on until you find what you need."

I took another long look at myself in the mirror before I slammed the door shut and turned to Laney. "Let's get her on the phone. Now."

4

An hour later, Laney and I were sitting on yellow silk couches, sipping tea in a huge dressing room of the personal shopping department of Saks on Michigan Avenue. The person that Laney knew wasn't working, but another woman, named Melanie, had proclaimed it a slow weekend and told us to come in immediately.

Melanie was a willowy frosted-blonde who could have been anywhere from thirty to fifty. She exuded calm and elegance as she sat across from Laney and me, handing us photos and opening pages of fashion magazines, pointing to styles she thought might look good on me. We'd already established that I wanted mostly casual clothes, since I didn't have a job, but Laney thought I should also get a few dressy things in case something came up. Since I'd been a hermit for the past five months, I couldn't imagine what would "come up" to cause me to need a beaded silver gown, yet I told Melanie I'd try it on.

"All right, ladies," she said, standing up and tucking a lock of her perfect blond hair behind her ear, "I have an idea of what you're looking for, so now I need to measure Kelly."

I stood on a pedestal, while Melanie's arms flew around me with a cloth tape measure, hugging my hips, slipping around my breasts, my waist. "All right," she said, "we'll get you mostly fours and sixes."

"*Size* four and six?"

"Definitely," Melanie said, rolling up her tape measure.

This should have been a cause for celebration, since I'd always been an eight or a ten. Always. My whole life, no matter how hard I tried to lose a few pounds for bathing suit season, I always hovered around the same weight, the same sizes. Laney and I glanced at each other briefly, neither of us acknowledging exactly how or why I'd lost that weight. I reached down and felt my hipbones through the baggy jeans and sweater. They were prominent for the first time in my life. I must have been either eating like crap or barely eating at all.

"You ladies relax," Melanie said with a calm smile, making notes on a small leather-covered notepad. "I'll be back shortly." Before she left, she poured us more tea, replenishing the biscuits she'd laid out on a silver tray.

"I could get used to being waited on like this," I told Laney, making my voice light, trying to instill some levity back into the situation. I made a point of breaking a biscuit in half and popping it into my mouth.

"No shit." She sipped her tea, holding her pinky out for effect, and we both laughed, relieved.

"I love you, you know." I was suddenly struck with how amazing Laney must have been to me over the past months.

"I know." She gave me a little smile over her teacup.

It scared me to think about what could have happened if Laney hadn't been there for me, but if I thought too much about the last few months, they might come back. I might remember. And as odd as it felt to have this gap in my brain, it was better than the alternative.

"So tell me," I said. "Are you still dating Archer?"

"Archer? Archer was eons ago!"

I imagined Archer in my head—a tall, skinny bass player in a jazz band, with stringy blond hair—but I couldn't remember learning they weren't dating anymore. Not that Laney and he had dated very long—not that she dated anyone for very long—but he was the last boyfriend I could recall.

"Is there someone new?"

She nodded.

"Name, please."

"Well, his real name is Gary."

"And what's his not-so-real name?"

She smiled and did that whistle of hers. "Gear."

"Excuse me?"

"Gear, okay? He calls himself Gear."

"And what band is Gear in?" This wasn't a hard question for me to come up with. Laney nearly always dated musicians. I think she'd done it initially to piss off her four older sisters and her parents, but after a few years of music men, Laney had begun to take guitar lessons, and now she was hooked on the whole scene. Her dream was to be in a band herself.

"High Gear."

"Excuse me?"

"You heard me. High Gear. They're very talented, actually."

"I'm sure. And how did you meet Mr. High Gear?"

"Well…" She nearly sighed. "I was taking a lesson."

She looked at me for confirmation that I remembered the guitar lessons she took at the Old Town School of Music, and I nodded.

"So I was taking a lesson, working on this song I'd written."

"You're writing songs now? That's amazing!"

"Lyrics, too. So anyway, the door was slightly open and I played this damn song for probably the whole hour, and when I opened the door, he was just sitting there in the hallway."

"Gear?" I asked, trying not to giggle at the name, although Laney probably wouldn't have noticed. She looked positively dreamy.

"He told me I was talented. He told me he thought my song was beautiful, and that was about three months ago. Three great months."

"Wow." I was struck by how romantic their meeting was. There was something so Shakespearean about him being drawn by her song.

It was completely different from the way I'd met Ben—a handshake at work when he started two years after me, and then an awkward, sloppy kiss a few weeks later following a Bartley Brothers happy hour.

I was about to ask Laney what kind of music High Gear played when Melanie sailed into the room holding aloft an armload of hangered clothes. "There's more coming," she said, "but this should get us started."

For the next hour and a half, I tried on more outfits than I knew existed—black pants and jeans of every style, silk sweaters, wool pantsuits ("Good for job interviews, if you decide you want one," Laney said), trendy skirts with splashy prints, clingy tops, leather boots, suede boots, short boots, high boots and every other shoe under the sun.

Ben used to like me in pastels—pink, powder-blue, lilac. "Soft and sweet," he'd said. Although I didn't despise those colors, I didn't love them, either, and yet little by little my closet had become full of them. I wasn't one of those women who would just change everything about herself in order to keep her man happy, but I *had* changed minutely, piece by piece. It was enough to eventually alter most of my wardrobe, to leave me feeling as if I didn't know what colors I liked anymore.

I noticed now that I was gravitating more toward the basics, sturdy, elegant colors like black, tan, cream and gray. Colors you could build a whole wardrobe around.

Meanwhile, Laney sat on the couch, offering a running commentary on each piece. The problem was that she liked nearly everything.

"Lane," I said, spinning around to face her. "I can't buy every single thing."

"I don't know why not. You've got money to spare from your severance package, and you look amazing in everything."

I turned back to the mirror and looked at the soft camel pants I had on with an ivory turtleneck and a pair of high-heeled camel boots. Okay, Laney had a point. It wasn't that I thought I looked so fantastic, but the clothes were fitting me better than ever before. Where I'd been curvy in the past, I was more angular from the weight I'd lost—*angular* being an adjective I'd only dreamed of applying to myself in the past.

"The trousers look fabulous on you," Melanie said. By this time, she had realized that I was definitely in a buying mood, and champagne had replaced the tea. She stood now with two other assistants, all of them studying me, nodding along with her.

I shrugged. "Okay, I'll take the pants."

"And now," Melanie said, floating toward me with a garment bag hanging gingerly over her arms, "let's try this."

It was the gown from the photo, and it was stunning. I slipped it on, stepping into the high sandals they'd given me. The lining was silky and smooth. When I zipped the dress up, it felt like a second skin.

I came around the curtain, and as I stepped onto the pedestal I heard a gasp—Laney's. I looked into the mirror and saw what she meant. It was spectacular. The dress was sleeveless and formfitting. It was cut so well, with its high neck and equally high slit, that it could have made anyone look good. The silver bugle beads glimmered with each movement as I turned this way and that. It was the most beautiful dress I'd ever seen.

I looked down at the price tag and tried not to swear. It was half a mortgage payment—if I'd still had a mortgage to pay off.

"You *have* to get it," Laney said, a hand on her chest. "You look fabulous."

"But it's crazy money."

"Don't care." Laney raised her champagne flute.

"Where would I wear it? I mean, what are the chances of me going to a gala or something if I've been needing anti-depressants just to get out of the house?"

Melanie and her assistants sent each other questioning looks, probably wondering if they were dealing with an es-capee from a mental hospital.

Laney shook her head and gave them a smile as if to say *She's kidding*. "Kelly, it's perfect on you. You *have* to have it. And who knows what will happen? Maybe there'll be a black tie wedding."

"Yeah, maybe Ben and Therese's." The thought almost made me fall off the heels.

Laney must have seen my stricken face because she jumped up, putting her arms around me from behind. "Look, this is a special dress. You probably won't ever again find something this amazing. Think of it as a treat to yourself after everything you've gone through. And I'll make you a deal. If after a year you haven't found someplace to wear it, I'll buy something fabulous, too, and we'll take each other out for an outrageous night in our dresses."

I looked at myself in the mirror again. I'd been so frugal for years, saving up to buy my town house, the one where Ben and I would start our lives together, and what did I have to show for it? Not a goddamn thing. I smoothed the dress over my stomach, although it hung perfectly. I watched the light glinting off the beads.

"Deal," I said to Laney. I turned and hugged her back.

Fifteen minutes later, I was ready to go and wearing a new outfit—a silky, bronze sweater, a pair of dark jeans and tall, black leather boots. As I bent over to sign the credit card slip, I flipped my hair over my shoulder and got a rush of that damn-I-look-good feeling. It'd been a while. But then I got another rush, this one much more panicky, and my hand froze over the slip. What if Laney was wrong about how much money I had? What if I'd just rendered myself penniless?

"Everything all right?" Melanie said.

"Uh…" I tried not to focus on the grand total at the bottom. If Laney was wrong, if I was broke, I'd just have to return everything. "It's fine," I said, and I scrawled my signature with a flourish. "Thanks for everything."

"Oh, it was a pleasure," Melanie said. "A real pleasure."

I'm sure it had been a *great* pleasure, since my whopping purchases had probably provided Melanie with her sales quota for the month, but I kept my mouth closed. Despite the moment of panic, I was entirely too pleased. I knew that this frivolous shopping spree couldn't provide answers about my memory loss or stem the depression I feared might return; yet it had made me feel a hell of a lot better.

"May I make one more suggestion?" Melanie said.

She turned me around to the mirror and fingered my dull hair. "Can I send you to a friend of mine at Trevé?"

I knew what she was trying to say. My hair was hell. Something needed to be done. But Trevé was the hottest salon in the city.

"I'm sure I wouldn't be able to get in there anytime soon," I said.

"Let me try."

She whipped out a cell phone the size of a Tic Tac box

and raised it to her ear. "Tommy," she said. "It's Melanie from Saks. Tell Lino I'm calling in my favor. I need an appointment today."

She paused, listening.

"No, it's not for me. A client. Kelly McGraw." Another pause. "Perfect," she said with a smile. "Kisses to Lino."

She clicked her phone off and looked at her watch. "You'll have to get a cab. Lino is expecting you at Trevé in twenty minutes."

We could hear the music pumping even before we walked in the door. A huge doorman with a bald head held the glass door for us. "Welcome to Trevé, ladies."

"You'd think they'd have somebody with hair," I said as we muscled my Saks bags through the doorway.

Laney laughed, or at least I could see her laughing, although it was hard to hear her above the thumping music. The front desk was at least six feet tall and spray-painted with gold graffiti. I stood on my tiptoes and screamed my name to the collagen-lipped receptionist, who led us upstairs to the stylists' stations, where the music was, thank God, being played at a much lower volume.

I was seated on a chrome-and-leather chair, my bags piled high in a closet, while a stool was pulled up for Laney, and two more glasses of champagne were delivered to us.

"Feel free to lose your memory every Saturday so we can do this once a week," Laney said.

I knew she meant it in a kidding way, but it reminded me of my horrible morning, of that sheer fear I'd felt when Beth Maninsky opened my door.

"You okay?" Laney looked a little chagrined at her comment.

I shook my head, shaking off the thoughts at the same time. "I'm great."

I was leaning forward, my glass outstretched to toast with

Laney, when I heard a cry. I swung around to see a short, deeply tanned man with dark hair and at least two coats of mascara around his dark eyes.

"My God!" he said, before he rattled off a litany of what sounded like Italian words. "Melanie didn't tell me it was this bad."

He spun my chair around so that I faced the mirror, and began pulling up strands of my hair, studying the split ends in the light.

"I take it you're Lino," Laney said. She put her champagne glass down on his station with a clunk. She had that defensive tone in her voice, the one that said, *I'll break your legs if you mess with my friend,* and I loved her for it.

"*Signorina,*" he said in a heavy Italian accent, "I mean no harm." He squeezed my shoulders and I looked at him in the mirror. His long lashes batted a few times. "You're gorgeous," he said to me. "*Bellisima.* Look at your body, your clothes. Beautiful! But this hair! I have no time for this." He shuddered and turned to a boy who looked all of seventeen. "Get her shampooed. Now."

After my head was scrubbed and then massaged until I was in a near dreamlike state by the underage minion, I was caped and back in front of Lino, who began furiously working away with his scissors.

"Shouldn't you ask her what she wants?" Laney said, the snippiness in her tone matching the sound of the scissors.

"No." Lino gave my hair another decisive clip. "I have no time for talking. I decide. Clearly, she does not know what is right for her hair. We'll do a little cut, *molto bene,* and then you two ladies will be gone."

"But that's ridiculous!" Laney said. "You have to take your time. This is her hair we're talking about! You need to find out what she wants. She's an adult, she should decide—"

"Lane," I said, holding my hand out. I couldn't actually

see her, since Lino had my wet, wonderful-smelling hair hanging in front of my face like a curtain. "It's fine."

"You don't care what he does?"

I considered her question for a second. Usually, I was concerned about what Ben would say if I did something nuts with my makeup or hair, of what they would say at work, but that didn't matter now, and I found myself pleasantly surprised. I was in for a change, and I told Laney as much.

"Mmm-hmm," Lino said.

"So where are you from in Italy?" Laney asked. She sounded like she was trying to be nice, which I appreciated, since this guy had both my head and his sharp silver blades in his hands, but I sensed something mischievous in her voice. Although "Laney Pendleton" might not sound Italian, she was. Her mother's family came from Milan. Laney herself had been to Italy at least ten times.

"Napoli," Lino said, the scissors flying furiously.

"Oh, so you've been to Ravello, right?" she said.

"Mmm-hmm." This time there was no smugness to his tone.

"Have you been to that hotel—what's it called—Palazzo Mazzo?"

"Of course."

Laney kept peppering him with questions about the Amalfi coast, about Positano and Capri and Sorrento. Lino grew more terse with each query, his scissor-snipping growing faster and faster until I felt I had to put a stop to it.

"What's going on here?" I said, ducking my head away from the approaching blades.

Laney had a sadistic-looking grin on her face. "He's not Italian."

"Mon Dieu!" Lino said, slapping his hands to his chest so that the scissors were pointed at his neck as if he might off himself. "That's not true!"

"Oh yes it is." Laney's face was smug, almost triumphant.

"First of all, *mon Dieu* is French, not Italian. Second, there is no hotel named Palazzo Mazzo in Ravello, and Salerno is *not* right next to Capri. You're a fraud!"

Behind me, Lino froze, the scissors poised at his neck for a long moment. Then he leaned over my shoulder, toward Laney. "Keep your voice down, you little hussy," he said in a clear Southern accent.

Laney and I both gasped. "Where are you from? Mississippi?" I asked.

"Tennessee. And don't you say a word."

"What's it worth to you?" Laney still wore that sadistic smile.

Lino glanced around, then leaned back into our little circle again. "I'll give her a free color, I'll pop for a makeup application and then you two get the hell out of here."

"Done!" Laney said, and they shook hands over my cape.

Two hours later, I emerged from Trevé, my hair a gleaming, coppery-caramel color and styled in a chunky, layered bob that made me feel cutting edge (no pun intended) and gorgeous. My face had been cleansed and moisturized and powdered and plucked; my eyes were smoky with brown shadow; my lips glistened with gloss.

"Girl—" Laney looked me up and down as we stood trying to hail a cab "—we are going to have one hell of a night."

5

We went to Laney's, since I had no desire to go back to the high-rise I couldn't remember, and I had enough clothes now to last me a month. Laney had a loft apartment in Old Town, with lots of exposed brick and artsy charm.

She cranked up a Rolling Stones CD and tossed me a beer. It was dark outside, but the apartment seemed to be glowing. Because of our afternoon champagne infusion, we were feeling a little goofy, and we danced around her kitchen for a while, singing into our beer bottles.

"All right," Laney said after a few songs, "I need to redo my makeup and find an outfit that's going to make me look half as amazing as you. Come to my room and help me decide what to wear."

"Sure."

As I walked through the living room toward the bedroom, my eyes caught on the baskets of photos Laney kept by her fireplace—one for childhood and family photos, one for high school and college, and two more for recent pictures.

"I think I'll flip through these for a second," I said, sinking onto her couch and picking up the high school/college basket.

"No problem."

I think she sensed what I wanted—to test my memory, to make sure it wasn't only the last five months that I couldn't remember.

She turned the music down a little, and soon I could hear the slide of hangers and the opening of drawers from the gaping door of her bedroom.

The few photos on top of the basket were of Laney's college friends, people I'd known vaguely from when I visited her during that time. Normally, I would have flipped through all of them, but I was more focused now. I was looking for pictures of myself.

The first one I came to was a shot of Laney and me in Tijuana, and I got a swoop of relief through my belly, because I could remember that time perfectly. I could even remember the hot Mexican guy who'd taken the picture. We'd been in San Diego for spring break, and we took a day trip into "TJ," as all the San Diegans called it. We were giddy with the exchange rate and spent the day buying bright, coarse Mexican blankets and silver jewelry before we spent the rest of our money on tequila shots and margaritas. The photo in my hands was taken right before the last bus back across the border, and both Laney and I were rosy with drink, huge careless smiles playing on our faces.

As I dug deeper, I hit on smaller photos, rounded at the corners, taken when 3x5 was the usual photographic dimension. One of my favorites was there—Laney and I standing in front of a row of gray lockers, my Nikon on a strap around my neck, Laney clutching a clipboard to her chest.

It had been taken only three days after we'd met, and once again, I had a near perfect memory of that day. We'd been just outside the yearbook office when someone had said they needed a photo of us for the staff section. Both Laney and I wore too much makeup and tidal wave bangs—bangs that arched above our foreheads and came to rest below one eye. Right before the photo was taken, Laney leaned in and threw her arm around me, a gesture that made me nearly weak with relief. I'd hated being new in the school, but after that moment, I knew I was going to be okay.

I picked through the basket, looking for pictures of my old boyfriends, thinking that maybe the breakup with Ben had something to do with the memory loss, and maybe I wouldn't remember my exes. But I easily found and remembered a picture of my high school boyfriend, Ted, whom I'd lost my virginity to in the stockroom of the convenience store where he worked, and Steve, my college boyfriend, who looked stoned as he posed in front of one of the landscapes he'd painted.

Laney has always called me a serial monogamist, but it's not really an accurate term. While it's true that I've had almost as many boyfriends as I've had first dates, I don't go from one to another to another without a break. In fact, I've always tried to avoid that pattern, having seen my mother date a long string of guys, only to end up with heartbreak. Instead, I have serious boyfriends, and if we break up, then I'm alone—no blind dates, no pickups in bars—until I find someone I truly, truly want to go on a date with. Laney claims this trait has weeded out far too many candidates and leaves no room for flings. Her point is that flings are, by design, to be had with completely inappropriate men—the ones you find attractive, but would never date for one reason or another. And yet the whole fling thing has always seemed a waste of time to me, particularly given my goal of being married with one kid by the time I'm thirty-five.

I picked up a stack of pictures toward the bottom of the

basket and quickly discarded them one by one onto the coffee table like a blackjack dealer. With each slap of a picture, I mentally listed the who, where and when, building up a confidence that most of my memory was intact. *Senior prom with Ted, me in a hideous chartreuse gown that make me look jaundiced; Laney and me after a football game, clearly about to pass out; on the beach in Florida with Laney's sister, Sophia; Laney's kleptomaniac college roommate, Tara.* When I came to one of Laney, Dee and me, my hands froze. I'd been a senior in college, full of myself and how cool I was. Dee was still in high school and had used the trip as an excuse to "check out the campus," when what she really wanted was to drink beer and hang out with me.

In the photo, Dee's light brown hair is short, and she's laughing—as she so often was—sandwiched between Laney and me, her head turned slightly toward mine. The pain of losing her rushed in like a hurricane.

According to Ellen Geiger, the psychiatrist I'd seen, everyone who suffers the loss of a loved one ruminates (her word) on the last time they spoke to or saw the person. I was not the patient to change that pattern. For months afterward, it was all I could think about—the last time I'd spoken to Dee and the last time I'd seen her, in January.

Dee had driven up from the University of Illinois to visit me, and we'd spent the weekend in our usual way—shopping during the day with Mom for clothes and boots and jewelry we didn't need, and at night going out with Ben and Laney, regaling them with stories of the astounding mix of freaks and psychopaths our mother used to date. Ben and Laney adored Dee as much as I did. It was hard not to. She had a little-girl way of holding her head down and drawing her eyes up that made you want to take care of her, and yet she could drink like a Russian soldier. And that laugh of hers was impossible not to love—a buoyant, soft-at-first chuckle that grew into a belly laugh.

On Monday morning, when Dee was supposed to leave, it was a silver-gray day, the sidewalks slick with ice, the city covered in a freezing fog. I had an early meeting, and so I was gone before she got up, leaving a note to help herself to breakfast and have a safe trip back. The usual banalities. She called me at work, though, wanting to chat, telling me about some dream she had about lobsters, relating a story she'd seen on the news that morning, and finally asking me where I kept the coffee filters.

"Third cabinet from the fridge." I tried not to sound annoyed. Dee loved long, chatty phone conversations (I didn't) and she was always calling me at work during her study breaks, hoping for an hour-long talk.

"What about bagels?" Dee asked. "Do you have any bagels?"

"I don't know, Dee, look around." I scrolled through my e-mails, anxious to get back to work. My meeting had been disastrous, and the market had just opened.

"Maybe I should visit Mom at work before I leave. What do you think?"

"Whatever you want."

"I haven't even seen her office yet. Where's the building? It's somewhere on Michigan, right?"

"Michigan and Randolph."

"Yeah, maybe I'll just stop in. Although I do have two papers to write."

At that point, Ronald Han, my boss, who was known around the office as Attila the Han, stopped by my desk and stood over me with a frown, brandishing a stack of faxes. He drew a line across his neck with his finger.

"I've got to go, Dee."

"Oh, all right. But what do you think? Should I pop in to see Mom?"

Attila slapped the faxes on his palm.

"I think you should just get on the road." I deduced that

if she stopped in to see Mom, she might very well "pop in" to see me, too, and it was proving to be a much too hectic day for visitors.

"Yeah, you're probably right."

"Okay, see you then," I said, and hung up.

Two hours later, I got a call from the state police, and two hours after that I saw Dee for the last time when I identified her bloody body at Cook County Hospital.

The memory of that morning reverberated in my brain now until I had a hard time breathing, wondering if maybe I was going under again, if I would soon forget this moment, too. But after a second, the air was a little clearer, and I was still there, still holding her picture, still missing her like crazy. At least, I consoled myself, I remembered. I seemed to recall everything about myself and my history except the very recent past.

With that thought, I picked up Laney's latest basket of pictures, the ones taken during the last few years, and sure enough, I seemed to recognize all those as well. Actually all but one—a photo of Laney and me leaning together at a lunch table. I recognized the restaurant, a brunch place where we frequently met on Sunday mornings to dissect our weekends. Based on our clothes, the photo had probably been taken in summer…but I couldn't remember having this picture taken at all. My earlier confidence evaporated, leaving a hollow feeling in my stomach.

I noticed how odd I looked in the photo. It wasn't my hair, which was pulled back the way I used to often wear it, or my outfit of khaki shorts and a T-shirt. It was my face, and the utter lack of a genuine expression on it. My head was next to Laney's, and she was smiling widely, but my face was frozen. Sure, I was smiling, but it was forced and tight, the grin failing to reach my eyes.

Laney slid into the room then, holding her hands away from her body for an outfit inspection.

"Adorable," I said. She wore a shorter black skirt, a sweater in a deep wine color and matching lipstick.

"Thanks." She dropped her hands. "What's that?" She came around the couch and stood behind me, looking over my shoulder.

I lifted the photo so she could see. "It doesn't even look like me."

A second went by. "It really wasn't you," she said. "You hadn't been you for a long time."

I looked at my grim image one more time before I tucked it, facedown, into the bottom of the basket.

"Where are we going?" I'd been so distracted by my haunted face in that picture that it hadn't dawned on me to ask the question until we were already in a cab, flying down Lincoln Avenue, past lit-up bars and restaurants and outcroppings of brick town houses much like the one I used to own.

"Tarringtons," Laney said.

Tarringtons was one of our old haunts, a place where we used to know each and every bartender. I couldn't say when I'd last been there, but I was sure it had been over a year. Ben and I had fallen into that relationship stage where we didn't go out that often, happy to stay home, tucked away in the town house, making linguini and watching movies (weird little independent films if it was my night to pick, *The Godfather* or some other mobster flick if it was his). The problem with that stage, of course, is that when you come out of the relationship, as I apparently had, you feel odd going back into the old stage, the go-out-every-night-and-make-witty-small-talk stage. I hoped I was up to it.

The smoke hung like nimbus clouds from the ceiling as Laney and I walked in. Tarringtons was a long, thin, oak-lined place with a wooden bar to the left, the rest of the place scattered with stools and tall round tables. At the front, a shaggy guy played acoustic Van Morrison tunes.

We made our way to the bar and snagged the last two empty stools. Laney ordered margaritas, our cocktail of choice. I started to ask her for more details about Gear, but we were soon interrupted by a shout and a round of hugs from Jess and Steve, two friends of ours from Laney's days at an advertising agency. Jess and Steve both still worked there (at least as far as I knew), and they both still did everything together, but for different reasons now. For years, while they were "just friends," we were constantly telling Jess that they should have sex and get it over with, but she swore they weren't like that. Then one day, a year and a half ago, they'd announced that they were, in fact, like that. They were in love, they'd discovered, and a few months later they were engaged. We'd been hearing about the wedding plans all year and in fact, if I remembered correctly, it was coming up soon.

"Oh my God," Jess said. "Is it Kelly McGraw, blast from the past, or is it a vision?"

"It's me," I said, letting myself be pulled into another one of Jess's surprisingly strong hugs. Everything about Jess was tiny—her miniature frame, her rosebud mouth, her hands and feet—and although she hated being called "cute," she was probably going to be stuck with the term her whole life. Steve was just the opposite. Tall and gangly, with an unfortunate resemblance to Ichabod Crane.

"You look unbelievable," Jess said. "Where have you been and what have you done to yourself?"

"We had a little makeover day," Laney said. "Shopping at Saks and then the works at Trevé."

I smiled at her, thankful for her answer and the diversion from the question about where I'd been for so long. I wasn't prepared to broadcast my memory loss, and I couldn't very well use Ben as an excuse for not being around, since everyone probably knew we'd broken up months ago.

"I won't even ask what you spent," Jess said, "but whatever it was, it was worth it. You look beautiful!"

Behind her Steve nodded, and I thanked them profusely, the compliments making me sit taller on my bar stool.

"So the wedding's soon, right?" I asked as Laney turned to the bar and ordered drinks for Steve and Jess.

"One week from today," Steve said. "According to the schedule Jess set, we should be home right now writing out place cards, but we needed a break."

"*He* needed a break," Jess said. "Anyway, Kell, we're so bummed you can't be there."

I couldn't be there? Why not? These were two of my good friends. An uncomfortable silence fell.

"Right. Well, I was going to be busy." I glanced at Laney for some help.

"With that charity thing," she said.

I had no idea what she was talking about, but by her expression and the way she was nodding slowly I could tell that she was making it up. I had, apparently, declined the wedding invitation because I had another date with my couch and my antidepressants.

"Right," I said. "The charity thing. But I'm not doing that anymore, am I?"

"No," Laney said. "It got cancelled, right?"

"Right. So I'll be able to go, after all. Is that okay?"

"We'd love it," Jess said, but she and Steve exchanged worried looks. "The thing is we already turned in our seating chart. I don't know if we can change it."

"I've got an idea," Laney said. "I was planning on bringing Gear, but he was going to have to leave early to go to some gig, so why don't I just bring Kelly as my date. Would that work?"

"That would be perfect!" Jess said in a relieved voice. "I'm so glad you'll be there."

"Me, too." I squeezed Laney's hand.

I loved being out and about like this, loved seeing my friends. So why hadn't I done it for so long? Why had I holed myself up in that apartment and turned down a wedding invitation? I wouldn't think about it. Not now—maybe not ever.

I helped Laney order another round of drinks, then more cocktails when other friends arrived. We made a tight circle near the bar, shouting over the music, laughing at old stories, clinking glasses. And then I felt him. My mouth slowed down, my head turned. Ben. Pushing through the crowd. He looked handsome in a thick wool sweater, his brown hair tamed and combed away from his face, his cheeks a little flushed from the cold outside. Behind him, another Toni look-alike trailed along, and when I looked closer, I could see they were holding hands. Therese. The girlfriend.

Ben was smiling, looking right at our group, and I was panicked at how I was supposed to act. From what Laney had told me, I'd been trailing after Ben like a puppy for the last few months. But if Ben or Therese were unhappy about seeing me, they didn't show it. They walked up to us, calling hello, hugging a few people, while Laney glared at him. Ben knew Steve from college, but clearly Laney hadn't expected him to be here tonight.

When he reached us, Ben nodded at Laney. I felt my heart beating hard under my new bronze sweater, and I wondered if anyone could hear it. Laney gave him a terse nod back, and then Ben turned to me with an expectant smile.

"I'm Ben," he said, apparently not recognizing me. He started to raise his hand to shake mine, but then froze, the smile dropping from his face. "Kell?"

"Hi, Ben." *Be brave. Be brave.*

He gave a little shake of his head, the one that reminded me of a dog shaking water off its coat, the gesture he made when he was trying to clear his brain of something he couldn't make sense of.

"Jeez." He stared at my hair, my face, my clothes. "What…ah…what happened to you?"

He made it sound as if I'd been mauled by wild dogs.

"I'm sorry," he said. "I didn't mean it like that. You just look so different, especially from this morning."

Was it only that morning that I'd stood in front of his apartment, frenetically pushing the buzzer?

"You look great, though." His words came fast now, almost tripping over themselves. "You look better and beautiful, and I'm glad to see it, and—"

Just then the woman I assumed to be Therese wedged herself into our conversation and cast a look of disdain at me, then one at Ben for good measure.

"Hi," I said, as politely as possible. "I'm Kelly."

"I know who you are." She raked her hands through her sandy, streaked hair and shot me an expression of pure disgust.

I felt myself falter. It had been such a shock to be so close to Ben that I'd forgotten for a second that I'd met this woman sometime over the last five months while I was hounding her boyfriend.

"I need to use the powder room," Laney said in a too loud voice. "Kell?"

"Sure," I said, grateful beyond belief.

"Are you all right?" Laney asked once we were in the safe confines of the tiny pink bathroom. She gripped my shoulders and peered at my face.

"I was just surprised, that's all." It was true, and I was also surprised to find that I didn't feel like falling apart. I didn't feel like crying or shrieking. I had just been so startled to see him, the guy whose kids I thought I'd have, whose underwear I thought I'd wash for the rest of my life. How strange it was to have known him so intimately—to know the way he squeezed his toothpaste tube into a triangular roll and the way he liked to have his forehead rubbed when he had a headache—and yet not to have a relationship with him anymore.

Laney hugged me, then proceeded to give me a rousing pep talk about not letting him get to me, how I was gorgeous and smart and starting a new chapter in my life that didn't involve him.

By the time we made it back to the bar, I was better. We ordered another round, and I was just starting to enjoy a chat with Jess about their honeymoon plans when Ben interrupted.

"Can I have a second?" He shot me his meaningful look, the one he'd probably given me on my birthday before he'd handed me my walking papers instead of a diamond solitaire.

Jess patted me on the shoulder as if to say good luck, then left us alone.

"So." Ben looked me up and down again. "You must have had some day."

"A great day, actually. A little shopping with Laney."

"And a new haircut."

I said nothing. Did he really want to talk about my hair?

"You really look amazing."

"Thanks." I hated myself for being flattered.

"Well, anyway," he said, with another doggy shake of his head, "Therese asked me to speak to you about today."

I looked over my shoulder at his girlfriend who was pre-tending to be engrossed in a conversation with Steve, but I could sense her antennae pointed in our direction. "Yeah, I'm sorry about that."

"This coming over to my place really has to stop."

"I know. It's done. It won't happen again."

He gave me a look of patent disbelief. "Seriously, Kell, Therese is getting upset. This can't keep happening."

His mouth continued to move, talking on and on about how poor little Therese could barely sleep, how I needed to get on with my life, et cetera. The more he talked, the more I wanted to laugh, because right then the thought of wait-ing for Ben at work or calling him repeatedly or buzzing his apartment was ludicrous to me. He'd dumped me, the asshole, and although I still had a hard time wrapping my mind around that, I wasn't stalker material. I couldn't believe I'd ever gotten close to it.

Finally I interrupted him, putting a hand on his arm. "I can't even remember doing those things you're talking about, but I promise you, it won't ever happen again. I've had a little memory problem…." I let my words trail off, suddenly unsure whether I wanted to admit to anyone other than Laney my loss of memory. Would people think me crazy? *Was* I crazy?

"What are you talking about?" He actually looked concerned, his gray-brown eyes worried and blinking, and that expression got to me. I found myself telling him the whole story of my day, explaining that I had no recollection of us breaking up or the way I'd been unwilling to let him go.

"Are you joking?" he asked a few times, his eyes skeptical now, as if this might be another one of my crafty ploys to get him back.

"It's true. I can't remember my birthday or anything after that until today. But I feel okay."

"Well, shouldn't you go to a doctor or something? Get yourself checked out?"

I made a show of holding out my arms, looking down at my legs. "Everything else is intact, so…" I shrugged.

"I don't know." He fingered the dark-brown freckle on his right cheekbone. That freckle had always made him self-conscious, because it resembled a speck of dirt, and people were forever telling him he had something on his face. But I used to love that spot. I'd kiss it whenever he walked in my door.

"You do look good." His eyes trailed over me again.

I wanted to make a snappy retort, something like *Yes, I look damn good and you're not getting any of it,* but I kept quiet.

"So how's Bartley Brothers?" I didn't want to talk about us or my memory any longer, but wanted to occupy Ben for a while, just to piss off Therese. "How's Attila?"

"Demoted. He's pushing paper," Ben said.

"No!"

Ben nodded. "Lots of people are getting moved around or let go."

"Yeah, so I heard."

"Well, obviously. You'd know that since you…"

"Got fired."

"Right."

There was an uncomfortable pause.

"So tell me what happened to Attila," I said.

Ben launched into a story about Attila being investigated for insider information right around the time of the budget cuts. From there, our conversation was easy, catching up on all our co-workers—my *ex*-co-workers—Ben telling me stories about trades gone awry, and bringing me up-to-date on the market.

We were laughing about another Attila story when Therese sauntered up to us and placed a proprietary hand on his arm.

"Benji," she said—and I couldn't help it; I snorted. Benji was a nickname he hated, the name Ben's brothers used to make fun of him. Both of his brothers were much bigger. They excelled at football and other bone-crunching sports, while Ben had been relegated to running and tennis.

Ben sent me a look as if to say, *Shut up, please.* I tried to quell the giggles.

"I'm ready to go," Therese said, shooting me little knives with her eyes. "It's getting *way* too uncomfortable in here."

"How about one more and then we'll head out?" Ben said.

Therese's bottom lip dropped a little. I got the impression that she wasn't used to Ben saying no to her. "I want to go now. We've got to be at my mother's for brunch tomorrow, remember?" She sent me a look of triumph, clearly expecting me to be crushed by this news. Strangely, I wasn't. In fact, I felt so much better now that Ben and I had had a normal conversation.

"Sure," Ben said, "I was just updating Kelly on what's going on at Bartley."

"Great. Did you tell her that you made partner?"

Ben sent a quick, guilty look in my direction.

My good mood, my ease at talking to Ben, evaporated like steam. "What? When?"

"Last week," Therese bragged.

I fought hard not to smack her.

"Is that true?" I said to Ben. *I* was the one who was supposed to make partner first. *Me.* Ben had started at Bartley two years after me. I was next in line. How had I gotten the ax while he was elected to goddamn partnership status? I felt my neck go red.

Ben nodded sheepishly.

"He deserves it," Therese said. "He's worked really hard and—"

"Excuse me," I said. "Could you shut up for one minute?"

Her eyes narrowed, and she sent a glance at Ben as if to say, *Are you going to let her talk to me like that?*

"Kell," he said. "Take it easy. It just happened. I didn't even know it was coming."

Something about the way he had said that, the way his words got incrementally softer at the end of the sentence and the way his mouth became tight, told me that he had damn well known it was coming. He probably knew back in May. For a horrified moment, I wondered if he'd known that I was going to be fired, too. I stood there, completely stumped for words, wishing my temper would take over and do something rash that I would later regret—something like head-butting Ben—but nothing came. Finally, Therese tugged on his sleeve.

He drained the rest of his beer. "I'm sorry, Kell. Good to see you."

I searched my brain for a witty comeback, something that would erase the smirk from Therese's face, but once again I came up blank. A pregnant quiet enveloped us.

"Ben, let's go," Therese said.

He hesitated, still standing before me as if he might say something else.

"Oh, please," Therese said, before he got the chance. She clamped a hand on his arm and dragged him away.

When they reached the door, Therese disappeared through it, but Ben turned around and for the longest moment held my eyes.

My temper flared *after* Ben left, obviously the wrong time, but I was immune to a cure, and so I sat at the bar, boring poor Jess and Steve and Laney about the manipulative machinations of Bartley Brothers and the treachery of Ben, all the while trying to douse my anger with cocktails. Laney eventually wrenched the conversation away from me and back to Jess and Steve's wedding, and they were happy to prattle on about place settings and invitations and the band vs. DJ debate until we got the "last call" shout from the bartender.

After Tarringtons closed, and Laney had convinced me that no convenience store in the city sold margarita mix, she and I lay snug in her king-size bed, gossiping maliciously about Therese, giggling about Ben not recognizing me, and rehashing—at least fifty times—my conversation with him. Although still pissed off about him being made partner ahead of me, about him possibly knowing that I would be fired, I felt much better now that I'd gotten my dose of rage. And oddly enough, I felt a tipsy contentment around me. It'd been eons since Laney and I had had a late-night chat like this, a fact that made me sad. It was Laney who'd been with me every step of the way though the traumas of high school, the newfound freedom of college and the often painful days of early adulthood, and yet it was Ben I'd ended up spending so much time with. Ben, who'd eventually decided that the time meant nothing.

"He is such a fucker," I said, the margaritas making my tongue loose, causing me to repeat myself over and over.

Laney gave me a light smack on the arm. "Stop already. It's unhealthy. Let's talk about something else."

"Name it."

"Are you sure you're all right with this no-memory thing? I mean, you've had a lot going on today, and it's all right to fall apart."

I turned on my side to face her. "I feel better than I ever have."

"Well, don't think that you have to put on a tough act. You can still fall apart if you want."

"Nope. I've done enough of that."

Laney was silent for a second, and I could hear the whoosh of cars passing by her building. "It's just that something was definitely wrong. Something more than Ben and the job," she said.

"It was obviously something that didn't matter."

"Maybe."

Her tone made me feel a little chilly, and I buried myself deeper under her duvet. What was it that I hadn't told anyone? Did it matter now? On one hand, if whatever it was could explain *why* I couldn't remember this summer, I wanted to know it. For some reason, I truly wanted to learn why this odd memory loss had happened to me. But on the other hand, if I remembered those five months, wouldn't I just slip back into that depression? I wanted the whys and the hows of the situation, but I feared the details. I felt as if my memory was a house of cards, wobbly and shaky and hollow inside. I was afraid that if I came too close to that emptiness, that missing time, everything would fall in on me.

"Look, Lane," I said, "I've already spent too much time on whatever it was, and maybe that's why I feel so good now, because I let myself be depressed until I couldn't be depressed anymore."

"Shouldn't you try to figure out more about what was going on with you during that time? I could help you, you know. We could go talk to Ellen or somebody, maybe do some research." Laney's voice sounded so sweet, so helpful and slightly worried, and it made me tremble a little inside.

I squeezed her arm, as much to reassure her as myself. "It's okay. As far as I can tell, nothing good happened during those months, right?"

"Right," she said, a hint of doubt lingering in her voice.

"Right." I rolled over, turning my back to her. "And what you don't know can't hurt you."

6

On Sunday, I suffered an intense headache. I usually didn't feel so bad after a night of drinking, but I probably hadn't been drinking much for five months. I tried not to think about the headaches Laney had told me about, the ones I suffered during those months I was holed up in my apartment.

After Laney plied me with ibuprofen, she and I joined Gear and the rest of his High Gear band to watch the Bears game at a little corner pub. I'm not sure what I expected of Laney's latest boyfriend—maybe heroin at halftime?—but he wasn't exactly the stereotypical dude in a heavy metal band. Oh sure, he had the requisite tattoos on his arms (barbed wire on the right, some Chinese lettering on the left) and he wore a ripped black T-shirt and black army boots, but Gear was warm and friendly, too, which surprised me.

"So this is the infamous Kelly," he said when Laney introduced us.

"Infamous? I hope that's a good thing." I held out my hand, but he pulled me into a hug. He smelled like shaving cream and cigarettes.

"You're infamous because Laney Bug is always talking about you."

"Laney Bug?" I looked over my shoulder at Laney, who groaned a little, probably realizing that she would never be able to live down this nickname. I could almost see us at age ninety, me taunting her, *Oh Laney Bug, can you bring me my tea, please?*

The rest of Gear's band weren't quite as outgoing or sweet, but we spent a happy afternoon with them eating pizza, watching football and screaming at the TV when the Bears messed up. I drank a few beers in a hair-of-the-dog effort, and didn't think about anything else for hours—not Ben or my town house or my lack of employment.

Monday morning, I rolled over in Laney's bed and stretched, feeling, once again, intensely headachy from the alcohol. Apparently, I couldn't hold my liquor like I used to. I heard the hum of Laney's hair dryer from the bathroom, followed by the clatter of makeup on the tile floor and Laney's curse.

"You okay in there, Laney Bug?" I yelled, stretching my legs under her comfy duvet.

"Late," she called back, ignoring my use of her new nickname. "Totally late."

A second later, she tore out of the bathroom, yanked open her closet and stepped into a pair of shoes.

"What time did you get up?" I asked.

"Six."

I turned and squinted at her bedside clock. It was eight-thirty. "And what have you been doing?"

"Answered e-mail, did a Tae-Bo tape, returned a few phone calls."

"Okay, now I feel like a lazy ass."

"You need to take it easy." She picked up her purse by the bedside and squeezed my shoulder. "Stay as long as you want, all right? And call me at work if you need anything."

"Thanks." I watched her run into the kitchen and grab an apple out of a bowl. "Have a good day!" I called, but she was already out the door.

With Laney gone, the apartment seemed empty and vast. I swallowed some Advil, then took one of the books from her shelf, a memoir about a woman who'd followed the Grateful Dead. I figured that maybe I'd lie in bed all day and read. The book wasn't that interesting, though, at least not after the first three acid trips, and within an hour I was antsy. I knew I should probably go back to my own apartment, but the thought brought only a queasy feeling.

To thank Laney for everything she'd done for me lately, I ignored the pain in my head and the nausea in my stomach and cleaned up her place. Then I made myself a bowl of granola and decided I'd just spend a lazy day in front of the TV.

The first few hours went okay, especially after my headache eased. I watched the news and business stations, trying to catch up on the market, studying the Bloomberg as I used to for the ticker symbols that signaled the retail stocks. There were a couple of surprises, a few stocks that were way higher than when I'd followed them, and I found myself analyzing the rest of the market and how it might affect these companies. After a while, though, I didn't care all that much. It was a relief just to flip the channel.

Next, I tried the talk shows and the soaps, which kept my interest for a whole forty minutes. What, exactly, was I going to do with the rest of my day? A better question— what had I done when I was *home* for five months? I couldn't fathom it.

A thought came to me. Laney had said that I had more than enough money to live on because of the severance pay from Bartley Brothers and the sale of my town house. But what if I'd somehow spent that money during those five months? Laney had *assumed* I was holed up in that high-rise, but what if I'd actually been blowing the cash on God-knows-what, maybe a sailboat or a Porsche for Ben or a diamond engagement ring for myself?

I found Laney's cordless phone, dialing the number for my bank's automated system. Leaning against the kitchen fridge, I punched in my social security number, relieved that I remembered it, then my banking code, which came just as easily. A second later, an inflectionless voice informed me that I had a nice chunk of money in my account, more than I'd ever had at one time. Laney had been right, after all. I hadn't blown it. I didn't have to work right now if I didn't want to.

But what did people do if they didn't work? I put the phone on the counter with a clunk. Most women I knew who were officially unemployed were unofficially working their asses off in their own homes, raising their kids. I didn't have kids, obviously. Wasn't even on the path to eventual children. So what to do?

I could do anything I wanted with my life, I realized. It was mine to shape. I suppose that had always been true, but before, I'd felt the invisible constraints of the need for money, or my relationship with Ben, or the partnership track I thought I was on. Yet none of those concerns existed anymore.

My life was a clean slate. What did I want to do with it?

I found a pad of paper in Laney's desk and settled on the couch again. "New Possible Careers," I wrote at the top. I sat there for a full five minutes staring at the paper. Why wasn't anything coming to me? *Anything,* I told myself, *write anything that comes to mind.* I shook my hand to relax it and scribbled the following list:

Journalist
Clothing Store Owner

Music Video Dancer
Ambassador to France

A good list, excellent really. These were the jobs that I'd always thought so glamorous and cool. I could almost see myself as a political journalist, a pen tucked behind one ear, the president at the podium, pointing to me and saying, "Kelly," because of course I'd know the president. The problem was that in reality I had no writing skills to speak of and it probably took twenty years of hard-core newspaper journalism to get on the White House beat.

All the other possible careers I'd listed had impediments, too. I'd love to have my own clothing store, to be able to change outfits in the middle of the day just because I could, but I knew that owning a store was a massive amount of hard work. And as much as I'd been interested in the retail stocks and my own shopping, I really couldn't envision myself standing in the same shop day after day.

As for the music video career, well, I couldn't imagine what would be more fun than wearing a don't-fuck-with-me face and shaking my thing behind J.Lo or whoever, but I could dance about as well as I could remember the last five months. Ditto for the ambassador to France gig. I couldn't speak French.

I crossed out the list and tore the paper off, giving myself a fresh sheet. I would concentrate on the things that I *could* do, the activities that truly gave me pleasure, whether or not they could lead to a career.

The thing that came immediately out of the pen was "Photography." Ever since my stepfather, Danny, had given me that Nikon, a gift I later heard my mother say was "probably hot," I'd loved taking pictures. As a kid, it was something to do, something to play around with, a way to let myself be part of a crowd while still hiding behind the safety of a lens. As I got older, I realized that I was a natural at it. I could study the light on a sidewalk and realize how it would appear as a pattern in a black-and-white photo, and I knew how to take portraits from different ranges and angles to make the subject appear more studious or glamorous or thoughtful. Ben had even given me classes at a local university as a gift, and for the last few years I'd been taking them weekly. Was I still taking those classes?

I made a note to follow up on this issue, then wrote, "Shopping." Definitely one of my great loves, something I'd already made into a career of sorts, but I wasn't a retail analyst anymore, and I'd already done enough shopping on Saturday. I could probably get an analyst job at another investment firm—I knew enough people in the business; I could work my way up *again*—and eventually I'd be a partner somewhere else, just like Ben. Yet, even as I thought this, the realization came to me that I didn't *have* to work right now, and that knowledge took away all my drive to be in the market again. Maybe I'd never had the drive, or I'd only been driven by money.

What else? I lowered my pen and scribbled, "Walking." I wasn't much of a runner. I hated the way my breath came ragged and hard when I tried jogging, but I loved to walk. Again, I couldn't imagine why I had holed myself up in my apartment during an entire summer in Chicago, a city that was made for walking along the lake and through the zoo and down the Mag Mile. That's what I would do today, I decided. I'd take a huge walk.

But first I wanted to finish my list. What else, what else? It came to me, the answer, but I had a hard time putting it on paper. Finally, I wrote in small letters, so fine that you could barely read them—"Family." My mom had given me the best life she could muster, but it was one filled with random men, alternating cities and a series of small apartments. For as long as I could remember, I'd been jealous of the typical family—the husband and wife in the country with the 2.5 kids—and I'd sworn I'd get that for myself someday.

And so I'd always been concerned about the ticking of my so-called biological clock (although to be truthful I couldn't hear a peep), pointing out to Ben time and again that if we were going to get married and have kids, we had to do it soon—a belief that led, in part, to the ultimatum I'd given him. But now I didn't really have any family at all. Dee was gone in an instant, in a tangle of metal and rubber on the Dan Ryan Expressway, and Ben was gone now, too. And the children I was supposed to have one day? Far, far away.

My mom was still around, of course, but she and I had been family in name only since Dee had died. We'd handled Dee's death differently, to say the least. Me, well, I had my tantrums, my not-so-occasional flashes of anger when I tossed picture frames and broke dishes. Ben, after quietly watching me shatter more than half of my Pottery Barn bowls, had bought me a big brown candle and taken me into the bathroom one day.

"Throw it," he had said, opening the shower curtain and pointing to the wall inside the tub.

"What?" I looked from the candle to Ben and back again, irritated at this cryptic directive.

"Look." He took the candle from my hand, hurling it at the wall. It bounced off, a mere dent in the brown wax. "See? You can throw it and smash it. Do whatever you want, but it won't break."

"I *want* it to break."

"No, you don't." He kissed the top of my head. "You just want the feeling."

He was right. I turned to that candle often. I threw it against the bathtub wall over and over until the wall was splotched brown and the candle beaten into a misshapen lump. And one day I put the candle away, tucked it far under the sink, just in case. But I hadn't needed it anymore.

My mom, on the other hand, broke nothing, smashed nothing. She'd seemed to shut down after the accident. She didn't want to talk about it, she said. She wanted to leave Chicago and forget. And so off to L.A. she went, only one month after the funeral, and without Dee's death to talk about, all our conversations felt like disingenuous, twenty-first-century versions of the "Emperor's New Clothes." They were five-minute chats we both looked forward to ending. I had no idea when I'd last spoken to her.

I looked down at my watch. Right now, Sylvie Custer was probably at her desk on the set of *The Biz,* an entertainment "news" show that reported on the minutiae of celebrity activity—"*Tom Cruise considers sideburns! Tonight on* The Biz!"

I called information to get the general number, and the receptionist routed me through to my mom's desk. She answered with a crisp, "Sylvie Custer."

"Mom, it's me."

A little stretch of silence followed, and I knew what had happened. She'd been taken by surprise, and she'd thought for a moment it was Dee.

"Kelly," I said in a softer voice.

"Hi, honey. How are you?" Her words were mothering, but her tone slightly formal. It was the way we talked to each other now.

"I'm okay. You?"

"Crazy over here. Some starlet got arrested for shoplifting a pack of gum, and I'm trying to convince the LAPD to release her name. Meanwhile Mella, that Swedish fashion model—you know her?"

She made it sound as if I might have had martinis with Mella last night. "Vaguely," I said.

"Well, she's gained a few pounds, so I need a quote from the restaurant near her apartment."

I listened to some more Hollywood gossip, wondering how my mom could do it. She used to produce news segments on political corruption, double murders and Middle

East violence, and now here she was, digging up info on Mella's calorie count.

"So how's Ben?" my mom said in a swift topic shift, and I wondered, frantically, if I'd told her anything about our breakup. It didn't sound like it. I half wanted to tell her about my memory gap, but I didn't want to give her any more worries. I honestly didn't know if she could handle it, and it had been so long since I'd confided in her. And I was fine, wasn't I? Better than fine, actually. I'd admit to the breakup, I decided. I couldn't hide that, but I wouldn't mention the memory issues.

"Ben?" I said. "Well, you know we broke up, right?"

"What?"

Okay, she definitely hadn't known that, which either meant that I hadn't spoken to her for a long time or I'd avoided talking to her about that subject. It didn't surprise me, really. Our phone calls since Dee died were so few and so brief.

"What happened?" my mom said.

Great question. "He didn't want to get married." That was the simplest, most truthful answer I could deduce. I'd given him the dreaded ultimatum, the give-me-a-ring-or-I'll-walk speech, and it'd slapped me right in the face.

"Oh, honey, are you all right?" I could hear that anguished, parental tone in her voice, the one that made me feel warm and taken care of, but it scared me a little, too. I was always worried that she was close to a breakdown after Dee, and even now I wasn't sure what would make her snap.

"I'm fine. I really am. I saw him this weekend, actually, and we had a nice chat."

"What a little bastard. He probably wanted more time to run his races, right?"

"To be honest, I think he just didn't want me." Saying that out loud forced the breath from my lungs.

A pause. "Well, do you want to visit me? Maybe you

should leave Chicago for a while, take your mind away from it. You could probably get some time off work, right?"

Shit. Apparently, I hadn't talked to her about work, either. "Um, I got laid off from Bartley Brothers."

"Oh my God!"

"But it's a good thing, Mom," I said quickly, making sure to keep my tone light and untroubled. "They gave me a severance package, so I don't need to work for a while."

"Then you should come out here. Spend some time on the beach, eat lunch on the boardwalk. It would do you good."

"I'll think about it."

"You need to keep busy, Kelly. Are you still taking those photography classes?" I could tell she was struggling for a way to help me, one that wouldn't require any intimate revelations, but it dawned on me that she had a very good point.

I reached down and wrote on my list, "Go to school, *today.*"

7

I struggled a bit with my new hairstyle, my hands sticky from the pomade that Lino had insisted I use, but I finally shaped it into some semblance of the chunky bob he'd given me. I was able to render a toned-down version of the makeup job, too. Meanwhile, my new camel trousers looked great with a soft black sweater and my old leather jacket, although I still stood in front of the mirror for an inordinate amount of time. My body looked odd to me, smaller and sharper, as if it wasn't my own. As much as I liked my new look, it gave me a flash of that feeling I'd had when I was trying to shove my key into the mailbox Saturday morning.

I finally shut Laney's closet door on my reflection, ready to walk the city, to find out if I had taken any photography classes over the summer or was currently enrolled in one, and if not—sign up for a boatload of them.

I wandered down Wells Street past the amalgamation of

storefronts—an old-fashioned tobacconist, cute but over-priced boutiques, a couple of sex shops—until the beacon of my mother ship called me. It wasn't a Saturday, but what the hell? I ordered a White Chocolate Mocha, anyway. I sat in a plump velvet chair in Starbucks and sipped my coffee, happy to be there, to be paging through the *Tribune,* which I couldn't recall reading in ages. The news hadn't changed much in the time I'd been gone.

"Being gone" was how I'd begun to think of the months I couldn't recall. I pretended, at least to myself, that I'd simply been away on a long trip to somewhere, maybe Nepal or a remote South Pacific island, and now I'd returned with a touch of culture shock. This I've-just-been-on-a-long-vacation kind of mentality made me feel much better, edging me away from my fears about the need for a straitjacket or a fall back into the depression I couldn't remember.

I took my cup and continued strolling along Wells, then up Lincoln Avenue, and finally west on Fullerton, window-shopping here and there, sometimes poking my head in a store. Finally, after about thirty minutes of walking that left me feeling vibrant and healthy (although I suppose it could have been the caffeine), I reached the patches of brick buildings and green lawns that signaled the university. As usual, I felt like the oldest person on the premises as I made my way to the registrar's office, but it bugged me less today, since I was feeling rather saucy in my new outfit.

The registrar's office was a cramped little room with stacks of paper everywhere, making it look as if they hadn't discovered computers yet. The harried woman behind the counter did manage to unearth a keyboard from the mound of documents on her desk, and she confirmed what I had feared: I hadn't taken any classes since last spring. Actually, I supposed this shouldn't have disappointed me, since I wouldn't have remembered the classes even if I had taken them, but still the news raised the image of me in that strange apartment all by myself, an image I'd been trying to avoid with my vacation mentality.

I was flipping through the course guide, looking for classes that might allow late entry, when I heard my name being called. I turned and saw Rita Denny, a professor who I'd taken a few classes with already. A statuesque black woman, she always seemed confident and pulled together.

"Where have you been?" Professor Denny said.

"I took a break, but I'm ready to get back into a few classes if anyone will let me start late."

"Well, let's see." She took the notes from my hand and began reading over them. "Do you have any of mine here?"

I pointed to the seminar on portrait photography, which Professor Denny was conducting.

"Of course you can take it, but have you thought about an internship instead?" She glanced at me, and I must have worn a blank expression, because she laughed.

"It's just that I take classes for fun, not for a degree," I said, "so I didn't think any internships would apply to me."

"You might be surprised. You could probably learn more with an internship than you could in school this semester. Go to the placement office, and they'll show you the listings."

I thanked her and headed over to the placement office, fairly bouncing on the toes of my new camel boots. Maybe the Art Institute would need an intern, someone fresh, someone with vision to capture a new exhibit. Maybe the ambassador of France had turned to the university to help document his tour of America.

The realities were not so interesting. Most of the jobs were posted by companies looking for cheap labor to photograph and catalog merchandise, another by an insurance agency seeking someone to shoot brochure photos.

I stepped outside the office and decided to call a few of them anyway, just to learn a little more. Ten minutes later, I dropped my cell phone back into my purse and sagged against the wall. Despite Professor Denny's assurances, the fact that I wasn't a degree candidate had eliminated me from each position I called about, and one was already filled.

I dragged myself back into the placement office and paged through the rest of the listings, scribbling a few notes, although most positions looked as unpromising as those I'd already called.

Finally, I came to the last listing, which, according to the date, had been posted there for at least six months. I couldn't imagine why, since it sounded like the best one of the lot.

"Established photographer seeks assistant for work with commercial campaigns, magazine shoots and artistic portraits. Call 555-6754."

It was short and sweet, but it had my attention. I used my cell phone again and was surprised when a man answered immediately with a slightly belligerent, "Yeah?"

"I'm calling about the assistant job?" I hated how my own voice came out meek and questioning. I hadn't applied for a job in almost a decade, and making these calls was foreign to me.

"Yeah. Okay," the man said, and this time I could tell he had a British accent. "What's your name then?"

"Kelly McGraw."

For whatever reason, this drew a chuckle from him. "Kelly, Kelly, Kelly. Bet you're Irish then?"

"Half." Was this standard questioning for a photography internship? Did heritage and nationality count somehow?

"Well, Kelly Kelly. I'm called Cole. Want to come round to my flat tonight then? Say seven o'clock?"

"Uh…" Was this supposed to be a date or an interview?

"Oh, now don't be scared, Kelly Kelly. I just don't have time to talk at the moment, and I'll still be working tonight. There'll be others here. You'll see."

"Well, I guess so," I said, thinking that I'd make Laney come with me. Safety in numbers.

"Lie down on the washer!" Cole shouted away from the phone. "No. *Over* it, please. There you go. Now, Kelly, where were we?"

"The address to your studio," I said, while at the same time saying a silent prayer that he wasn't some kind of pornographer.

"Right, right. Got a pen?"

After I left the university, there was little to do. In one day, I'd watched TV, had my Starbucks, read the paper, taken a walk and followed up on my photography interests. And now I had an interview—something that hadn't even seemed possible this morning. What else was there?

Then it dawned on me. I needed to get ready for the interview. I should probably bring my own camera and portfolio. And that thought brought the reality I'd been hiding from—I'd have to go back to that apartment on Lake Shore Drive. *My* apartment. There was nothing stopping me except my fear that spending time there could somehow boomerang me to the depressed state Laney had told me about. At the same time, a little interest tickled at the back of my mind, because maybe if I went back to the apartment I could figure out *why* I couldn't remember.

I hopped into a cab, and in less than fifteen entirely too short minutes I was in the circular drive. The building was tall and imposing as I got out and gazed up at it, the huge gray blocks cold and aloof. The same doorman who'd been there when Laney brought me on Saturday was at the front desk inside.

"Miss McGraw," he said, dipping his head at me.

What was his name? What was his name?

"Afternoon," I said. Then I hesitated a second, feeling as if I had to be granted access to the building. *Keep walking.*

The doorman crinkled his eyebrows together, but I managed to get my feet moving again. I walked down the hallway, knowing his eyes were on my back, wondering if he would shout at any second and accuse me of breaking into someone else's apartment, because it felt very much like I was trespassing. I forced myself to take careful footsteps, until I reached the double doors that led to the anteroom and the elevators. As I pulled them open, I glanced back, and sure enough, the doorman was still watching me. I gave him what I hoped was a nonchalant grin before I ducked through the door.

Once upstairs and standing in front of apartment 1204, I hesitated as I held the key to the slot. Keys hadn't worked so well for me lately. What if this key was wrong, too? What if I'd somehow forgotten again? What if I didn't live here anymore? But no, that couldn't be right. The doorman had recognized me, after all. I shook my head and before I could freak myself out any further, pushed the gold key forward. It fit perfectly, turning the lock with a smooth click.

8

Walking around my apartment, tiptoeing really, reminded me of the way Dee and I used to prowl through the newsroom offices when my mother took us to work. As a single mom, she was often unprepared when a baby-sitter quit or we didn't have school on a given day, and lacking any other options, she'd schlep us to the station with her, bringing along a bag of toys and books. She worked in the newsroom, a massive, busy place with ringing phones and running people, a place that fascinated Dee and me. But the newsroom wasn't for kids, Sylvie would say. And so she'd find an unused office—one normally occupied by a station executive or newscaster who was out of town—tell us not to touch anything, and leave us there for the next eight hours.

Our books and Barbies would occupy us no more than a few hours, then the temptation to prowl and pry would overtake us. We'd peek through drawers, study photographs and read letters, looking for "clues" about the person whose office we were desecrating.

Now I was opening drawers in my *own* apartment, reading crumpled receipts from the garbage and peering cautiously into closets. The apartment itself was still so foreign and devoid of character. And yet so many things I came across, things I'd owned before my birthday, were fiercely familiar, like the Waterman pen given to me by Attila the Han, which I found next to the phone, or my favorite red T-shirt crumpled at the side of the bed. The whole snooping-on-myself experience brought back that house-of-cards feeling, rendering me nervous and nauseous and slightly claustrophobic.

It occurred to me that the claustrophobia might be partially due to the closed drapes and the dust hanging in the air, and so I decided to tidy the place. I threw the drapes open, letting in the bright fall sun, then dusted, vacuumed and scrubbed the apartment clean. Along the way, I came across nothing particularly alarming. No cryptic notes or receipts for odd purchases. The apartment seemed more like a way station, a place where a human being had merely subsisted for a few months. One of the most disheartening realizations was that there were no new outfits in the closets or drawers. No new clothes for five months!

I went searching for my date book, something I used to carry with me at all times. Unlike the rest of the analysts at Bartley Brothers, I'd never used a Palm Pilot or other electronic calendar. I liked turning the pages of my date book and seeing my weeks spread out before me, reading the notes on what I'd done in the past, looking through the upcoming appointments to remind me what shape my future would take.

When I found it in the top drawer of my nightstand, it was all but empty for the last five months. There were none of the usual notations such as, "Drinks with Laney, 9:00," or "Work out, 5:30." Instead, I saw only one appointment listed over and over—"Ellen Geiger, 2:00." It appeared that

I went to see her every Monday and Thursday at the same time. So Laney had been right. I'd been keeping my psychiatrist in business.

I looked at my watch. It was four o'clock on Monday afternoon. Was I supposed to have been at Ellen's office a few hours ago?

I left the bedroom and went back to the kitchen. The answering machine next to the fridge was blinking. When I hit the button, the voice that rang out of the machine was Laney's. She was just checking on me, she said. She hoped I would get out today and get some fresh air. The automated woman who came on at the end of the message told me that Laney had left the message Saturday morning, probably right about the time I was in Lincoln Park, trying to pick up my nonexistent dry cleaning.

No one else had called me the rest of the weekend, which struck me as sad. I used to be one of those people who had too many messages—from Ben, Laney, Jess, friends from work, Dee, my mom. I used to get irritated by the number of calls I had to return, trying to squeeze them in on my cell phone as I hurried about town.

There was one more call on the machine, though. It had been left today, and as I expected, it was from Ellen Geiger.

"Kelly," she said in a soothing voice, "you were scheduled for two o'clock as usual, and it's two-thirty now. Please call me and let me know you're all right."

She did sound a little worried, which made me feel guilty, so I picked up the phone and hit the speed dial for her number.

I could picture Ellen's elegant office from the few times I'd been there last winter. I could see her perfect ash-blond hair pulled away from her face by a headband, her hands holding a thick ink pen, gently jotting a few notes as I talked. She was perfectly nice, and I'm sure perfectly competent, but after a few sessions I didn't see how paying her more than a hundred dollars an hour would help me get over Dee's death. I wasn't in denial about it; I was just heartbroken and angry.

But if I stopped seeing her after my sister died, what had made me go back this summer?

As Ellen answered, I sat on one of the bar stools in the kitchen.

"Oh, Kelly," she said. "Is everything okay?"

"Great." I swiveled back and forth on the stool, wondering if I should explain the weekend, my whole memory loss. The problem was that I didn't remember seeing her twice a week for the last few months, so the thought of confiding in her felt somewhat awkward.

"Mmm-hmm," she said, and I remembered that murmur she uttered when she was thinking, that frequent "Mmm-hmming." "What happened with this afternoon?" she said. "Why didn't you show up?"

"Well...I forgot my appointment." There. That was true enough.

"You forgot?"

"Right."

"Mmm-hmm. Do you want to reschedule for tomorrow?"

"No. And I won't need to come in Thursday, either." I opened my date book on the counter and crossed out Thursday's appointment.

"Excuse me?"

"Actually, I don't think I need to see you for a while." I felt as if I was breaking up with her and should try to let her down easy. "I appreciate all your help."

"Mmm-hmm. Kelly, are you having suicidal thoughts?"

"What?" I stood up from the stool.

"Are you having thoughts about suicide?"

"No! Why would you ask that?"

"Well, you've been depressed, as you know, for some

time, and now you call me, sounding like you're putting your affairs in order, so to speak."

I laughed. I really did. It struck me as ludicrous and funny. "Ellen, look. I can promise you that I've never had a suicidal thought in my life." I stopped for a moment, wondering if that was true. Had I had any inklings over the last five months? No, no matter how depressed I'd gotten, I knew, somewhere down deep, that I would never think of taking my own life. "The thing is," I continued, "I've had a bit of a memory loss, but I feel fantastic. I really do, and so I don't think I need to see you anymore."

"Mmm-hmm. What do you mean by memory loss?"

How could I explain in a short and easy fashion? I gave her a brief rundown of my weekend, ending with how wonderful I was feeling, and reasserting again that I didn't need to see her.

"I have to insist that you come for at least one more session. Amnesia is nothing to be taken lightly, and it can be the cause of other psychological or physical damage. What about tomorrow? I can fit you in at the end of the day. Say seven-thirty?"

I was about to protest. I didn't want to spend money on therapy, when for all practical purposes I was feeling better than ever. And despite the tentative snooping I'd done around my own apartment that day, I was truly scared to remember the months I'd lost. Wouldn't those memories bounce me back to that depression? It was as if I was finally standing on solid ground, but could sense an abyss only a few footfalls away.

Despite my fear of that abyss, though, I was more and more curious about *why* I couldn't remember, about what had caused this whole strange episode in my life. Maybe Ellen could shed some light on that.

I opened my date book again and flipped to tomorrow's date, then wrote in, "Ellen Geiger, 7:30."

* * *

I met Laney for drinks near her office in the Loop, and we joined the masses of people looking for alcoholic sustenance before their train rides home. We found a tall, high table in a corner of a bar, and I ordered a beer, but barely sipped it since I wanted to be fresh for my interview. I hadn't been on an interview since the one for Bartley Brothers eight years ago, right after college graduation. I wasn't sure what to expect. I had my Nikon in my camera bag with me, along with a small portfolio of my stuff, and I'd flipped through my multitude of photography magazines, which I'd located in my apartment. What else to do, I wasn't sure, and "Cole," whoever he was, hadn't been much more explicit.

"I have to tell you that I'm jealous," Laney said, after she listened to what I'd done with my day. She took a sip of her margarita and cocked her head at me.

"Why would you be jealous?"

"Well, maybe not jealous—that's too harsh—but envious."

"Still confused over here."

She sighed. "You've got a whole new lease on life, and you're following a dream by interviewing for this assistant job."

I played with my beer bottle, thinking about that for a second. "I don't know if this Cole guy could ever fulfill a dream for me. Sounds a bit wacko."

"That's not the point. You're trying to break into a profession that you're passionate about."

"What about you? You've already broken into your profession and you love your job."

"No, I don't."

"Sure you do! You're always telling everyone how much you love it. You always say—"

"Kell," she said, cutting me off. "When I say that, I'm talking in relative terms."

"What do you mean?"

"I like my job enough. I like the people I'm working with, and I consider myself lucky to have a gig like that, but I don't *love* it."

"Really?" For some reason, this disappointed me.

"Did you love your job at Bartley?"

I was quiet.

"See," Laney said. "You didn't love it, either. You were kicking ass and taking names, and you said you wanted to be partner and all that, but you never loved it."

"This is so depressing. Do we know anyone who loves their job?"

We were both quiet now, taking sips of our drinks, struggling to come up with someone, *anyone,* who adored what they did.

"I know!" I said, pointing at Laney. "You're passionate about music. You love that, and you're taking guitar lessons."

Laney scoffed. "That's hardly the same thing."

"It is, too. Instead of thinking about the fact that you'd love to play guitar, you're actually learning how to do it."

"But it's not my job. I mean I wish it was, I'd love to be in a band, but that will never happen."

"One step at a time, right? Maybe you will be someday. Maybe Gear will ask you to join them."

"Never. That's the problem with the guys I date. They invite me backstage and to the studio, but only as arm candy."

"Gear seemed nice."

"He is. He's nicer than the rest, but…" Her voice died away.

"But what?"

"He's got his band and his buddies. He really doesn't need me for much except—sex, I guess."

"Hey, at least you have someone." I thought of the load

of Ben's belongings—the grubby flannel pajamas he loved, his financial books and the sunglasses he'd spent $200 on— that I'd stuffed in a Hefty bag and thrown down the garbage chute that afternoon.

"Well, you could have *someone,* you know," Laney said. "You could date someone just to date, instead of thinking where it might lead. You could have a fling for once, instead of being a serial monogamist."

"Don't start, Lane."

"I'm just speaking the truth."

"It's entirely possible that I might have a fling," I said.

Laney guffawed.

"Seriously. I'm a different person than I was a few days ago. I might have a one-night stand tonight."

"Yeah. Right."

"Maybe this Cole guy. Maybe I'll sleep with him."

I wasn't sure why I was protesting so much, except that sometimes I found myself woefully embarrassed about the fact that I'd never picked up a guy and slept with him. It wasn't as if I was living at the turn of the century. Everyone I knew had had a few one-night stands—at least—so why not me? It wasn't for lack of opportunity—the bar scene was filled with men looking for action. But Laney was right. I had those set plans in my head about getting married and having a kid by a certain age. I was always looking to see if a guy could take me somewhere, if he might be something special. On the other hand, Ben certainly hadn't turned out all that special. Maybe a fling was exactly what I needed.

"Your new potential employer?" Laney said, still laughing. "You're going to have a one-night stand with your new boss?"

"It's entirely possible!"

"All right then," Laney said, throwing some bills on the table, "let's go get you some sex."

* * *

"This has to be it," I said, checking for the third time the scrap of paper where I'd written Cole's address.

Laney and I were standing in front of a large warehouse, just south of the Loop near Printer's Row.

"He said it was his 'flat.' Isn't that British for apartment?" I said.

"Maybe *flat* means dump."

It was true. The warehouse was no prize. Thick bars guarded grime-covered windows, and the brick was flaking and crumbling. It was a long way from the marble and mahogany of the Bartley Brothers' offices.

"Maybe we should go get another drink and forget this." I shifted my camera bag to my other shoulder. Orange light from the sunset hovered behind the Sears Tower and the other skyscrapers. Soon it would be dark. Why wasn't I in my old plush office right now, tying up the day's loose ends, still drawing a hefty paycheck? I'd worked my ass off for almost a decade and had nothing to show for it.

Laney took the address from my hand. "What the hell? We've come this far, and you still might get laid tonight."

"You know I'm not going to sleep with him," I said, irritated for pretending a one-night stand was in my repertoire.

Still, I followed Laney around the side of the warehouse, where we found a huge metal door that was propped slightly open with a wooden block. Inside was a dreary little foyer with a set of buzzers. Laney looked at the address once more and pressed the button for number 3. There were no names by the buzzers, and I wondered if we were about to stumble into some sort of pornography den. Maybe that's why Cole had asked me about my nationality. Maybe he was doing a Paddy-and-the-Irish-Girls kind of a flick.

After a second, the intercom came on and the same abrupt, British-sounding "Yeah?" that I'd heard on the phone today bellowed into the lobby.

"It's Kelly McGraw. I'm here for the interview."

He buzzed us in, and Laney and I took a rickety freight elevator to the third floor.

"How do I look?" I said, pulling at the ends of my hair.

"See? You do want to sleep with him."

"*Lane,* please."

"Sorry. Not what you were looking for, hmm?" She peered at my face, then tucked my hair behind my ears. "Perfect. Absolutely perfect. If he doesn't hire you he's nuts."

The elevator creaked to a stop and opened onto a massive room that must have taken up the whole span of the building. One end housed the living quarters, judging from the rumpled bed and tiny yellow kitchenette overflowing with dirty dishes. To our right was every photographer's dream— a wide-open space with tall (clean) windows that would surely let in tons of light during the day. The hardwood floors were scarred but beautiful, and the exposed brick and ductwork gave it the perfect studio feel. The problem was that my pornography fears appeared to be coming true.

In front of a white backdrop was a topless model sitting on a shiny white washing machine. Her arms were crossed over her chest, and she was smiling demurely at the spiky-haired man photographing her.

He must have heard us come in because he yelled, "At ease," to the model, who dropped her arms—along with her demure smile—and leaned back on her elbows. I looked to the floor, trying not to stare at her breasts. "And Vicky, you can go," he said to a woman, who was apparently a make-up artist.

"So, which one of you is Kelly Kelly?" the man said, walking toward us.

He was lean and wiry, probably in his mid-thirties, although the sharp lines around the jade-green eyes made him look a little older. The lines, combined with his disarming smile, gave him a somewhat wicked appearance. He reminded me of Chaz Miccelli, a guy from high school who used to smoke pot between classes and slump at the back of the room. Laney and I would roll our eyes and mutter "gross," whenever we passed him, but Chaz had a way of looking at me, a devious way of smiling, that made me go home to my four-poster bed and fantasize about him.

"I'm Kelly McGraw." I stretched out my hand.

"Cole," he said, shaking it. He looked at Laney. "And who, may I ask, is this?" he said.

"Laney Pendleton." She stepped forward with a little swing to her hips. "Official friend."

They shook hands, both smiling at each other, until I felt I had to say *something*.

"Look. Thanks for having me up, Cole, but this probably isn't the position for me. I'm not prepared to work on these kinds of shoots."

His eyebrows shot up. "What on earth do you mean by that?"

"You know." I waved an arm at the model, who sighed loudly. "Ethically, I can't be involved in something like this."

Cole glanced back at the model, then at me. "I see. You're ethically opposed to washing machines then?"

"No, of course not. It's not that. It's…"

"Come have a look," he said.

I hesitated.

"I won't bite," he said. "I promise."

He led us down a few stairs toward the studio area and picked up a contact sheet on a table, handing me a loupe to look through. The shots, featuring the topless model in various poses across the machine, were surprisingly tasteful. None of them showed her breasts, or her spread-eagle as I'd feared. In fact, the way he'd shot them, in black and white, from below, and with the model's hair hanging over her face, made them artistic.

"You've heard of Spring Clean Washers?" Cole said.

I nodded, raising my head from the contact sheet.

"They're trying to sex up their image a bit." Cole gave us another wicked grin. "But look, you're obviously involved in some sort of antiwasher movement, so you're right. You're probably not the one for the job."

"No... I... It's just—"

"Hey, Beckett," the model called, interrupting my stammering. "Let's get the show on the road." She threw her brown hair over her shoulder, her breasts swinging with the movement.

I leaned forward as if I could somehow confirm what I'd heard. "Did she just call you Beckett?"

He turned away from us and picked up his camera again. "Thanks for coming by," he called over his shoulder.

I looked at Laney, who appeared amused with the whole situation.

"Did she just call him Beckett?" I said in a fierce whisper.

"Sounded like it. Why? Will that make you want to sleep with him?"

I gave her my sternest, meanest look and took a few steps toward Cole. "Are you Coley Beckett?"

"I'm called Cole now." He snapped a shot, the flash booming, making me blink.

The model had her arms over her chest again, but she smirked. "Just don't ask him why he's not in New York anymore," she said. "He doesn't like that question."

"That's right, Michelle," Cole said. "Now keep your mouth shut and smile."

I could do nothing but stand there, helpless, wondering if my "ethical" talk had prevented me from being an assistant to one of the most famous photographers of the last decade. Coley Beckett was a fashion photographer—or at least he had been—and he was as renowned for his antics and bad-boy image as he was for his work. In college, we'd studied his photographs, spread across the pages of *Vogue* and all the other glossies, my professor gushing about how *insightful,* how *sensory* Beckett was for someone so young. I didn't know about insightful and sensory, but I knew that his pictures always made me feel something—not always good emotions, but always something. That's what I wanted to do, too. I wanted to take pictures that made people feel. After college, I'd followed his career. He was in the press because of his partying, his steady stream of model girl-friends…but then something happened a few years ago, something big that got him blacklisted from the business, but no one seemed to know what his grievous crime actually was. He'd dropped out of sight, as far as I knew, and now here he was in a warehouse studio in the South Loop.

Beckett snapped another few shots and told Michelle they were finished. The model stepped into her clothes and, as she went to leave, leaned in to kiss him on the lips. Beckett turned his head quickly so that the kiss landed on his cheek. The woman sighed and strode past us to the elevator.

Beckett began cleaning up his lenses, putting them in a large black case. I was still too stunned to know what to do.

"Kell," Laney said in a low voice. "Are we staying or going?"

I looked at her, then back at Beckett. "Excuse me," I said, practically tiptoeing toward him. "I'm sorry if I said anything to upset you, but—"

He gave a sharp, caustic laugh, yet said nothing.

"So can we talk about the assistant job?" I took a few more steps toward him.

"Why?"

"Look. I love your stuff. I always have, and I'd like to learn from you, if you'd let me, and help you at the same time."

He looked up from packing his lenses. "Do you have a portfolio with you?"

I handed it to him.

He flipped through my prints, too quickly it seemed.

When he was done, he took two out of the bunch and placed them on the table. One was a picture of Dee, taken a few months before she died. She was holding a wineglass and laughing, a candle flickering in front of her, the light making an oval halo. The other was taken at North Avenue Beach, the sand rippled from the strong Chicago wind.

"Which of these," Cole asked, "do you prefer?"

I pointed to the one of Dee.

"Why?"

"Because of the subject. That's my sister. Or it was." I shook my head. "Anyway, it's not technically the better photo of the two. The texture is better in the other one, and the lighting, but I like this one the best."

Cole placed the two photos back in my portfolio. "You're absolutely right. The one of the lake is much better. Do you know what ambient light is?"

Was this a quiz? If so, his questions were easy. "Sure, it's just natural light."

"And aperture?"

"It's the opening of a lens."

"And the size of the lens is controlled by what?"

I had to think about that one. "The diaphragm?"

Another nod. "Which lets in more light, an f/8 or an f/5.6?"

I thought for another second. "The 5.6."

Cole leaned his head back, perusing my face. "Well, you seem brighter than the coeds I've been interviewing, and I've been without an assistant for seven months. Also, I need someone with an 'official friend.'" He leaned past me and gave Laney that wicked smile. "So you're all right," he said, looking at me again.

"All right? What does that mean?"

"It means you're hired. I'll see you tomorrow at noon."

9

Laney invited me to stay with her again, but I knew I couldn't do that forever. I hailed a cab back uptown to the Lake Shore Drive apartment I'd come to consider my new place. In my mind, I tried to pretend that I'd chosen it knowingly, that it had a sort of hominess to it, some feelings of coziness and comfort. Once I was there, though, I was restless and antsy. I had a photography job! Starting tomorrow! Granted, this Cole character wasn't my dream boss, but everyone had to start somewhere, right? I was partly nervous, partly excited and partly nauseous at the thought that I was nervous and excited about a job that an eighteen-year-old could get when I should have been moving into a partner's office.

My stomach churned at the thought of Ben getting his own partner office. I'd taken down the shrine of Ben photos that afternoon, and I felt like defiling one of them now, maybe cutting his head out and pasting it onto a picture of a goat, but I knew I'd regret that someday, the same way I regretted so many other graceful gestures I'd decided to make when I was pissed off. (The time I "accidentally" spilled coffee on Attila's keyboard comes to mind.)

So I sort of drifted around my apartment. The fact that it was now free of all my clutter and junk made it feel even less like my home, as did the fact that my furniture seemed to be in the wrong place. I went into my bedroom where my other framed photos were and brought them into the living room and kitchen, sprinkling them around on the end tables and the countertops, so that my mom, Dee, Laney and Jess smiled out at me from all corners of the apartment. While I did this I wondered why all the photos were in the bedroom to begin with. Was that where I'd spent most of my time?

I went back in the bedroom and looked around for anything that might give me the answer to that question, or, even better, the answer to the bigger question of why I couldn't recall this past summer. I suddenly focused on my jewelry box sitting on the end of the bureau. What if I'd been pawning off family jewels to buy drugs? Maybe I was a coke whore and I simply couldn't remember it. But I didn't seem to be craving anything. I looked through my jewelry box and ruled out that possibility. There weren't really any family jewels, anyway, at least not anything that other people would be interested in. Just my mom's modest platinum ring with the small inset diamonds that had been her wedding band when she married my father, and the pearl earrings that my mom's mom had left to me in her will.

Lacking anything better to do, I put on my favorite flannel pajamas, the blue ones with the white fluffy clouds, and got in bed. Leaning against the headboard, I picked up one of the three spy novels I had on the nightstand. It was dog-eared but I had no memory of ever reading this book. I started reading and got sucked into a tale of a young man traveling through Russia who stumbles onto a college where they train Russians to act and talk like Americans so that they can infiltrate our country. The novel was written during the Cold War, and as a result, no longer had the urgency or scary undertones to it, but it did get me to thinking about my own situation. What if *I,* not Beth Maninsky, was the covert operative for the CIA? Maybe I'd been involved in a shoot-out during an undercover investigation or maybe I'd seen something horrifying that could change the world, and as a result, I'd lost my memories of the past five months. I liked this potential. I liked the thought of myself in black leather, packing heat, sneaking around the Kremlin or some such place. The problem was that I could recall my whole life prior to these last five months, and I was quite sure that I had never been a spy.

Another potential came to me: maybe as part of my job in the financial industry I'd stumbled onto an explosive international secret. It was possible that they'd surgically removed a part of my brain so I couldn't recall it. What secret I might have found while studying retail stocks and who "they" were I wasn't quite sure, but I rather liked this theory, as well. It took any blame away from me.

I slid my fingers through my hair and felt around my head for healed incisions or telltale bumps, and I discovered absolutely nothing.

Okay. What kind of job starts at noon? I'd been too startled to really think about it when Cole had said I was hired, but by nine-thirty Tuesday morning it seemed ridiculous that I didn't have to be at work yet. By the time I would get there, most people would be halfway done with their day.

I hadn't slept well the night before, and as a result, I felt a little like Laney. I'd been up since five, and since then I'd cleaned my camera and all my lenses. I'd picked out a professional yet casual outfit of black pants and a crisp white shirt. I'd dug out my coffeemaker from a cabinet, made myself a pot, and now I still had two hours to go.

Earlier this morning, from my living room window, I'd watched the normal people bustle by in their suits or their business casual, all heading to the train or bus that would take them to their jobs, ones that paid more than the few bucks an hour I'd get from Cole. By now, everyone was gone except for a few beer delivery trucks and a couple of stragglers.

I'm not sure why I was so concerned about the measly hourly wage that Cole would pay me. I had enough money to last for the next few months at least, and it wasn't as if I was worth much in the photography field, with my limited experience. I guess what was bothering me was the thought of the salary and bonuses I used to make at Bartley Brothers. Strangely, I hadn't gone into the financial world for the money, but in the end it was what had held me there, like a pair of golden handcuffs. It was what was drawing me back even now. Most of my old colleagues, Ben included, were fascinated by money, by the thought of making a lot of it, and that's what brought them to Bartley Brothers. I was the exception to that rule.

I'd wanted to be an analyst in the financial world because of my father. He'd taken off when I was just a baby, which made him a mysterious figure to me. My mom must have sensed that and, maybe wanting to compensate for the fact that I had no dad, often made him sound clever and intriguing.

"Your father played the stock market," she would say, "and he was the best." For years, I imagined a Monopoly-like board game called The Stock Market that my dad was an ace at. I pictured him deftly moving bright plastic pieces around the playing field, everyone else groaning at his brilliant maneuvering. Eventually, after my seventh-grade class learned to track stock prices in the paper, I'd realized what the market really was, and that's when I decided that I wanted to be a stock picker, just like my dad. I fantasized that by going into his field, I would get to know him some-how, maybe give him a reason to stick around. I knew bet-ter than to mention this to my mom, who by that time never had anything positive to say about him, and so I grew up, always secretly knowing what I would do with my life. I got a business degree from the University of Chicago and landed a job with Bartley Brothers. It wasn't until I'd been there three years that I'd confided to my mom the reason why I'd chosen my profession.

She'd looked at me as if I'd slapped her. "Kelly, I never said he was in the stock market."

"Yes, you did. A bunch of times."

She thought about that for a second, and then sadly shook her head. "I didn't mean for you to take it literally."

"Are you saying he didn't play the stock market for a living?"

"Well, he was in banking."

"What, exactly, did he do in banking?"

My mom scratched at her scalp. "He sold blank checks to banks. And he wasn't even very good at that."

I don't think I ever forgave her for shining such a false light on my father, the light that made me follow his phan-tom form into a world he didn't even work in. But by then it was too late. I was on my way up, I was making a shit-load of money and I'd gotten used to it.

I turned away from the window and began to clean my apartment, but it was already spotless. I tried to watch TV, but like yesterday, as I flipped and flipped and flipped, there was nothing on. I began to feel more and more jittery. When I could no longer convince myself that it was the coffee, I muted the TV and called Laney at work.

"Laney Pendleton," she answered, sounding out of breath and rushed.

"Hey, it's me."

"Hi, hon. What's going on?"

"I think I'm having a panic attack."

"What? Hold on, I'll close the door." There was a pause, the sound of Laney saying something to Deb, her assistant, then the thud of a door closing. "Okay," she said. "Shoot."

"What am I doing taking this job? That Cole guy used to be famous, but c'mon, I'm not a photographer. I'm not some freshman living in a dorm. I'm thirty years old, for Christ's sake, and—"

"Hold it," Laney said, her tone brusque now. "Are you kidding me with this?"

"No. I don't even have to be in until noon. What kind of job starts at noon?" On the TV, Oprah was consoling a crying woman. I flipped to CNN.

"I meant the panic attack, Kell. You're not really having one, are you?"

"It's an expression." Why was she being so technical?

"It didn't *used* to be an expression for you."

I took a quiet moment to process this. "Oh, shit. I'm sorry. Did I really have panic attacks?"

"A few times."

"Jesus." Just the thought of myself having a panic attack was depressing. I was suddenly glad that I had an appointment with Ellen Geiger tonight. "I'm really sorry."

Laney sighed. "That's all right."

"No, it's not. I've put way too much pressure on you this last year. You've had to do too much. I'm sorry. I really am."

"You'd do it for me," she said.

"I would, and I want to do it for you right now, so tell me what's happening over there." I clicked the TV off with a firm press of my thumb. I would give Laney my full attention. Something she'd been doing for me for months.

"It's nothing. It'll be fine."

"C'mon. Tell me. You're just not used to confiding in me anymore and you sound frazzled."

"Well, I am, if you want to know the truth. I've just about had it. Deb has completely dropped the ball on our tampon ad campaign."

"Mmm," I murmured to keep her going, deciding not to mention the funny fact that she had a lot of genitally related marketing projects—the herpes and now the tampons.

"She *said* she was going to type up my notes and arrange a meeting with the clients and coordinate it with Creative, and I've seen her on the phone around the clock, but it turns out she's been interviewing caterers and florists for her wedding! And I can't fire her, not now. She's the only one who knows how to read my handwriting, and she understands everything in this department if she'd just get off her ass and do it. And…"

Laney went on for a good fifteen minutes, during which time I murmured my understanding and finally made some suggestions to deal with the wedding-obsessed Deb.

"I feel so much better," Laney said. "Thanks for listening."

"No problem." Actually, it had been a treat to get out of my head for once.

"Okay, so tell me what's up with the job," Laney said, "and please do not use the words *panic attack*."

"Deal. Here's the thing. I'm way too old for something like this."

"Like what?"

"A frigging *assistantship*. Being an assistant is something you do when you're just starting out."

"Aren't you just starting out in photography?"

"Yes, but maybe it's too late to begin something like this. I should have done it a long time ago. It's embarrassing to be making a paltry hourly wage at thirty."

"Why?"

I struggled to find an answer for that one. I finally settled for, "People will talk."

"Who?"

"Well, the Bartley people for one. I had a 401K and insurance and a pension plan over there. And now look at me!"

"I'm looking, but I don't see what you're talking about. This is an opportunity of a lifetime."

"But I'm giving up the path that I was on, the one I worked so damn hard at."

"Can't you climb the corporate ladder after you've done this for a while and gone through the money you have? Couldn't you get another analyst job then if you want it?"

"And what am I supposed to say at an interview? That for a year or so I've been lying on my couch, going to therapy and probably making coffee for a crazy, washed-up Brit?"

Laney sighed again. I could hear the door open and Deb saying something to her. "Kell, look. Do you want to do this?"

"I don't know. I mean this guy *used* to be famous, but who knows if he's even any good anymore?"

"That's not what I mean. I'm asking you, in a perfect world, would you want to make a living doing photography?"

"Yes." I didn't have to ponder for even a millisecond.

"Then listen to me. It doesn't matter that you're doing grunt work or that you wish you'd done this in college— or that people will talk. What matters is that you've got a shot, and you've got some time to do it. Granted, it might be harder to get back into the investment banks later, but you'll always be able to be an analyst. You might not make as much money as you did before, but you know it's true."

Though she couldn't see me, I nodded. "Thanks, Lane. Again. You're my savior."

She chuckled. "Tell that boss of yours I said hi."

* * *

Cole's building was no less scary in the daylight, and the closed blinds inside his place made it seem like nighttime again.

"I'll finish shooting the washer ad today," I heard Cole say when I was a few steps out of the elevator.

I still had my coat on, my eyes hadn't adjusted to the dark and we hadn't even greeted each other, so all I could do was blink and say, "Okay."

When my eyes started working again, I saw that he was standing near a tall butcher-block table, the kind most people would have in their kitchen, only his was covered with film and notes and contact sheets. He flipped through a few of the sheets. "I'm not happy with the light in here."

I looked around, thinking, *What light in here?* Even the shades in his living quarters were pulled down.

He lifted his spiky-haired head and looked at me. "I'm going to need you to hold the strobe."

"You don't have a stand for it?"

"I do, but I want *you* to hold it." His tone had a faint snippiness to it, but it could have been just the British accent. Or maybe this strobe-holding thing was some punishing ritual similar to fraternity hazing. I was a photographic pledge in the house of Beckett.

Since he obviously wasn't going to tell me where to put my coat, I slung it over a chair just outside the elevator. I walked down the few steps to where he stood and looked over his shoulder, seeing that each little rectangle in the contact sheet showed the topless model and her best friend, the Spring Clean Washing Machine. As I glanced at the sheet, I noticed, out of the corner of my eye, that Cole's hair was wet, as if he'd just gotten up and taken a shower. Then I realized why we'd started so late—Cole was apparently still the bad-boy of the photography world, even though he was in Chicago now. He'd probably been out all night boozing with a gaggle of models.

"I need a soft-focus effect." Cole peered at the contact sheets.

"Couldn't you move the lens or shake the camera?" Those were two of the tricks I'd learned in my last class, and I felt ridiculously proud of myself for being able to dredge them out of my head.

"Hypothetically," Cole said, the British snippiness creeping back into his tone, "but I'd rather have you holding the light."

"I'll never be able to keep it perfectly still."

"That's right, Kelly Kelly," Cole said, sounding distinctly bored with me. "The light won't be as static, and it will soften the effect."

I'd never thought about that approach. The pledge had already learned something.

Unfortunately, the pledge obviously hadn't lifted weights or done any kind of physical activity in her five months on the couch. Within two minutes of holding the lights, my arms began to shake. Michelle, the same model from the night before, was back in her black bikini bottoms, this time on her stomach over the washer, her knees bent, her feet crossed. I had to give her credit for her abilities. When Cole was snapping pictures, her face was smooth and serene, as if lying on a household appliance made her the happiest woman in the world. When he took a break, she dropped the serene look and said things like, "Shit, it's cold in here. My nipples could cut glass." There was no stylist on this shoot—apparently too low budget—but Vicky, the makeup artist, would scurry up to Michelle, hand her moisturizer to massage into her breasts and ply her with pancake foundation. I took those opportunities to drop the light for a second and massage my arms instead of my breasts.

"Right," Cole said an hour or so into it. "Let's go again, shall we?"

I took a deep breath, like an Olympic wrestler about to enter the ring, and raised the light above my head again.

This time, I watched Cole instead of Michelle, searching for any of those British stereotypes from the *Austin Powers* movies. Bad teeth? It was hard to tell since he rarely smiled, but soon he grinned at something Michelle said, and I could see that they were white and quite straight. Bad dresser? No, I wouldn't say bad—rather, interesting. Today he had on black pants, black Doc Maartens and a navy-blue shirt with a French word in bright orange. I wondered what the word meant. And what about the stereotype that British men say "shag" all the time and do, in fact, want to shag everyone they come into contact with? Well, Cole must have been the exception because it was clear that Michelle was hitting on him, and he seemed oblivious. During a break, she sauntered up to him all cute and naked, ostensibly to look at the contact sheets from the day before, but he barely seemed to notice her brown, "glass-cutting" nipples hovering mere inches from his face. And he certainly wasn't hitting on me. If anything, he'd forgotten I was there, a fact that made me focus again on the thought that an uneducated, eighteen-year-old could have done my job. Hell, a particularly strong twelve-year-old could have done it.

At about four o'clock, Cole announced that he'd gotten enough shots and thanked us for our time. The makeup woman left first, then Michelle. As she had the night before, she strolled toward the door, threw her hair over her shoulder and tried to kiss him on her way out. But he turned fast on his Doc Maartens and thanked her very much for her good work. Maybe he hadn't been out with a gaggle of models last night. Or maybe he was gay. I didn't get that vibe from him but my vibe meter was notoriously inaccurate on this subject.

I had initially noticed my deficient gaydar in college with the first guy I dated there, Remy Stanson.

"Oh, he's *so* gay," Laney had said when she came to visit on a football weekend. We were in my dorm room filling flasks with pink schnapps, and Remy had just gone down the hall to use the men's room.

"He is not!" I said indignantly. Remy was only the second guy I'd ever slept with, and Laney's proclamation seemed a slam against me as well as him.

"Yes. He is," she said, still concentrating on pouring the thick liquid into the silver metal opening.

At the football game, I watched Remy yelling, "Defense, defense!" just like every other male, and I knew Laney was wrong. He met none of the gay stereotypes—he wasn't effeminate, he wasn't a particularly sharp dresser and he wasn't prettier than I was. But a month later, while I was searching for a pair of socks to wear home from his apartment, I came across a stash of gay porn at the bottom of a drawer, and I had to admit to Laney she was right.

Unfortunately, my gaydar didn't get any better. After Remy, I refused to see the light about George Michael, whom I'd had a crush on since his *Wham!* days. Again, Laney kept telling me that I was an idiot, that he was clearly homosexual.

"But he says 'Wake me up before you go, *girl*,'" I protested.

"It's 'Wake me up before you go, *go*,'" she explained, yet I remained unconvinced until he was caught in that bathroom.

So now I knew that I certainly couldn't make any judgments about Cole.

"All right, Kelly Kelly," he said when Michelle had left. "I need you to clean something for me."

"Sure." Finally something other than strong-arming the lights. "Your lenses?"

He looked up at me, then back down at the camera he was disassembling. "No. And don't ever touch my lenses unless I tell you to."

I swallowed down a snappy retort. This was my first day on the job. As Laney had said, I had to start somewhere. "Okay. What then?"

"The floor."

"Excuse me?" I covered the strobe light with a sheet and came a little closer to him.

"I need you to mop the floor," he said, in a tone that suggested *What else would you be doing?*

I thought of my job at Bartley Brothers, where the hardest manual labor I'd ever done was raise my Starbucks cup to my mouth. "Don't you have a cleaning service?"

"Not until the weekend, and I've got another shoot starting tomorrow."

"Well, cleaning really isn't part of my job description, is it?"

He scoffed. "Your job description is whatever the hell I tell you to do, so go." He made a shooing motion with his hand. "The supplies are in the closet."

I hesitated for a very long moment. *What was I doing here?* I had a business degree from the University of Chicago. I had worked for one of the most respected banks in the world. I wasn't a goddamn maid. If this was what it took to "start over" in a new career, I didn't know if I wanted it that badly.

"Kelly, go," Cole said, shooing me with his hand again.

I hated him right then. I knew he was doing this to test me, to see if I'd walk out the door as I was contemplating doing. He was demeaning me on purpose.

Well, I wouldn't let him win. I turned and stomped toward the closet, but my irritation slid into something darker. "Jesus fucking Christ," I muttered as my boots clomped on his hardwood floor.

Using Jesus's name as a nifty expletive told me that one of my temper flares was looming on the horizon. Usually I tried to fight them when I got that initial feeling. I would take deep breaths, à la my meditation tapes. I would tell myself to calm down and get over it. I would dig the brown candle from under the sink and hurl it. Today, though, I didn't even make the attempt to quash the instinct. It was familiar, the red angry flush that came over me, making me feel like I was the same person I'd always been—not at all someone who would sit in a dark apartment for months or stalk her ex-boyfriend. A token of my original self. And so I held on to it, letting it fill my head.

I kept stomping and slamming around with the broom and the bucket until I heard Cole call out something about watching for streaks.

"Mother-fucking asshole," I muttered. Unfortunately, it came out louder than a mutter. In fact, there was nothing truly muttering about it. I held my breath for a second to see if Cole had heard me. Silence. I glanced over my shoulder and across the room. I saw his stunned face, mouth a little open. Humph. Served him right. I stood a little taller, knowing he wouldn't be messing with me anymore, but then I heard him laugh.

It was sort of a chuckle at first, but it quickly skidded into outright belly laughing.

"Oh, God," Cole said, between snorting and slapping his thigh. "Did *you* just call me a mother-fucking *arse*hole?" This, apparently, was the funniest thing he'd ever heard. "God, that's priceless!"

Before I could come up with what to say to my employer, albeit an unconventional one, who'd just heard me call him a filthy name, he turned and walked into his darkroom, where I could still hear him laughing.

His laughter was like water to my temper tantrum. It completely squelched it, leaving me crabby and embarrassed, with nothing to do but quit or clean. I went to the sink and filled up the bucket.

The mop was noxious and stringy, and it gave me shivers. As I maneuvered it around his bed, I thought about pouring the bucket of water on his sheets. When I swabbed around a table that held a few lenses, I felt an overwhelming, childish urge to drop one on the floor. I restrained myself, knowing that if I did, I'd be dropping the job, too, a possibility that didn't seem so horrible anymore. I decided that I'd give Coley Beckett until the end of the week. If this gig didn't somehow get better, I was out of here.

"Mind the lenses," I heard Cole say from behind me. I hadn't heard him leave the darkroom.

I swiveled around and leaned on the handle of the noxious mop. "Excuse me?"

"Mind the lenses," he repeated. He was slumped in a beanbag chair now, not really looking at me. He flipped through a black book that looked like an appointment calendar. Back to his usual surly personality.

"I know how to mop a floor."

"Excellent. Just take care around the equipment."

I resumed my scrubbing, moving the mop in hurried, angry strokes.

"Christ, you missed a spot," I heard from behind me.

Deep breath in, deep breath out. "Where?"

He nodded toward a dark circle on the floor.

"It won't come out."

"Try harder."

"Is this asshole behavior the reason you were run out of New York?"

He froze. I could tell by the way his finger was poised in midair over his book. Finally he looked up at me, silent.

"Is it?" I said, not caring that I might be fired.

The lines around his eyes seemed to deepen, and suddenly, Cole looked like a sad little boy. "You wouldn't know anything about that," he said, in a low, almost inaudible voice.

There was a weird, melancholy air around us now. I wasn't sure what had happened or what to make of it. I finished the mopping without comment from Cole, and spent the rest of the time breaking down the washing machine set. I didn't know what kind of shoot was happening the next day, and Cole had barely spoken to me except to tell me where to put things. After a few hours of silence, I actually missed the sarcastic snippiness.

"You can leave now." Cole called to me from inside the darkroom.

"Okay, thanks," I yelled back. Why was I thanking him? The silent hours had unnerved me, I guess. Still, I was excited to escape the place. Maybe I'd talk Laney into getting a margarita at Uncle Julio's Hacienda, or maybe I'd go see a movie.

But then I remembered that I had other plans. Ellen Geiger. I had half an hour to get uptown to see my shrink.

10

Ellen Geiger lived on the first floor of an elegant graystone on State Street, one of those places built at the turn of the century, with iron carriage posts out front and stone lions guarding either side of the door. At least I assumed Ellen still lived there and was still using the front room as her office. I checked the name by the doorbell just to be sure.

As I waited for her to answer, I glanced up the street toward Lincoln Park, which was lit up by tall round lights. I wondered if Ellen's practice was lucrative enough for her to own this house so close to the park and the lake. Maybe it was a family home, or maybe she had a wealthy husband. The problem with therapy was that the conversation was so one-sided you rarely learned much about the person hearing your deepest secrets. As a result, Ellen probably knew more about my last five months than I did.

I heard the soft tap, tap, tap of footsteps, then a golden glow came from inside as the hall light was turned on.

"Kelly," Ellen said, opening the door. "Come in."

She was probably in her late thirties or early forties, and she struck me as someone who could look totally sexy if she wanted to. For all I knew she broke out the leather jeans and fuck-me stilettos on the weekends, but for work she nearly always wore conservative, secretarylike attire. Today she had on a wine-colored cardigan sweater over a white blouse and straight black skirt. She wore low, tasteful black pumps. Her ashy-blond hair was pulled back by a velvet headband.

"How are you?" She gestured for me to come into her office, a small but stylish room with a huge bay window. I assumed that window overlooked the street, but the heavy silk drapes in front of it were always closed tight and the place lamplit, like now. I wondered if Ellen threw open the drapes after her last client left, tore the headband from her hair and headed for a pitcher of martinis in the fridge.

"I'm good," I said, noting mentally that I was particularly curious about Ellen today. The few visits that I could remember with her after Dee had died, I'd just marched up the steps, fell into the couch and talked, talked, talked, not concerned about Ellen or her life. Maybe it was because I was feeling so much better now. I had more space in my thoughts for other people.

Another thought—maybe I was nervous about this meeting, about what Ellen might tell me.

She took a seat next to her desk and watched me in that expectant way of hers, waiting, I'm sure, for me to launch into a diatribe about all my issues. The problem was, I honestly didn't feel as though I had any that I wanted to discuss with her.

Someone had to break the silence, though, so I finally opened my mouth and said, "How are *you?*"

This caused Ellen to blink a few times. Apparently, she

didn't get asked that question very often. "Fine, fine, but I'm concerned about your loss of memory. Why don't you tell me about that."

"I pretty much told you everything on the phone, and as I mentioned then, I feel great. Better than I have in a long time."

"Mmm-hmm. What do you think caused this gap in your memory?"

A legit question. "I honestly don't know. That's one thing I am wondering about. Can you tell me about the different reasons that someone might lose their memory?"

"Well, psychologically and psychiatrically speaking there are a number of reasons. Trauma, alcohol abuse, senile dementia—"

"Dementia? Isn't that just another word for crazy?" I said defensively.

Ellen grinned. "We don't think of it like that, and I don't think you're crazy, Kelly."

"Then what do you think it could be?"

"Well, first we'd have to rule out a physical cause for your amnesia. Have you had any physical problems?"

"Nope," I said, deciding not to mention my alcohol-driven headaches.

"I'd still like you to see a colleague of mine at Northwestern. Dr. Hagar." She leaned forward and handed me a business card.

I slid it in my bag without looking at it. "You're an M.D., aren't you?"

She nodded.

"So why can't you give me your opinion?"

"Why are you so anxious about the cause?"

"Wouldn't you be? I can't figure out why I don't remember the last five months. I know I was down, depressed, whatever you want to call it. My friend told me that I'd been seeing you a lot—"

"Who told you that?"

She'd stopped me in midthought. "Excuse me?" I said. "What friend told you that?"

"Laney." I watched her face for a reaction that I knew she wouldn't reveal. The woman should play professional poker in Vegas. "Why?"

"Mmm-hmm. Just curious. Keep going."

I was frustrated now. "Can't I ask you some questions for a change?"

"Of course."

"I'd like to know your opinion about why I can't remember."

"Mmm-hmm." She pursed her lips again. "Kelly, I wish I could give you that, but I can't possibly, based on the limited information I have. All I can tell you is that although I saw you a few times last January, I've been seeing you regularly since…" she looked down at the notes on her desk "…mid-May. During that time, we've been dealing with your very natural reactions to your sister's death, the breakup of your relationship with Ben, the loss of your job, your mother's move out west. You've had an extraordinary amount to deal with. Your anger and sadness over these issues are nothing to be embarrassed about."

"I'm not embarrassed. Honestly."

"Then why are you focusing so much on the whys and hows of your current situation, rather than what you've been dealing with for the last half a year?"

I looked down at my lap, and, realizing I still wore my leather jacket, shrugged it off. "Here's the thing. If we talk about those issues that I was dealing with, if we talk about the depression I had, I might remember it, right?"

"That's possible. Memory is very tricky."

"Then I don't want to talk about it, because I don't want to remember any of it."

"Mmm-hmm. Why is that?"

"Would you want to remember that kind of a time? A time when you could barely get out of your pajamas?"

No response from Ellen.

"Look at me," I said, holding up my hands in sort of an offering. "I don't need a doctor. I feel great. Why would I *ever* want to recall that time?"

"I understand what you're saying, but I think it's dangerous to push that time away."

"I'm not pushing it away, I'm just not trying to remember."

Ellen looked at me for a long moment. "I think in your situation, that's the same thing. However, I see your reluctance to discuss this issue, and so I'm going to let it go. I just need to ask you a few questions for clarification."

I took a breath and nodded, relieved that she was going to drop it. As I waited for her to talk, I noticed that one of the lamps on the desk was sending a yellow ring of light over Ellen's blond hair, and that the headband had some kind of glitter on it. Maybe she did have those stilettos in the closet, the martinis in the fridge, after all.

"Are you still taking your meds?" she said.

I thought of the prescription bottles I'd found in my apartment, the ones that still sat in the kitchen cabinet. "No."

"You know, you really must wean yourself off those. You can't just stop."

"Too late. I don't even know the last time I took one."

"Just so I understand this completely. Do you not recall *anything* at all about those months?"

"Nothing." Great, could we move on here?

Ellen read something in her notes. She seemed to be going over and over one particular entry.

"What is it?" I said.

"Something had been troubling you," she said.

"I know, I know—Ben, Dee, the job." I tried to keep the irritation out of my voice. Were we going back to that again?

"Well, you were very caught up with Ben. You seemed

to think that if you could get back together with him, the rest of your life would improve, a notion I tried to rid you of. But there was something else that was bothering you, as well." Ellen glanced at me, that expectant look on her face again.

"What was it?" I blurted out.

She shook her head slowly. "That's the thing. I don't know, either. I can't be sure, but I often felt that you were holding back something. In fact, you essentially admitted that you were. You said you wanted to focus on the other issues, primarily your breakup and your desire to reunite with Ben."

I thought of what Laney had told me on Saturday—that a few weeks after my birthday something sent me from a sitting-around-in-pajamas kind of mood to an antidepressant-popping-and-stalking-Ben kind of mood.

"When did you first note that I was holding something back?"

She glanced down at the desktop. "May 22."

A few weeks after my birthday.

"I didn't tell you anything else?" I asked.

"I wrote here that you were concerned about someone's opinion of you."

My mind sped through a host of possibilities, the people whose opinions I cared about—Laney, Ben, my mom. But I'd talked to Ellen about all of those people.

"I got the distinct feeling," she continued, "that you were focusing so much on the other issues that we've already mentioned because you didn't want to deal with this person or their opinion."

"What was the opinion?"

"I can't say. You wouldn't tell me anything else about it, and ultimately, I had to respect that. It's possible that it was just a minor issue, and I'm making too much of it."

She smiled at me again. Something about the sympathy

in that smile made me realize that she didn't think it had been such a minor issue at all.

The next day, as I rode the El to Cole's place (a starting time of ten instead of noon) I puzzled over my talk with Ellen. Whose opinion was I so concerned about, and what was that person's opinion of me? I gripped a silver bar for balance, the train careening around a corner, feeling a wave of dizziness, an ache in my head. The faces of the other commuters seemed terrifyingly blurry for a few seconds. I could see the red of a man's baseball cap across from me, but it was fuzzy, almost as if the bloody color was undulating. I increased my grip on the bar, afraid of falling to my knees. But then, just as quickly, the dizziness was gone, the other people on the train restored. The dull throb in my head was still there, though. It was just exhaustion, I decided. I'd been going over the same questions all night, barely sleeping more than a few hours. Laney had no guesses for me, but she agreed with Ellen that there was something I'd been concerned about, something I wouldn't tell even her, something that had made me more depressed than I had been.

The train lurched to a stop and a pimply, teenaged kid vacated a seat. I saw another woman about my age eyeing it, but I dived and managed to grab it before her, fearing another dizzy spell.

As I settled into the curved plastic seat, I couldn't help but notice a coolness inside myself. It was separate from my headache, and it wasn't due to the temperature in the train because they had the heat cranked up. The cold feeling was coming from something Laney had said last night.

"I don't know what it was," she'd said on the phone, "but you hinted that someone had given you some news you didn't like, and it was after that you got worse."

Some news you didn't like… I'd gotten an opinion from

this mystery person, and according to Laney and Ellen, that opinion had sent me over the proverbial edge.

The whole thing scared me to death. I could deal with the other issues. I could hear about my birthday night with Ben and feel sad and pissed off. I could think about the fact that I'd lost my job and feel rightfully bewildered and, once again, pissed off. I often thought about Dee—crying when I found a sweater I'd borrowed from her or one of the little notes she used to leave me when she'd stayed the weekend. These issues produced all sorts of emotions in me—sadness, anger, confusion—but despite my hesitations, none of them threatened to return me to that dark place Laney had told me about. None of them truly scared me. This other thing, though, this thing I wouldn't tell Laney or Ellen or apparently anyone, terrified me. If it was enough to make me lose it at the time, couldn't it do the same thing now? As Ellen had said, memory is tricky.

The train stopped at the last station in the Loop, and most of the remaining passengers disembarked. An older, very dirty man with a collection of plastic bags stuffed with God-knows-what fell into the seat across from me and gave me a lecherous grin. I gave him a defiant stare before I looked away. That was my usual tactic—show 'em you're not scared, but don't tempt 'em.

Out of the corner of my eye, I saw the man groping around at something in his lap. I prayed it was one of his bags and not his fly. Still, I wasn't scared of the guy. Leery, maybe, but not scared. What I feared was that other thing that lurked in the city, in my mind somewhere.

"You're late," Cole said, when I walked into his loft at ten-fifteen. He looked pointedly at his watch, then returned his attention to the equipment he was setting up in neat little rows on the butcher-block table—lenses, filters, film.

"The El," I said, not bothering to explain further. In fact,

I had a perfectly legitimate excuse, since the train had come to a stop in between stations and sat there, inexplicably, for twenty minutes before we started moving again. I couldn't bring myself to relate this tale to Cole, though. It seemed beneath me. When I was at Bartley Brothers no one looked at me strangely if I came in fifteen minutes later than usual. No one even blinked, because I was a professional, damn it. I felt a little sinking in my chest. I wasn't a professional now. I was nowhere close to being a professional photographer, and that's why I had to take Cole's shit if I wanted to get anywhere in this business.

"Sorry," I said, mostly under my breath. "Won't happen again."

Cole didn't even acknowledge my half-assed apology, which made me want to retract it. Instead, I made a quick decision to do my best today. None of this thinking that the job was a crappy little gig that a twelve-year-old could do. None of this hostility toward Cole. It was entirely possible that if I changed my attitude for the better, so would he.

"What's on the schedule for today?" I said, throwing my leather jacket over the chair and walking into the studio.

"Commercial shoot." Cole was dressed in yet another pair of black pants and heavy black biker boots.

"You want to tell me what it's for, what we're shooting exactly?" I made my voice pleasant and curious.

He shrugged. "I'll tell you how I want to approach it, because I'll need your help."

"Okay."

"I want to approach the subject like a canvas." He looked up at me, and there was a flicker of excitement in his eyes.

"Okay," I said again, not wanting to ruin the moment, but not having a clue what he was saying.

"This isn't like the Spring Clean shoot, where the company knows exactly what they want the ad to look like. I've got a little more room to work with, you see? So I want to start out with the set as minimal as possible and then build the picture from there, element by element."

I nodded again, excited now myself. "It's like you'll be painting on film. You'll be adding different strokes, different props and backgrounds until you build the picture you want."

Cole gave me the first genuine smile I'd ever seen. "Exactly."

I felt a silly swell of pride. "What do you need me to do?"

"I need you to take down the white seamless and set up the light blue." He gestured toward the dark end of the loft, a place that was jumbled with old furniture and posing stands and other assorted crap.

"Seamless?" My mind whirred through all the information I'd gleaned from my photography classes. Nothing called "seamless" came up.

"Yes, the seamless."

When I responded with a blank stare, he pointed to the area where Michelle and her friendly washing machine had sat the day before. A long roll of white paper, about eight feet wide, hung from two silver posts and was unfurled onto the floor, creating a curved backdrop of sorts.

"It's the backdrop," I said.

"Well, right, but it's called the seamless. I need you to get the one that's light blue like a robin's egg. Can you do that?"

I nodded again, annoyed at his patronizing tone, determined to make a go of it before I asked for help. Besides, I was still excited about this ad that we'd be working on. Maybe it was for Tiffany's! Robin's-egg blue was their color, after all. Maybe they'd bring little goody bags for us, and I'd get that chunky chain necklace I'd always wanted. Maybe this was one of those really artistic ads that Cole would win an award for. Possibly I'd win one as well for being an assistant. Did assistants win awards like that? Probably not, but my contribution to a Tiffany's ad might be something I could talk about at interviews and put in my résumé.

I spent the next twenty minutes enthusiastically picking through rusty chairs, discarded film canisters and a host of strobe and back lights until I found a large roll of light blue paper. It was so long that just carrying it through the rest of the junk made me feel like one of the Three Stooges with a ladder. I spent another twenty minutes trying to set up the damn thing like Cole had said, but the silver stands were too tall, so even if I could launch one side up and get it to stay, I wasn't tall enough to secure the other side.

Finally, I called him over. "It's too high."

"I don't want it *high.* Didn't I say that?"

"No."

"I think I did."

"You didn't."

We glared at each other.

"Well, anyway, it's quite simple." Cole lifted the paper off with one hand, and using hand cranks that I somehow hadn't noticed, slid down the top section of each pole so it was about four feet high.

"You can't even have a model sitting on a chair in front of this. It'll be too short," I said.

Cole looked it up and down, then glanced at the notes in his hand. "It should be fine."

The buzzer sounded a few minutes later, and soon the elevator opened. A thin man with rectangular tortoiseshell glasses and long black sideburns burst into the room.

"Are we ready?" he said, marching straight toward me and my seamless. "Cole, everything ready?"

Obviously Cole and this guy had worked together before because Cole only nodded, a movement the sideburns guy couldn't see, since he was looking at me.

"Artie," he said, fast approaching me, holding out his hand, "I'm Artie Judd."

I grasped his hand, and he gave me a dry, quick pump of a handshake. "Kelly McGraw."

"Nice to meet you, Kelly. I'm the art director for the shoot today."

"An art director named Artie?"

"Yep." He gave me a pleased smile. "Perfect, huh?"

"Sure." Over his shoulder I saw Cole roll his eyes.

"Has Cole told you what we're doing today?" Artie said. His gaze stayed on me only a moment before it fluttered around the room, looking over my seamless, the lights, Cole's table of equipment.

"Not exactly." I glanced over Artie's shoulder again and saw Cole dip his head toward his notes, almost as if he was hiding.

"Well, it's very exciting." He moved around me and began playing with the seamless, rolling the sides up a little higher, but accidentally ripping the paper at the ends where I'd taped it. "Public service ads are our way to contribute."

"Public service ads?" I had a flashback of the well-dressed herpes sufferers in Laney's marketing campaign.

"That's right." He had completely dismantled the seamless as I'd constructed it, and the paper was now crumpled. "Sorry about that, but it's got to be sturdier. Animals are notoriously unpredictable. Everything's got to be solid, you know?"

Artie pushed past me, moving back toward the elevator. "Where is the handler?" he said in Cole's direction, but he didn't seem to notice when Cole said nothing.

"Animals?" I said, with a smirk in my voice. "This artistic picture you're going to build element by element is a public service ad with animals in it?"

Cole shot me a mean look that made me quash the laugh rising inside me. "If that's your attitude, you'll never make it as a photographer," he said. "You've got to take work where you get it, and you've got to do your best no matter what the subject."

He was right. Absolutely right. Everyone had to begin

somewhere, and I should know that by now, but the thought of the famous Coley Beckett shooting some kind of animal-farm ad that would probably run in the free homeless newspaper seemed strange. Obviously, though, Cole was starting over after whatever had happened to him in New York, and I, of all people, should be more sympathetic to that. Wasn't I starting over myself? Besides, it was probably an ad reminding people to pick up their dog poop, and I'd get to play with puppies all day.

I constructed my seamless again. A few minutes later, the elevator opened, and a tall, burly woman dressed in jeans and a sweatshirt stepped out.

"Cole Beckett?" She looked around the room, reading from a scrap of paper. She looked inordinately stressed out. Her brown hair fell in dirty clumps around her face, and her ruddy face gave the impression that she'd just run ten miles.

Cole came out from his living area and looked her up and down. "You're Tina?"

She nodded.

"Bring him in," Cole said.

Tina breathed heavily, as if she was preparing herself for major lifting. She stepped back inside the elevator, then with a grunt, pushed out a large, silver metal crate on wheels. Rustling and a low grunting sound came from the crate, and I found myself taking a cautionary step back. That was no puppy.

"Where do you want him?" Tina said, moving back and forth on her feet like a boxer.

Cole ducked his head down and looked inside the crate. "Right," he said, and pointed toward me.

Tina began pushing the crate in my direction. More grunting sounds came from within the metal cage. I wasn't afraid of animals—although to be truthful, I hadn't been exposed to much more than dogs, cats and mosquitoes—and yet I felt increasingly nervous as the crate rolled closer.

Finally, Tina reached me. "Where do you want him?" she said.

I lowered my head a few inches, bending at the waist, until I could see inside the tiny metal squares of the crate. Inside was something quite large, the size of a very fat German shepherd, but the thing had pearly pinkish skin. It swung around in the crate and looked right at me.

I stood back up, all my thoughts of a glamorous Tiffany's shoot, or at least a cute puppy shoot, screeching to a halt in my head. "It's a pig, right?"

Tina nodded. "His name's William."

William, it turned out, was a bigger diva than any model could have been. The picture that Cole built step-by-step started with plunking William's fat ass in a red toy car in front of my sky-blue seamless. Apparently, the public service announcement was an ad for road rage, which would read *Don't Hog the Road.*

"Get it?" Artie said to me at least four times. "Don't *hog* the road! Get it?"

I nodded and attempted to seem interested, but the truth was that William made me jumpy, so I tried to fade into the background, hoping Cole would forget that he'd hired me. Instead, he kept calling me to the set and asking me to add another item—a silk scarf around William's squirming, fleshy neck, a pair of sunglasses on his thick, snorting head. Each time, I approached the pig like Clarice approached Hannibal, sure that he was going to attack at any minute.

"Why can't Tina do this?" I asked Cole once as I tiptoed up to William with a different scarf.

"Because you are my assistant, not Tina."

That was true enough, but I hadn't signed up to be a pig whisperer.

"Hey, William," I'd say, sidling up to him. "Nice piggy…

Nice piggy, there you go, sweetie. I'm just going to put this little scarf on you. Won't that look nice?"

Inevitably, William would stare at me with eyes like two black marbles and then start snorting and squirming viciously in his little car. Tina, his handler, continued to disappear for cigarette breaks, and so I would wrestle the scarf around William's stout body, only to have Cole or Artie tell me that the tassels of the scarf needed to be realigned.

Strangely, thankfully, William didn't smell like a pig. Tina said she'd given him a bath before they drove into the city, and as a result William smelled a little like soap and a little like dirt, which was not altogether horrible considering that I'd expected him to smell like shit.

"For Chrissakes, Kelly," Cole said at one point. "The scarf should look like it's flowing back behind him."

I glared at him, then tried to readjust the scarf, but it just kept hanging limply over William's shoulder. I wondered absently whether pigs had shoulders, while trying to take my mind away from how much I was beginning to despise Cole.

"Kelly. *Please* get it right," Cole said, after I'd spent ten minutes with the scarf and with William's oddly sweet breath in my face. "It must be flowing."

"Why don't you just use a fan?"

Tina, who was actually nearby this time, and not outside sucking down a cigarette, coughed and held out her hands. "No, no. William doesn't like fans or high winds. At all."

Cole gave me a smug look, and since I didn't want to test William's patience, I flicked and fluttered the scarf, all the while listening to Cole's mutters and impatient orders and Artie's useless and contradictory suggestions.

As the day went on, Cole grew more and more irritated that he wasn't getting the shots he wanted. It wasn't apparent whether he blamed me, himself, the pig or Artie, who did little as far as I could tell, but either way it put Cole in an absolutely foul mood. Due to some animal labor laws or some such, we couldn't make William work two days in a row, so if we didn't finish the shoot today, we'd have to wait until Friday and start all over again. This wasn't such bad news to me, since I now smelled like dirt and pig soap and couldn't get the feel of William's squirmy, faintly hairy flesh off my skin.

By five o'clock, Tina had materialized from another round of smoke breaks and once again stood close to the set. "Cole," she said, her ruddy face even more red at the thought of hauling William back to wherever they were from. "I've got to get him in the truck before it gets dark or he'll freak."

Cole let out a huge sigh. "Bloody hell," he said. He bent over his butcher-block table, which held all his equipment, and picked up a large lens he hadn't used before, securing it to the camera. "Just one more shot."

Tina scurried close to me, getting ready, I supposed, to wrestle William into his cage. Meanwhile, I crossed my arms over my chest, relieved that my pig-whispering was about to come to an end, at least for the day.

"Ready," Cole said, peering into his viewfinder.

I watched his finger hesitate for a moment, then it pressed down on the shutter, and at the same time the flash, a huge burst of white, boomed from the strobe that was attached to his camera. I blinked to clear the light from my eyes, but instead of seeing William on the little red car, I saw a man. Not Artie or Cole, or anyone I recognized, actually. His face was close to mine, leaning over me. He was murmuring something, words I couldn't make out. His hair was dark and thick and rippled, like a pot of melted chocolate. His eyes were a brilliant blue, and there were two distinct freckles under one of them. His mouth kept moving. What was he saying? He seemed kind—I could tell that much from the way his eyes looked into mine, searching for some indication of understanding—but I still couldn't hear him properly. What was he saying? What was he—

"Kelly! Kelly!"

Kelly? Was that what he was saying? Was the man saying my name?

"Kelly, are you all right?"

His voice sounded British. His face got hazy. I blinked again, a few more rapid flutters of my eyelids, and then everything seemed clearer. There was a man leaning over me, and it was Cole.

"Kelly," he said, "are you all right?"

"Yes, sure."

Was it Cole the whole time? That didn't seem right. Cole's hair was inky-black and spiky, while the other man's was a rich, warm mahogany. Cole had brown eyes, not blue, and there were no freckles underneath the one.

"Can you stand?" Cole said.

I looked around and saw that I was slumped on the hardwood floor of the studio. Tina and Artie hovered behind Cole, their eyes concerned. Even William seemed to have his black-button eyes focused in my direction.

"Yes, I'm fine." I let Cole pull me up by the arms. "What happened?"

"You just sort of sat down on the floor and lay back," Cole said. "Your legs were flopping around a bit and then you didn't move."

"My legs were *flopping?*" I tried to imagine it, to remember it, but there was a blank in my mind, just like the space where those five months had disappeared.

"Are you all right, then?" Cole said.

"I'm fine." Truthfully, I felt rather lightheaded. "I'm fine," I said again to reassure myself more than anyone else. "I just need to eat something, I think. I didn't eat lunch today." That was a total lie. I'd brought a turkey sandwich and eaten it a few hours ago, but I needed an excuse for my tumble, and my stomach did feel nauseous.

"Well, why don't you go home now?" Cole said.

"Yeah, why don't we call you a cab?" Artie said.

"Or maybe you should go to the emergency room?" Tina suggested.

"No, no, I'm absolutely fine." And, in fact, the light-headedness was dissipating, and now all I felt was a growing embarrassment at the commotion I'd caused. "I'm really fine. I'll hail a cab home and go right to sleep."

"You're sure?" Cole said, and I could have sworn I saw real worry in his face.

"Absolutely. I'm sorry about that."

I put my coat on and grabbed my bag, mumbling more apologies and reassurances about my condition. A minute later, I was tucked in the back of a warm cab, wondering what in the hell had happened and whether I was starting to remember my lost months.

11

All night I tried to find him. My blue-eyed man with the two freckles.

I ignored the potential ramifications, too overcome with curiosity. I ignored the queasy feeling in my gut that wouldn't seem to go away.

I thought maybe the boom of light from Cole's flash had scared a memory out of my head, so I tried to recreate sudden light flashes to trigger another one. I stood in the doorway of my bedroom, flicking the lights on, then off, then on again, waiting expectantly, holding on to the door frame so I wouldn't fall again. This exercise got me nowhere.

Next I got out my Nikon and every flash I owned, which totaled only three. With each one, I tried the same process—I secured the flash, turned the lights off, pointed the camera at myself from very close range and clicked.

Each time, the light burst like a firecracker in my face, leaving me blinking, startled, frazzled, but with no new memories.

When I wasn't looking for the two-freckled man, trying to scare some image or memory out of my brain, I spent the rest of my night trying to figure out who he was and what he'd been saying to me. The first thing I did, of course, was call Laney, but I couldn't reach her at home or on her cell.

I wished desperately that I could call Dee, who had the keenest memory and the most annoyingly perfect sense of observation. I'd first realized that on my twelfth birthday, when Dee was only six. It was the first time my mother had let me baby-sit, a moment that she'd been waiting for longer than I had. She hated paying for baby-sitters and had thought for a long while that I was old enough to take care of Dee and myself on my own. But because of some news segment she'd produced on baby-sitters, where an expert had said that the sitter should be twelve years old at the very least, we both had to wait. My mom was smart enough to know that she wasn't a natural parent, and so she regarded words of such "experts" as law. The day I turned twelve, though, it meant she had a built-in baby-sitter, which would drastically open up her social schedule.

She'd had a party for me that day. It wasn't as if my birthday got ignored. We were living in Atlanta at the time, in a tiny apartment on the third floor of an old house in a neighborhood called Virginia Highlands. A few of my friends came home with me after school, and Sylvie provided the requisite cake and candles. But my classmates' parents picked them up at six, and by seven o'clock Sylvie was dressed and ready to go out for the night, her eyes bright.

I remember she was wearing some sort of Madonna getup

with black tights and a black short skirt and lots of those ridiculous rubber bracelets that were popular at the time.

"Here's the number of the restaurant," she said, tearing a page out of the phone book and circling a listing. She rifled through the book, ripped out another page, circled something there and handed me that, as well. "And here's the number of the bar where we'll be after that. You okay, birthday girl?"

I nodded, as happy about this as she was.

As soon as my mom left, I made sure Dee was all right in front of the TV, and I started going through my mom's things. I was, at the time, still curious about my dad and where he'd gone. Sylvie had always given me the he-just-disappeared-into-the-night kind of a story, which I now realize was probably true, but at the time, it only made Ken McGraw seem more mysterious. She'd shown me only two photos of him—a posed, stilted one of them on their wedding day ("I look so thin there," she would say) and a very out-of-focus shot of him holding me after I was born. He looked to me like most of my friends' dads, which mystified me all the more. If he was just like them, why hadn't he stuck around?

And so I spent that night digging through my mom's desk drawers, pawing past tubes of out-of-favor lipsticks and the multicolored matchbooks she collected but never kept in one place, paging through the stacks of work documents and leafing through the photo albums she was always half-heartedly trying to start. The only picture I found that I hadn't already seen was a closeup of him holding up a can of Budweiser the way others might present a bottle of Dom Perignon. His light brown hair was the same color as mine. His green eyes, the color of old grass, were mine, too, but after those few things, the similarities seemed to end. I couldn't remember him, and presumably we had nothing in common other than a few physical features.

After twenty minutes of staring at the picture, I tucked it back in my mom's denim-covered album and went to the living room where Dee was quietly building a Lego house while watching a made-for-TV movie. I ruffled her soft, curly hair, switched the channel to *Dynasty* and helped her with the Lego until my mom came home at ten that night. She was earlier than usual, and she hadn't brought her date inside, which meant it hadn't gone well.

"So what did you do tonight?" she said, pulling off the rubber bracelets and piling them on top of the TV like a slinky.

Dee looked up and spoke for the first time in over an hour. "I watched TV and played with Lego's, and Kelly was in your room and in your drawers. She looked through your picture book, and she stared at one picture for a long time."

My mom and I were both silent for a moment, just gazing at this kid who rarely put two words together.

"Kelly, is this true?" my mom said at last.

I gave Dee the nastiest glare I could muster, which, as intended, brought an expression of terror and teariness to her face. She ran off to her room and piled pillows on her head, something she did when she was scared or upset. I found her that way after Sylvie's lecture on respecting others' privacy. By that time, I felt horrible that I'd upset Dee when all she'd done was tell the truth. True to her nature, she forgave me immediately, but she never forgot. She never forgot anything, and that would have helped me immensely now when I couldn't remember a chunk of my life.

The fact that I couldn't call Dee to ask whether she remembered the two-freckled man, that I could never call Dee again, made me feel even more confused that night in my Lake Shore Drive apartment, even more lonely. But thinking about my twelfth birthday had given me an idea. I could

look through my own photos, just the way I'd rifled through
my mom's that night.

I settled on the couch with a glass of merlot, a candle
on the coffee table and a pile of mismatched photo albums at my side. Like last weekend, when I'd gone
through Laney's photos, I found I could recall perfectly
the pictures from before my birthday in May. I could remember where each one was taken and names of the people in them. But there was no sign of a blue-eyed guy
with two freckles, and the photos were only making me
feel worse. So many of them were of Ben and Dee and
my mom, people who were now, for one reason or another, gone from my life. I also felt a strange distance
from the person I was in those pictures. The Kelly Mc-
Graw who smiled out of those photos knew who she was
and where she was going.

I picked up my wineglass and sat back on the couch for
a minute. I wanted more than anything to just shut the albums and put them away, to put away all the memories and
any possible reminders of the time I couldn't remember.
Because I really didn't want to remember the summer
months, after all. Hadn't I been saying that all along?
That the memory loss was the best thing that had happened to me, since it had led me to my new life? The problem was that my new life wasn't feeling so fabulous right
now. I was alone, living in an apartment devoid of character and working as a pig wrestler for an asshole Brit. But
the flash of that man had intrigued me. So I took another
sip of the warm, spicy wine and again started paging
through the album.

I stopped at a shot of Ben and me, taken at Ben's cousin's
wedding a few years ago. Ben looked confident and gorgeous in an olive suit I'd found on sale at Field's. I was wearing a sleeveless black dress with a boat neck. We both had
goofy grins on our faces, which were slightly pink from

dancing and the infusion of bubbly we'd had by that time. I'd been so happy that night. Dee hadn't died yet, things with Ben were wonderful—or so I'd thought—and I was reasonably content every morning to head for work.

I slipped the photo out of the plastic and raised it close to my face, wondering whether it had all been so perfect back then. Did I really have it together, the way I wanted, or had I simply decided that was the case? I liked my job, thought it was decent enough, and that made me feel fortunate because I knew people who absolutely despised their jobs. I also felt lucky because I had Ben. I'd gotten past the period where I needed to go out and get loaded every Thursday, Friday and Saturday, and I was ready to be a little more adult. I was ready to spend Thursday nights at a nice restaurant with a man, rather than at the local bar with a few hundred other people. I wanted to rent a cabin with Ben on the weekends and spend our days antiquing and cozying up to a fire.

I had assumed, though, or maybe I'd just decided, that becoming an adult and slowing down my lifestyle were synonymous with a certain loss of passion. So when my job became more routine than challenging, I made partnership the ring to attain. And I'd all but demanded a ring of a different sort from Ben. My reasoning there was somewhat convoluted. First, there was my self-imposed goal of marriage and a kid by thirty-five, a deadline fast approaching. There seemed to be no reason not to get a jump start on that. I did love Ben dearly. I loved having sex with him, loved talking to him about work, loved traveling with him and just generally having him around. And yet there was the fact that last year, long after that night at Ben's cousin's wedding, things had staled slightly. We had fewer items to talk about at the end of the day, and we had sex less and less often. The usual, I supposed. That's what I told myself—that it was common. But then on Christmas, Ben gave me a raincoat and a set of Kohler sink handles I'd wanted for my master bathroom.

I flipped through the album until I found those pictures. In them, I'm sitting with Ben's parents, his brothers and their wives, all of us wearing red flannel pajamas in keeping with the Thomas family tradition, and I have, on my lap, an orange goddamn raincoat and a pair of faucet handles. They seemed the kind of gifts a husband would give his wife of forty years. And I was no better. In the picture, Ben is holding up the gifts I'd bestowed on him—a charger for his Palm Pilot and a juicer. After that day, I convinced myself that the complacency was okay, it was natural somehow since we were together for the long haul.

I stuck with that rationalization until Dee died, and the ground seemed to crack and split under my feet. Suddenly I felt the need to make sure I was right—that Ben and I would be together forever, that I would reach the safety of my goal by thirty-five. I decided that it was time. Time to get married, to think about having kids, to grow up. It was a certain sense of duty, a squaring of my shoulders to the world, and that's when I gave him the ultimatum.

I really did want to get married, and I truly did want to marry Ben, but as I gazed at those Christmas pictures now, I wondered if it was for all the wrong reasons.

I turned the pages of the album and made myself work quickly through the rest of it, as well as the other albums by my side. Nothing surprising there. No photos from the last five months at all. Certainly no pictures of that man who flashed in my memory.

By the time I put the albums back in the closet, I'd started to doubt whether he really was a memory, and instead I started wondering, not for the first time that week, whether I was just plain crazy.

* * *

Cole had been asking me to come to work anywhere between ten o'clock and twelve, and although I loved sleeping in and not having to rush around like crazy while still groggy and stupid, I also missed the early mornings in Chicago. I used to be at Bartley Brothers by seven-thirty without fail, and I loved my morning routine. Walking the four blocks to Starbucks, taking in the orange glow that rose over the lake and the city's east side, hearing the call of birds, even in the winter, and just breathing in the fresh scents of a new day. People think you don't get these things in the city, but you do. You just have to look for them.

So on Friday morning, even though I didn't need to be at Cole's until ten-thirty, I was up and out by seven, loving the crisp feel of the morning, smiling at the commuters I passed. It amazed me how much better I felt from the night before. Sometimes all it took was a solid eight hours in the sack.

An alarming thought dawned on me after two blocks, though—I didn't know where the nearest Starbucks was in this neighborhood. After circling around a five-block perimeter I began to get alarmed again. No Starbucks. By then my brain was fighting against the early hour and screaming for caffeine.

Just then I spotted a little place up the street with thick maroon curtains in the two front windows and a small maroon sign above the door that said Katie's Coffee, with an actual coffee mug hanging from the letter *C*. A little too cutesy for me, but it would have to do.

Inside, the place was even cuter. It was full of old wood tables and fat velvet couches, the rust-colored walls making it feel cozy and warm. At one end was an old decorative fireplace, the kind you see often in the city, but there was actually a fire in this one—at seven-fifteen on a Thursday morning. Amazing. I ordered a latte, tucked myself into a table by the front window and happily whiled away a few hours with the morning papers, thinking that Katie's might give the mother ship a run for its money.

"You're all right then?" Cole said when I walked into his loft.

"I'm fine." I'd had a terrible headache since I'd left Katie's, but I wasn't about to tell him that.

"Good." He resumed his typical demeanor—rude, short and impatient—giving me rapid-fire instructions.

After making me spend half the day rearranging his props closet, Cole introduced me to the darkroom. Developing film was the phase of photography I'd had the least experience with, but every time I'd done it, it never failed to awe me—that magic moment when an image appears.

I asked a number of questions because the whole point of working with him and putting up with his high and mighty attitude was to learn, after all, and I didn't want to botch the shots. Unfortunately, my questions only seemed to irritate him further.

"Jesus bloody Christ," he said at one point, exhaling pointedly. "These shots I'm having you develop are personal to me. You can't muck them up!"

"The shots of William are personal to you?" And what self-respecting man said "muck"?

"These are *not* from yesterday's shoot. I send out most of the commercial work. It would take too much time otherwise. Look, maybe I should just do this myself."

"No, I can do it." I wasn't sure why I was so keen to prove myself to him. Probably some corporate gunner part of myself that had stuck around even after I'd gotten the ax from Bartley Brothers. "Just a few more questions."

"It's not rocket science, is it?"

After a silent showdown, Cole exhaled again, then said, "Let me explain one more time."

I tried to act like Rainman and make speedy mental notes

on his explanation of the englarger, the fixer, the agitating process and the stop bath. I wasn't sure I understood it all, but when he finally left me alone, I was relieved.

As I sifted the heavy paper in the developer solution, waiting for the images of God-knows-what to appear—maybe Cole decked out in S&M gear, or a photo of a vodka bottle—I let my mind sift, too. There was something so calming about the process, something so soothing about the golden-red gloom and solitude of the darkroom, that I found I could relax and let my brain roam. I found myself thinking first of Bartley Brothers, how I missed the luxury of that job. The private office, the free snacks, the two-hour, wine-laden lunches with brokers, the self-esteem shot in the arm I got when I told people I was an analyst for one of the most venerable banking institutions in the country.

Inevitably, when I thought of Bartley Brothers, I thought of Ben, and I realized that I missed the camaraderie I had with him. We used to leave work together nearly every night and rehash our triumphs and failures over dinner or cab rides to the gym. I loved having someone who implicitly understood my job and my co-workers.

Now, of course, I was completely on my own as Cole's slave du jour. There was no one who could truly understand my passion for photography alongside my disdain for my boss.

I tried to focus on what I did like about my new job. Hmm. Well, I was wearing faded jeans, a black turtleneck and my new high-heeled black boots, an outfit that would have been way too funky for Bartley Brothers.

Was that the only thing I enjoyed about this job? The clothing? There had to be something else. Otherwise, what was I doing here besides pissing away my early thirties?

I glanced at the tray and saw that something had started to appear. I felt a quickening of excitement in my stomach, which reminded me that *this* was what I liked about my new gig—the fact that I was doing something with photography every day. Despite the tickle of anticipation in my belly, I made myself keep the paper moving as Cole had ordered—twist, turn, twist, turn. Something pale appeared first. Someone's pinkish skin. The expanse of paleness grew. Then there were two eyes. A tickle in my belly again. It was so amazing the way this picture of someone was growing right before me.

I leaned over and saw, emerging under the left eye, two freckles side by side.

I stood up and gulped at the air, which seemed stifling now. Was it him? The man from my memory? Did Cole know him somehow?

I kept my hands moving, kept agitating the paper, since I didn't want to ruin the shot, but I couldn't look at it anymore. It scared me, the image of this guy. On one hand, I wanted to know who he was and what he knew, if anything, about why I couldn't remember. At the same time, I was afraid that by giving me answers, he might bring with him all the memories of this summer, and I could lose myself again.

Finally, I had to remove the photo or risk overdeveloping it. Without looking into the tray, I lifted out the dripping shot and dropped it in the stop bath. Later, I transferred it into the fixer and finally clipped it to a line hanging over my head, all the while managing to not look directly at it. When it was secure, I couldn't avoid it any longer. With another deep breath, I raised my eyes and stared directly at the photo.

I laughed.

It wasn't the man with two freckles. It was a close-up of a little girl maybe three years old. She had dark, shiny hair that hung to her chin, big round eyes and a sprinkling of freckles over her nose and both cheeks. I laughed again. I'd let my imagination get the best of me.

There were other photos of the little girl, a number of

them taken from a distance with a large lens, shots of her playing by herself in a sandbox, crouched on her little legs over a bucket.

When I was done, I took a few out to Cole, who was sitting at a kitchen table that doubled as a desk, judging from the notes and papers he had spread over it.

"Did you want to see these now?" I asked, blinking rapidly in the light of the studio, which was blazingly bright after the darkroom.

He took them from my hand without a word and studied them.

"Who is she?" I said.

"My niece." He didn't look up.

"Does she live around here?"

"Outside of London."

"She's adorable."

"Yes."

I glanced at my watch. I'd given up on a thank-you or a comment about how well I'd developed them. "I'll be heading out then, unless there's something else you want me to do."

"No, no. You can go."

I left him there, sitting at that table, still staring at the little girl.

12

"The two-freckled man?" Laney said. "That's what you're calling him?"

I nodded and sipped my margarita, thinking back to that image I thought I'd seen in the tray. I must have been in the darkroom too long, the dim, eerie lighting affecting my thinking or my vision.

"You know," Laney said, "you're making him, whoever he is, sound like a circus freak with that name."

"I know, I know, but it makes it more amusing than scary."

We were at Uncle Julio's Hacienda, our favorite spot for dinner and margs. The place was packed that night. The crowd spilled into the bar area, where everyone jostled for a spot at the long rectangular tables or at least a handful of chips from the baskets on them.

"Well, it is scary, this memory thing," Laney said. "You really should see Dr. Markup or someone."

"That's not what I mean," I said, slightly irritated that she was bringing up the doctor bit again. "What I mean is, who the hell is this guy? It freaked me out last night when his face just came to me like that. Maybe he's a serial killer. Maybe I witnessed a heinous crime, and that's why I can't remember. Maybe he's looking for me right now!" Through my tequila buzz, I noticed my voice had gotten rather shrill.

"Let's not be melodramatic."

I shot her a look.

"Seriously," she said. "It could be someone you saw on TV or in the paper. He might be a model you saw in an ad, and for some reason you're getting this flash of him like you do in dreams sometimes. You might not know him at all."

It was possible, but what Laney was saying didn't seem right. I had the feeling I'd known this guy somewhere, at some time.

"Why didn't you call me about this last night?" she asked. She put her glass down on the table, her eyes down, her dark bangs falling over her face.

"I did. I tried you at all of your numbers. Where were you?"

"Out with Gear." She gave that nervous chuckle of hers.

"Everything all right with him?"

She waved a hand. "Oh, sure."

"So what is it?"

"Well, you didn't even call me today to talk about it."

"I was at work, if you can call it that. *You* were at work, too."

Laney ran a finger around the wide mouth of her glass.

"What? What is it?"

She shrugged again. "Normally, you'd call me right away about the slightest thing."

"I *did* call you right away."

"But you didn't leave a message."

"No. I've put you through enough over the last year. You don't need to deal with me all the time. I just figured I'd fill you in when I saw you, and that's what I'm doing."

"You're not bugging me, you know. You can call me anytime."

"I know that."

"Okay." She picked up her glass again. "Well, let's consider the possibilities then for Mr. Two Freckles. Was he cute?"

I thought about his rippled dark hair, those kind blue eyes. "Oh, yeah."

"So maybe he *was* a model you saw in an ad."

"Maybe, but I'm not convinced."

"Well, I'm not convinced that the serial killer possibility has legs, so what could it be?"

I thought of how, in my first flash of him, the man's face was close to mine and his mouth was moving, saying something to me. It seemed intimate somehow, and that gave me a great idea. "A one-night stand!"

"What?" She looked at me skeptically.

"Seriously. Maybe I was sleeping with him."

"Honey, you were in that apartment all the time."

"But you don't know that for sure. You weren't there the entire time, were you?"

"No, but—"

"And you don't know who I had visiting. So maybe I was sleeping with him. Maybe he was my first one-night stand!"

I'm not sure why I felt so sophomorically pleased with this possibility, but I didn't have the opportunity to think about it anymore, because two guys angled themselves into our space, probably drawn by my loud ramblings about one-night stands.

"Could we share your end of the table?" one of them said. He was cute enough, with brown hair cut short, wearing khakis and a yellow sweater. His friend wore black pants and a black shirt, making me think of Johnny Cash.

Laney shot me a look that said, *Just say the word and I'll get rid of them.*

But if I hadn't slept with the two-freckled guy that meant I probably hadn't had sex for about six months. Here were two nice, reasonably attractive guys flirting with us. Why not talk with them? Who knew what could happen?

So I gave them a smile and made a little space on the table for their drinks, and started chatting with the Johnny Cash character. There was no doubt about it. He was flirting with me. He gave a toothy, knowing smile while he shook my hand and introduced himself. He leaned forward and spoke in my ear, asking if he could buy me a drink.

And with that, I promptly got cold feet. I struggled to remember what I used to talk about all those nights, before Ben, when I trawled the bars, trying to meet guys. What moves did I make? Did I have lines that worked like a charm? It all seemed so long ago.

I gave Johnny Cash another smile, but I could feel it come out bitter and frozen. The giggle I attempted sounded more like gunfire. My confidence evaporated. I couldn't believe I'd ever liked flirting. Meanwhile, Johnny seemed less and less interested, his eyes reaching over my head to scan the room while he took a tiny step back to create distance between us. Within five minutes, I was giving Laney the big-eyed nod-of-the-head signal that said, *Get me the hell out of here.*

She did. And shortly thereafter, we were at Laney's place, having a quiet little girls' dinner of Subway sandwiches and Amstel Light.

* * *

A headache woke me at six the next morning, and by seven-thirty I was at Katie's Coffee, hoping to chase it away with caffeine. I dumped my stuff in the window seat and ordered a mug of hazelnut latte from the Rastafarian dude working the counter. So far, I hadn't met anyone named Katie, but everyone she had working there was unbelievably nice, always coming by your table to give you a refill or to see if you wanted a muffin. As much as I loved the mother ship, I could get used to this kind of service.

As I sat in the window, under the velvety curtains, I watched the commuters passing by on their way to the El or the bus. The early ones were usually slower moving, rubbing the sleep out of their eyes, their chins tucked down into their scarfs, but by the time the nine o'clock hour came closer, they were ramrod straight and rushing, rushing, rushing forward with expressions bordering on panic.

Instead of the papers that morning, I'd brought two of my photography textbooks, which I flipped through, trying to learn more about light and lenses and developing and such. It was clear that whatever I was going to learn from this job, I would have to gain from watching Cole. He hadn't turned out to be a very good teacher thus far, and so I needed to augment what I'd seen with my textbooks. I was determined to get *something* out of this experience, even if it was a passionate dislike of pigs and Brits. But my headache kept pounding, the print swirling in front of me.

When I got to Cole's at ten that morning, I was feeling better and bright with caffeine. Of course, the minute I entered the studio and saw the sneer on Cole's face, the brightness flickered.

"What?" I said. I'd decided to forget common pleasantries. I didn't get them in return, after all.

Cole looked down at his butcher-block table, which was,

this morning, covered with prints of William. "Look at these," he said with disgust.

I walked to his side. He had color shots lined up there, as well as black-and-white prints, and I had to laugh when I saw them. William actually looked as if he was having a great time in the little car—a pair of sunglasses on his head, his snout turned up so it seemed like he was smiling—and in a few of them, I'd been able to get the scarf just right so it looked fluttery and fluffy.

"What the bloody hell is so amusing?" Cole said.

I sighed. "It's a pig in a car. I mean, c'mon, that's funny."

"God, you Americans have no taste. Look closer, please," he said. "Try not to be so enticed by the subject matter. Look at the composition of the photos, look at the light."

I leaned over the table and studied them, and I started to get his point. "There are weird shadows."

"That's right," he said patronizingly, as if I was a two-year-old who'd just announced that the sky was blue. "And why do you think that is?"

I peered closer and studied the dark cast behind William's pointed, floppy ears, the shadows to the one side of his snout. "We needed to light him better."

Cole nodded, his face scrunched up tight.

"What?" I said. "You're the one who did the lighting, re-member? I did the seamless and—" I was about to go on about the pig wrestling I'd performed, a pretty big effort for the team, if you asked me, but Cole cut me off.

"Kelly Kelly," he said. "As my assistant, I need you to be aware of everything—*everything*—even if I don't tell you to do it. Do you understand?"

"Yes, but—"

"Yes but what?"

I was truly irritated now, so I just decided to tell him the truth. "You're not the easiest person to talk to, so if I see something that's off, it's a little hard to approach you."

Cole stared at me, expressionless. "Try it. All right?"

When Tina, William and Artie arrived an hour later, everything was ready to go, with extra strobes set up at Cole's direction. Once again I adopted my pig whisperer personality, sneaking forward to put the sunglasses on William or adjust his scarf. I was a little more used to him this time, but because of the added lights, it was hotter than the equator, making William slick with sweat.

"Powder!" Cole or Artie would call from behind the camera.

I would take a monstrous breath and scoot forward with an oversize puff and a tin of powder and proceed to powder William's snout, his rounded little rump, even his hoofs. Unfortunately, the sweating made William smell much more piglike than before, and so I had to breathe through my teeth as I patted him down. To distract myself, I fantasized about cocktail lunches at Bartley Brothers and the trips to Manhattan for meetings with the New York office, my elegant room at the Four Seasons. With each foray near William's sweating, plump body, I missed being a financial analyst more and more.

"It's still not right," Cole said, a few hours into the shoot. "He's getting shinier, Kelly. Go into the closet and see if you can find some pancake makeup. We should have some left over from one of the fashion shoots."

I looked at poor William, panting in the heat, his powder starting to clump in odd white patches. The thought of putting pancake makeup on the poor beast was more than I could handle, and, I'm sure, more than he could handle. Luckily, I had an idea.

I grabbed a towel and while whispering, "Nice, William. There you go, William," I gently swiped the powder from his coat, not wiping hard enough to remove the sheen of sweat.

"Kelly!" Cole said in a sharp voice. "What are you doing?"

"Just getting him ready for the pancake makeup," I lied.

I heard Cole grumble.

I kept wiping off the powder, taking my time so even more sweat would grow on William's pink skin.

"Any day now," I heard Cole say.

I put William's Ray Ban's back on his face, stepped aside and admired how slick with perspiration he looked. "He's ready," I said.

I turned to look at Cole. His gave me an evil version of his patented sneer. "Where's the pancake?"

"He doesn't need it."

"Kelly, I don't have time." His voice had gotten lower and ostensibly more civil, which led me to believe that if my hunch didn't work out, I was probably going to be fired. The thought could have terrified me, but I'd been fired from bigger jobs than this.

"Remember what you told me this morning?" I said.

Artie, who stood near Cole, raised his eyebrows and looked back and forth between the two of us, as if ready for and delighted about the fight he saw brewing. Tina, as usual, was outside with her cigarettes.

"I told you to get the pancake makeup."

"No. This morning. You told me that as your assistant, I needed to be aware of everything, even if it wasn't something you'd told me to pay attention to."

"And?"

"And," I said, matching his snotty tone, "the ad would look better if William was slick and sweaty looking. He would look more sinister."

Both Cole and Artie stared at me in silence. Hmm. Maybe my great idea wasn't so great. I tried one more time to sell it. "Look, this is an ad for road rage, right? We want people to realize that they're being pigs when they hog the road, when they yell at other drivers, all that stuff. So we don't need a pig that looks cute and adorable. That doesn't get the point across. We need him to look mean and cutthroat and sinister."

More silence. I was about to cross the room and just start packing my bag. It might be better to quit than get fired again.

But Artie spoke up. "She's right," he said. "She's absolutely right. Can we get a few test shots of William as he is now?"

Cole glared at me, then nodded. I scooted across the room for his old-fashioned Polaroid that he used for trial shots. As I handed it to him, he didn't even meet my eyes.

In complete silence, Cole took at least five test shots from different angles. Even William kept quiet, seeming to sense that an ominous moment might be upon us.

There was more silence as Cole, Artie and I stood around the drying Polaroids, waiting for William's image to come clear. When they did, Cole pulled them toward himself, so that I could only see them upside down. He and Artie studied them for a very long time.

Finally, Cole turned a few of them toward me. "What do you think, then?"

I looked down at the shots. To my mind, they were hysterical, exactly what we wanted. The car gleamed red, the steering wheel a shiny black and William an angry pink. You could almost imagine him tearing down the road, ignoring the Children at Play signs.

"I like them," I said, looking back up at Cole.

"So do I." He put the pictures down and picked up his camera.

That night, I did something I thought I'd never do—went out for drinks with my new boss. In college, when I mooned over his stuff in my photography classes, I certainly wouldn't have thought that I'd ever be chatting over cocktails with the great Coley Beckett. Since I'd started working for him, I couldn't imagine a worse way to spend a night. But taking my suggestion about William seemed to have given Cole a new respect for me. The rest of the shoot was ultrasmooth. William appeared to be happier in his sweaty state and was more cooperative, making Tina and me much happier. Cole and Artie became more relaxed, too, and when the shoot ended early at five o'clock, Cole thanked everyone for their hard work in the most cordial tone I'd ever heard from him.

After William was packed into his silver crate and everyone left, Cole came up to me, running a hand through his spiky hair, and said uncomfortably, "Nice work."

It was probably the closest I was going to get to a "thank you" from him, so I nodded in what I thought was a gracious manner. "Sure. I'll clean up and see you Monday."

He didn't respond right away. I started rolling William's shiny red car toward the props closet. I had to bend over to do it, and so my jeans-clad ass was in the air when I heard Cole say, "How about a drink, then?"

I froze until I became aware that I was basically displaying my butt to Cole. I stood up quickly and spun around to search his face. Was he hitting on me?

Seeming to sense my internal question, Cole held up his hands as if I was pointing a gun at him. "Not for any particular reason. Just to celebrate a good day, right?"

I mentally ran through my social calendar for the night. Nothing. "Okay. Where do you want to go?"

"You pick," he said. "You're the local."

I couldn't imagine Cole trying to mingle with the lawyers and traders at any of the Loop bars, so thirty minutes later, we were in Bucktown at Soul Kitchen, a hip Cajun place with killer martinis. Because the dinner crowd hadn't arrived yet, we were given a curved corner booth with polished orange seats. The booth seemed too big for us, though, and silence filled in around us with each stab at polite conversation. Meanwhile, I kept peering through the dimly lit restaurant toward the door, looking for Laney, whom I'd called from my cell phone and told to meet me ASAP. I needed backup.

Cole, with his black spiked hair and black clothes, fit right into the scene, but even he seemed uncomfortable that it was just the two of us. I didn't get the feeling that he was trying to flirt with me, yet still I couldn't figure out why he'd asked me to have a drink.

"Look," he said, when he was halfway through his gargantuan martini. I was barely sipping mine, fearful of bringing on another doozy of a headache. I'd had so many of them lately. "I have to tell you that I'm not always like…" Cole seemed at a loss for words, but I refused to help him out, so just looked at him expectantly.

He tried again. "I'm not usually such a complete arse."

"Hmm." I nodded, debating between, "Could have fooled me," and "What, you're usually just a prick?"

"I don't want to harp on about it," he said, swirling his drink with one hand, "but I've been going through a rough time. Professionally, I mean."

I nodded again, wondering if he'd tell me now why he'd been blacklisted from the fashion world.

"Things are looking up, however." He gave me a half grin, before dropping his eyes back to his glass. "I think I might be getting an assignment soon, quite big, actually. Well, I shouldn't say anything, not just yet, you never do know, right? But it would mean a lot, professionally anyway. But as I said, I shouldn't speak so much about it. Jinx factor and all that."

He looked up at me then with an expression that seemed uncharacteristically human and hopeful. Was he actually seeking some kind of reassurance or approval from me? Didn't he have model girlfriends for that? And what had he really said? Just some ramblings about an assignment.

"Well," I said finally. "It sounds like it could be…" What was the word? "Big."

"Right, right." Cole nodded like an eager puppy.

Another pall of quiet fell over us, but—thank God—just

then Laney blew through the door, looking gorgeous in her tall black boots and red coat. She waved when she spotted us, and started picking her way through the tables.

"Ah yes, your 'official friend,'" Cole said, watching her closely as she made her way toward us, not taking his eyes off her.

Laney and I hugged, and she and Cole shook hands and did the nice-to-see-you-again thing. She seemed lit up with a Friday-night buzz, and somehow, she'd brought some electricity to our table. Soon we were gabbing over a bunch of appetizers, Laney asking Cole where he'd grown up in England and how he liked living in Chicago. Cole seemed more at ease than ever, answering her questions and making us both laugh by imitating his mother's Cockney accent and the messages she left him on his voice mail every day.

"So," Laney said at one point, leaning her elbows on the table. "Kelly tells me that you were run out of Manhattan. Want to tell us about that?"

Cole froze, a croquette halfway to his mouth.

I shot Laney a look that said, *Shut the fuck up, please!* How could she? I'd just gotten the guy on my side, and now he was sure to hate me again.

She only shrugged as if to say *How bad could it be?*

Cole put his food down on his plate and looked from Laney to me and back again. "Well, ladies, I don't think we know each other well enough yet for that conversation. My memories of it are rather like having a full proctology exam. Not suitable for dinner conversation."

There was a short pause, during which I struggled in vain to come up with a new topic. But then Laney lifted her glass. "Let's toast then. To taking it up the ass…and surviving it."

Oh, God. I hung my head. I should have cut Laney off after the first martini. Vodka does strange things to her. But then I heard something even more strange—the sound of

Cole laughing. I looked up to see him shaking his head, his eyes crinkled happily.

"To surviving," he said, and we all clinked glasses.

13

The next morning I lectured Laney about her behavior during the Cole dinner, telling her that although it had gone surprisingly well, she should never, ever say anything to him again about Manhattan or what had happened there.

"Well, he's such a hottie that he makes me nervous," she said. "I was just trying to razz him."

"You think he's hot?"

"Definitely."

"Really? Hmm." I guess I could see Cole being Laney's type. "Well, you can't ever bring that up again!"

"Fine, fine," she said. "You've told me twenty times now, I get it. Next topic. What are you wearing to Jess and Steve's wedding?"

"Shit! Is that today?"

I'd been so busy despising my boss during the week (and then worrying that I'd pissed him off) that I hadn't given any thought to the wedding or the maddening fact that Ben would be there, looking, I was sure, gorgeous in one of the suits I'd spent hours picking out, with Therese on his arm, looking, I was sure, gloatingly beautiful in some fantastic dress.

I spent a few hours trying on everything in my closet, with Laney on speakerphone doing the same thing. Everything looked different on my new body. Dresses that used to cling to my curves hung baggy now. Others that were forever tight suddenly fit well. I finally decided on a chocolate-colored, raw silk dress with a deep V-neck that Laney had made me buy when we were at Saks. I'd kept the tags on, just as I had the silver beaded dress, sure that I wouldn't have a chance to wear either of them. But the chocolate number was absolutely perfect, I decided, because it showed off some cleavage, and Ben hadn't seen it before.

I put on a ridiculous amount of lipstick and gloss, trying to force myself into a sultry, seductive, make-the-bastard-miss-you mode, but too many emotions kept batting around in my brain. I hated Ben, I kept reminding myself. The asshole had dumped me *on my birthday.* But my thoughts kept sliding to my good memories of Ben—our ski trip to Telluride when we barely left the hotel room, the way he'd surprised me with my first photography classes at the university. Then, of course, there were the jealous thoughts, spurts of rage over him being made partner ahead of me, wondering what he'd known about my getting laid off, sick with envy that he was with someone else so quickly. Lastly, I kept seeing the way his eyes had showed concern when we'd talked at Tarringtons. Those eyes tugged at me the most. I could tell he still cared.

I finally made myself leave my lips and the thoughts of Ben alone, since I was already late to pick up Laney. Ten minutes later, she slipped into the cab looking gorgeous in a black dress with her red coat over it, her hair sleek and tucked behind her ears.

"Ready?" she said as we executed the air kiss that we only did when we were wearing huge quantities of lipstick.

"Ready," I said.

The wedding was, unfortunately, a lengthy, wallop-packing Catholic mass. Clearly, this was the only time in the week where the priest was able to deviate from his usual script, and so he waxed on and on about the "formidable" institution of marriage, which of course he knew nothing about. I turned my head discreetly every so often to search the huge, drafty church for Ben and Therese, but I couldn't spot them. Most likely Ben was playing his "reception only" card, because of some running engagement he had this morning.

The reception immediately followed the ceremony. None of that lounging-about-in-a-bar-way-too-dressed-up-waiting-three-hours-until-the-reception-starts stuff. It was held in an old restored building off Clark Street, in a huge ballroom with gold-painted ceilings at least two stories high. Waiters in tuxedos circled with champagne, and a jazz quartet played muted elegant numbers in the corner. Still no sign of Ben and Therese, I noted as I swiped a champagne flute from one of the trays. It didn't matter, anyway. I'd mustered up more of the hatred for him, and planned to stick with that emotion for the rest of the evening.

After waiting in the receiving line for forty minutes so that we could hug Jess and Steve, and uncomfortably congratulate relatives we'd never met, Laney and I made our way over to the place cards. We'd been designated table 7, and we immediately began surveying the room and the rest of the place cards to see if we'd gotten a good table. God love Jess, because she hadn't stuck us at a singles' table, but put us with the rest of the crew from the advertising agency where Laney used to work, a fun, rowdy bunch.

Pleased, we sat down and proceeded to get mildly blotto with the rest of our group. Our table turned into a team of sorts because Jess and Steve requested that no one clink glasses to make them kiss, but instead that the tables sing a song with the word *love* in it. I've always found this rogue wedding practice a little too cute and entirely too much like summer camp, but because of the amount of alcohol ingested by our table, we got rather competitive about it, leaning our heads in and whispering our suggestions in case the other tables sent spies over to deduce our next number. Not that anyone would have wanted to steal our song selections. While other groups got up time and again to harmonize sweet, or at least appropriate, songs, such as "Love Will Keep Us Together" or "I Just Called to Say I Love You," our little bunch, on the other hand, shouted drunken renditions of "Love Stinks" and "Love Is a Battlefield."

Jess and Steve, to their credit, laughed, shook their heads and got up and toasted us. Other guests weren't so forgiving. Jess's mother, for example, glared as if she wanted to vaporize us. Normally, this would have made me panic and crawl under the table. I was nothing if not a parent-pleaser. While I was growing up, my mother was more like a kid than I was, going out late on dates, trying to sneak back into the house tipsy. I was always the elder, the person who didn't want any attention drawn to her. As a result, I usually felt a kinship with other "parents," and I was always the good kid in high school, the one that the families felt okay about sending their children out into the night with.

But right after I saw Mrs. Ladner frown with disapproval, I saw Ben. He was behind her and to the right, and he was looking straight at me. So instead of ducking my head or maybe opting out of our saucy version of "Love Kicked Me in the Ass," I raised my chin and belted out the final lyrics, envisioning myself as some bawdy opera singer. As we took our seats, I snuck another glance at Ben. He was laughing and clapping, and he was still staring directly at me, almost as if he was a parent himself, one who had just proudly watched his funny little toddler stumble about in the school play. Therese sat to his left, and, seeing Ben applauding, she slugged down half of her wine.

I sat back in my chair and crossed my legs, feeling rather smug. I could do this. I could be near Ben and survive. Even better than survive, I could be fun and elegant. Well, something approaching elegant, anyway.

I had just started conspiring with the pudgy guy on my left about possible dirty love songs when I heard the words that all single girls fear— "Ladies and gentlemen, it's time for the bouquet toss."

Actually, since those words hadn't applied to me for so long, it wasn't until my pudgy friend said, "Well, aren't you going to head up there?" that I processed what was happening. Now that I was truly single and a friend of the bride, I would have to stand up and effectively announce to the entire ballroom that I was a spinster. When I was with Ben, although still technically single, I'd avoided this by clinging to Ben's arm and murmuring, "We're practically engaged." But now everyone at the table seemed to be waiting for me to get up, and I had no excuse.

I turned to Laney. She looked about as pleased as I felt.

"Ready?" she said.

I downed the rest of my champagne. "Ready."

"Now, I know you haven't done this in a while," Laney said, as we picked our way through the tables toward the dance floor. "Here's what you need to remember. First, the bouquet usually lands in the center of the group, so stay toward the back or the sides. Also, clasp your hands in front of you, and if it comes your way, just lob it away like a volleyball."

"Okay, okay." I nodded and concentrated, as if she were giving instructions on how to defuse a nuclear weapon.

"And most importantly—and I can't stress this enough— do not look embarrassed. Stand tall like you're the hottest woman in this room."

I elongated my spine and put a serene smile on my face.

"Perfect," Laney said, and we took our place on the fringes of the group.

The band leader was yammering about the tradition of the bouquet toss, as if some guests might be unfamiliar with it, and while he was going on and on, I sneaked a glance toward Ben and Therese. The bitch. She had appropriated my pose, her hands around Ben's forearm, and she was giving me a smile that said, *You poor pathetic girl.*

I grabbed Laney. "Go get Therese."

"What?" Laney pulled back and gave me a horrified look.

"She's not married. She needs to be humiliated, too."

"I can't just drag her out here."

"Please!" I put my hands together like I was praying. "Please, please!"

Laney shook her head. "It's a good thing I love you," she huffed before she turned on her heel and headed to Ben's table.

I couldn't hear what they were saying but I saw Therese's smile freeze when Laney reached them, and then I could see her shaking her head, and finally Ben laughed and gave her a little shove. And so Laney was soon walking toward me with Therese in tow. Therese had on a skimpy blue dress that looked more like a slip, her long, tanned legs stretching out of the short hem and into shoes so high and pointy I couldn't believe she could walk upright.

"Kelly," she said when they'd reached me.

"Therese," I said back, mimicking her somber tone.

I was so pleased we'd forced Therese onto the dance floor that I forgot Laney's warnings and was standing with my hands behind my back when suddenly there was a drumroll and Jess launched the thing. In a very fast few seconds, I saw with horror that the bunch of lilies was coming right at me.

Here's the thing: I've never had a desire to catch the bouquet. Even when I wanted to marry Ben and I got talked into taking part in the bouquet toss, or when I thought I might want to marry my previous boyfriend, Eric, I never wanted to actually catch the thing. To me, it seemed a monumental jinx. And so as the lilies arched above my head, I started to shift to the right. Excellent. I was getting out of the way. But then I glanced back and saw that I'd left Therese standing slightly alone and looking up at that bouquet the way a cat looks at a can of tuna.

Not on my turf, I thought, as if I was some beat cop on the streets, and that thought catapulted me into action. I lurched back to the left so that I was side by side with Therese, both of us jostling together, our arms upstretched. I knew it wasn't adult behavior, but I didn't have enough time to talk myself down from the ledge.

Therese was taller than me, especially in those shoes, and as she elbowed me in the shoulder, I thought that there was no way I could win. At the last second, though, I bent my knees and jumped a few inches, shoving her away with the movement, and when I came down, I had the bouquet in my hand.

The crowd broke into polite applause.

"Yeah!" Laney jumped around me and smacked me on the back as if I'd just scored the winning touchdown, as if she'd actually counseled me to try and catch the thing. "Better luck next time," she said to Therese.

"Doesn't matter," Therese said, cupping her cheek and sending me a look with her flinty brown eyes. "I'm the one that'll be in bed with him tonight."

Sometimes I'm good at snappy comebacks. I can usually dredge up something if I'm in a situation where I couldn't care less about whatever's happening around me. But that wasn't true for this situation. I was in a stare-down with my ex's new girlfriend, and so I opened and closed my mouth like a mute fish.

Luckily, Laney came to my rescue. "Better you than us, girlfriend," she said before she took my hand and led me away. It wasn't that good of a retort, all things considered, but at least it was something. At least I'd had the last word by proxy.

After posing for pictures and dancing with the guy who'd caught the garter belt, I made my way to the bathroom, still holding the bouquet like it was some sort of prize. I didn't know what had made me fight Therese for it, but I was inordinately pleased with myself just the same. It had something to do with retribution, I decided, as I picked my way down a deserted carpeted hallway off the ballroom. I had finally gone head-to-head with Therese, the woman who'd taken away the man I was supposed to marry.

But that was ridiculous, I realized. Therese hadn't taken him away. He'd taken himself away and then found her.

I came to a sudden halt. Was that really true? Had Ben broken up with me *before* he'd met Therese, or had she been one of the reasons he'd given me the ax? If he'd known about the partnership earlier than he'd let on, if he'd kept that from me, maybe he'd been dating Therese on the side the whole time.

I felt my neck growing red and blotchy. I made myself move again and spent ten minutes in front of the mirror powdering my face and neck, applying and reapplying lipstick and gloss, and growing more and more furious with Ben. He'd probably known I'd be laid off, that I wouldn't make partner and that *he* would, and yet he hadn't said a thing. To top it off, he'd been dating that bitch behind my back.

I must have muttered something out loud, possibly something profane, because an older woman at the mirror next to me gave me a disapproving frown.

"Excuse me," I said, back into parent-pleasing mode. "Sorry."

I skulked toward the door, dangling the bouquet at my side, not caring anymore that I'd been able to out-jostle Therese, and just as I swung it open, I saw him. He was standing across the hallway, looking very much like he was waiting for someone.

"Where's Therese?" I said, drawing myself up tall and looking around as if trying to say, *She better not be around these parts or I'll kick her ass.*

"She's in the kitchen."

"The kitchen?"

"She's getting ice." He pointed to his cheekbone. "You elbowed her in the face."

"Oh God. I'm sorry." But I wasn't. I was apparently some immature high school bully, because I laughed.

Ben snickered, too. "I'm going to pay good money to get my hands on that videotape."

That stopped me cold. "So you can see two women duke it out for you, is that it?"

"No." He lost his grin, and I knew I was right.

"Look," I said, poking him in the chest just to keep up the high school bully image, "I need to know something."

I was pleased to note that he looked a little scared.

"When did you meet Therese?"

"The second weekend in June." It was the truth. I could tell by the way his mouth was relaxed. When he lied or exaggerated something, he pushed his lips together.

"All right. Question two: When did you know you were going to be made partner?"

"I told you. Last week."

"No, that's when they announced partnership, but when did you first find out you were going to get it?"

He sighed. "Someone mentioned something in the spring, but—"

"In the spring?" I said, interrupting him. "Before you broke up with me?"

"Yeah, but it wasn't for sure, and I didn't want to count on it, so I didn't say anything."

"How convenient. Did you know that I wasn't going to make partner?"

"No."

I narrowed my eyes at him.

"I swear," he said.

"Did you know I'd be laid off?"

"No," he said, his voice emphatic.

I scrutinized his mouth. Still relaxed. I believed him, and for a second I felt a little better. Then a thought dawned on me.

"But you *did* break up with me on my birthday, on the same day that I got laid off!"

Ben stared down at his loafers, the ones I'd bought at Field's along with his olive suit. He said nothing.

"How could you do that to me?" My voice got high, and I had to warn myself not to cry.

Ben looked up at me with a pained expression, and I could have sworn that he was on the verge of tears, too. "What was I supposed to do, Kell? I'd finally made a decision that I couldn't give you what you want, and then you get laid off."

"Couldn't you have waited a few days? A few months?"

"No, I couldn't. You made it damn clear that you wanted a ring by your birthday or it was over. Those were your terms."

I huffed a loud, exasperated breath, but he was right. I'd given him that ultimatum, the one that seemed so stupid now. Why threaten someone you love about something so big?

"I'm sorry it worked out like this, Kell, but you've got to believe me. I didn't know you were going to be laid off. I really didn't even think I would make partner, certainly not ahead of you. You're one of their best."

"*Were* one of their best."

"Do you want some help finding a new analyst position? I could make some calls." His eyes brightened. "Actually, I think Tammon Investments is looking for a retail analyst."

A couple of women came down the hallway toward the bathroom, and Ben and I both stepped against the wall. He was close enough for me to smell the minty shaving cream scent of his face, the scent that used to make me want to kiss that dark brown spot on his cheekbone.

"I've actually got a job." I took a step back, away from how good he smelled.

"What? That's great! Where?"

"I'm a photographer's assistant."

"Kell, that's amazing! It's what you always wanted to do." Ben was beaming. There was no mocking look on his face, none of the hidden disparagement I thought I might find from him or the others at Bartley.

I nodded, failing to mention that my job with Cole involved intimate knowledge of porcine snouts. But Ben was right. It *was* amazing. It had been only one week since I tried to put my key in my old town house door, since that day I realized I couldn't remember, and already I had a new job—not to mention a new wardrobe.

"Wow," Ben said. "I'm really happy for you."

"Yeah. Thanks."

Suddenly our conversation ground to a halt. A man pushed past us into the rest room. Down the hallway, I could hear the band break into a banging version of "La Vida Loca."

"So…" Ben said.

"So I should go."

He nodded. "I'm just going to use the bathroom, and then I should find Therese."

"Right. See you."

"Yeah. See you."

I turned and walked down the carpeted hallway, the sounds of the music growing louder and more up-tempo while I felt slow and sad in comparison. At least I'd gotten some answers from Ben. I should feel better that I'd cleared the air.

It was only as I reached the ballroom that I realized that I hadn't asked Ben the most important question of all—why didn't he want to marry me?

14

On Sunday, Laney and I took a rumbling El train to her family's house for the weekly Pendleton lunch. I'd drunk too much wine at the wedding, particularly after my WWF match with Therese and my chat with Ben, so I was looking forward to a good, old-fashioned hangover food-fest with Laney's mom, her four older sisters and her younger brother, Timmy.

"I need Advil," Laney said. She was slumped in one of the curved plastic train seats, occasionally rubbing her eyes. She was wearing old Levi's and a navy parka over a huge turtleneck sweater. You never had to dress up for the Pendletons. It was one of the things I adored about her family.

I dug through my shoulder bag. Because of the nagging headaches I'd been getting lately, I knew I had some ibuprofen in there somewhere. These pulsing aches in my temples made me nervous, made me wonder if they were somehow connected to that depression I'd had over the summer, if another bout of it waited for me around the corner. I tried to tell myself that the headaches were simply a product of tense muscles brought on by having to wrestle with William, or maybe the stress of having to put up with Cole's attitude, but both seemed like rather lame excuses.

I pushed my fingers through my purse, past my photo magazine, wallet, sunglasses, a tampon, packets of sweetener and other assorted items until I located two stray orange tablets and put them in Laney's hand.

"You're a goddess," she said.

We smiled at each other, and I started thinking about the first time I had visited the Pendleton household, during my sophomore year in high school. It was amazing how sharp my memory was about that day, when I couldn't even remember the past summer. We'd taken the train after school, something I'd been afraid to do by myself, and then walked the five blocks to their modest bungalow home, which looked the same as everyone else's on their block. As we got closer, though, I realized that although the squat frame house and its low-hanging shingled roof might mimic that of their neighbors, there was something different about the Pendleton's place. A feeling, a vibe. We got closer, and I realized that it was more of a host of sounds. I stopped on the cement sidewalk in front of the house, trying to make sense of the sounds—a woman shouting, the bouncing beat of a pop song, some tinkling piano keys, a rush of laughter, the squeal of a little kid.

"What is it?" Laney said, stopping to look at me, her face genuinely puzzled.

"Nothing." I shifted my backpack to the other shoulder and followed her up the crumbling asphalt driveway toward the garage. I had met Laney only a few weeks before, my first real friend in Chicago, and I didn't want to insult her by pointing out the cacophony.

The noises grew louder as we picked our way through the discarded bikes, old newspapers and a cornucopia of toys in the garage, and entered through a door that led right into the kitchen. It was a bright room with wide sea-green tiles and cheap, dark-wood cabinets. It would have been a rather ugly place if it weren't filled with food—muffins still in their tins on the counter, bags of chips on the octagonal table, something wonderfully garlicky simmering on the stove— and people, mostly women, all laughing and moving about the kitchen.

Laney jumped right into the fray, stuffing a handful of Cheetos into her mouth, punching a little boy on the arm. I stood where I was, almost huddled in the doorway, tingling with a mixture of apprehension and awe. At our apartment, I might hear my mom giggling with a date or Dee talking softly on the phone, but we weren't a loud family. There were only three of us, after all, and none of us was particularly musical or rowdy. So that scene in Laney's kitchen, the sheer sound and activity, overwhelmed me, and yet I was envious of it. Even more, I envied the way they were all so comfortable with that noise, with themselves, with the other people in their family. They had their issues, but they worked well together. They talked over each other and kidded each other and handed out food. It was like watching a raucous but finely tuned circus with ten simultaneous acts under the big top.

The Pendletons invited me into the chaos that day, and I eventually grew more comfortable there. Still, I always had to prepare myself before I visited. I had to remind myself that it would be crazy, that I would leave exhilarated and stuffed with food but with ringing ears.

So as Laney and I walked the few blocks from the El station, I made those reminders to myself again. I took a few deep breaths and shook out my shoulders. It was cold, with mid-October bringing a sharp, chilly wind to the city, and we both had our hands in our pockets, our scarves around our necks.

"They'll be so glad to see you," Laney said, turning to look at me in that stiff-necked way people do when they're bundled up.

"Me, too. It's been a long time then?"

"Well, the last time was definitely before your birthday."

"I can't believe I didn't see your family all summer." It was like not seeing a nearby beloved grandma for five months. Laney's family had, in a sense, become my larger, rowdier extended family, an inclusion I cherished, since I had no extended family to speak of. My mom had fallen out with her parents after she married my deadbeat dad, much to their chagrin, and my dad's family never took any interest in me. At least that's what my mom had told me.

I've never told her, but I do have one memory of my dad's mom. I couldn't have been much older than four, possibly the last time I saw her. I think my mom had a date and no one to baby-sit, so she dropped me off at my grandmother's as a last resort. I don't remember much about the house or whether she played with me or whether she sang me any songs. All I remember is that she fed me lemons. She cut up a lemon into fourths and told me to bite into it. My face scrunched up at the acidic tartness. I felt the sting of the juice running down my chin, and she laughed. Thinking back on that time, she sounds cruel, and yet I loved that she was laughing. She had dyed brown hair, curled up tight from rollers, and she wore a pink sweater. And I loved how she laughed and laughed and laughed. I don't know why I've never told my mom that. I don't know why a woman would feed lemons to a child.

"The upside of not seeing my family," Laney said as we walked down her street, "is that you don't have to pretend you remember anything. I assume you don't want to tell them about the memory issue?"

"Nope. Too complicated, and you know…"

"I know, they'll all have their two cents to put in and they'll never let you forget it."

"Exactly."

We turned a corner and the house came into view. A few seconds later I was being hugged and smooched by a pack of women in the Pendletons' warm, crowded kitchen, which was filled with the inviting scent of spicy tomato sauce. Laney and her sisters look very much alike. They all have the dark hair and animated dark eyes of their Italian mother, with the fair skin and mischievous nature of their Irish dad. Their father, a wonderfully sweet and funny man, who I sometimes liked to pretend was my own dad, had passed away a few years ago from colon cancer, an event that darkened their sparkling household for a while, but they all seemed to be doing well again.

"Where the hell have you been, Kelly?" said Frannie, the sister who was only a year or so older than us. She was bouncing a baby on her hip, looking like a less fashionable version of Laney in her gray sweatpants and stained ivory sweater. "Are you helping Laney drink Chicago out of all its tequila?" She laughed.

I gave her a polite grin. Frannie is the one member of the Pendleton family that I've never liked very much. I think it has something to do with the fact that she's so close in age to Laney and me. In high school, being one year older is everything. Frannie ran with a crowd that Laney and I saw as achingly cool, and she'd mutter things like "yearbook geeks" when we patrolled the bleachers on a Friday night, interviewing people.

After we grew up, I disliked her even more, but for different reasons. I no longer felt that Frannie was superior to me. In fact, once she got married right out of college and popped out three kids in quick succession, I felt superior to *her*. I think it was some kind of coping mechanism, some response to what she represents—the ugly side of marriage and kids. Her husband is the prototypical pompous ass who spends more time with his buddies than he does his family, and their kids are not the nicest tykes I've ever met. Her eldest, Nick, Jr., a boy of six, threw up on me last year and then giggled like a hyena. Is it wrong to hate a child?

I know it doesn't have to be that way. I know that some people get married and have children and then blossom. They have even more fun than they did before, albeit in a different style. But here's the thing—how do you know which group you'll fall into? You don't. And so last year, the closer Ben and I came to being engaged (at least in my mind) the more I disliked, even feared Frannie, as if her unhappily married and mothering self could somehow rub off on me.

Laney doesn't see Frannie the same way. She's always felt like we did in high school—inferior. In fact, Laney feels inferior to all her sisters because they're grown-ups, she says, and they don't take her seriously. They have families and responsibilities and perfectly furnished suburban homes, while Laney's eight-piece set of margarita glasses is the only matching kitchenware she owns.

Two of Laney's sisters sat on the countertop now, yelling to their kids, when they tore through the kitchen, and giving Laney shit about dating yet another musician. Laney's eldest sister, Nancy, stood near the stove laughing with their mom, a sweet woman whose curvy body and wavy hair managed to be both sexy and comforting.

Timmy, who had just turned twenty-one, ambled into the room, oblivious after all these years to being one of the few males. "Yeah, Kell," he said, "what've you been doing lately?" Timmy had grown out of his gawky teenage self and into a man who knew that his tall frame and broad smile were undeniably appealing. He flashed me a rather sexy grin, and I wondered for a second what it would be like to fool around with a twenty-one-year-old. Not Timmy, of course. He would always be a kid brother to me, but maybe I could have my first one-night stand (if that hadn't already happened with the two-freckled man) with a sexy younger guy. Maybe I should try the bar scene again. Maybe Timmy had some friends who would stop by. Maybe I'm getting a little carried away here.

"I haven't been doing much," I said, trying not to think about sex with Timmy's buddies, most of whom probably lived in their parents' basement, as Timmy did.

"Sorry to hear about you and Ben," Nancy said, looking over her shoulder as she stirred a red sauce on the stove.

"And the job," said Mrs. Pendleton.

I waved a hand as if it were no big deal, but I felt embarrassed at the thought that Laney had been coming home every Sunday with tales of woe from my life, probably telling the family what a depressed psychopath I'd been all summer.

Laney, who must have read my thoughts, whispered in my ear, "They only know the basics."

I smiled at her. "Yeah, I've just been taking it easy for a while."

"I almost called you a few weeks ago," Nancy said. "Rob and I were going out of town for a weekend, and I thought you might want to baby-sit for some extra money. But we found someone in the neighborhood."

"*I* would have baby-sat for you," Laney said, before I could reply. "And you wouldn't have had to pay me. Why didn't you call me?" She sounded hurt. Laney was forever offering to watch her nieces and nephews, but no one ever seemed to take her up on it.

Nancy waved a wooden spoon in the air. "You're busy. You're always going out, and you've got your boy-friends."

"That doesn't mean I wouldn't have cancelled my plans to help you out."

"No big deal," Nancy said, but as Laney slumped into a chair, I could see that it was a big deal to her.

"So seriously, what have you been up to, Kelly?" Frannie asked.

I leaned over and squeezed Laney's shoulder. "Just staying home a lot."

"Well, I saw you when we ran into each other in front of the Radisson Hotel," Frida said from her perch on the countertop.

I looked at Laney's sister, drawing a blank. "What?"

"Yeah, I forgot to tell you, Lane," Frida said, "but you remember that, don't you, Kell? It was at the beginning of the summer."

I tugged the scarf away from my neck. The room was hot, and the tomatoey smells were cloying now. "I, uh, I can't remember." It was true, of course.

Frida's forehead creased. "We talked for a while. I can't believe you don't remember. You were meeting your friend."

"What friend?" I exchanged looks with Laney, knowing we were both thinking the same thing—the two-freckled guy. Was he the friend I was meeting?

Frida chuckled. "I don't know who it was, but I was thinking that it was probably someone who was helping you get over Ben."

"Why would you think that?"

"You were so secretive. You didn't seem to want to tell me anything about this friend or what you were doing, but you were coming out of the Radisson Hotel, after all."

Timmy made a knowing sound as if to imply that I'd been having an afternoon of crazy hotel sex, and all the sisters laughed.

I helped myself to a few crackers from a tray and fake-laughed along with them, wondering if Timmy was right.

* * *

That next week at work, I actually began to enjoy myself a little. Cole was still generally a sarcastic "arsehole," as he would say, but there were some subtle changes, due, I supposed, to him taking my suggestion about William's sweat and the fact that we'd had a drink with Laney. For one thing, he was suddenly using the term "we" very often, as in, "We don't have a shoot until Thursday," or "We should get some more red gel for the back lights." He also seemed to trust me more, not hanging over me all the time and shooting me snippy instructions. He even gave me a compliment one day.

I was on the phone making production calls for a shoot that would involve catalog work for a lingerie ad. I'd been surprised to learn that Cole, as the photographer, had to do nearly everything for these shoots, including casting the models, ordering food for the crew, scouting locations if it was in a remote site, obtaining the necessary permits, setting rates for the models and himself, and so many other things. For this particular lingerie shoot, Cole had asked me to arrange for the food, and lacking any other thoughts, I immediately called the caterer that used to stock Bartley Brothers with bagels and fruit for our Friday-morning meetings. The quote they gave me was astronomical. No wonder I'd gotten laid off; Bartley Brothers needed to make room in the budget for three-dollar bagels and fifty-dollar tubs of melon.

Next, I called a number of small restaurants I used to frequent in the Loop, figuring they'd jump for joy at a catering deal. I found a Greek restaurant that would supply us with feta eggs and fruit in the morning and Greek salads and gyros for lunch. It was a tad tricky deciding how much food to order, since so many people at the shoot would be models, and although I knew the whole anorexia thing might be a cliché, I'd starve myself too if I was going to be photographed in a thong. Finally, I secured the amount, the pricing and the delivery schedule, and I typed the whole thing up for Cole on his computer.

I was on the phone again, this time with a booker from one of the modeling agencies, when Cole walked over to me, reading the printout.

"Great work," he said when I hung up the phone. "You're so much better at this than I am."

I was proud despite myself.

Later that day, I could hear Cole on the phone, talking fast and excitedly to someone, although I couldn't make out what he was saying. When he got off the phone, he was more animated than I'd ever seen him.

"What's up?" I said.

He bounced around on his feet, moving from his butcher-block table, where some equipment was lined up with militarylike precision, to where I sat. "Can't say. Don't want to ruin it, if you know what I mean, but soon. Maybe soon."

That's all I could get out of him, but he was in such a charming mood that he let me leave at three o'clock. When I got home that day, I was feeling good about my new job and wanting to try out some of the photographic techniques I'd picked up by watching Cole. I dug my camera bag out of the closet by the kitchen, making sure that I still had battery power. I checked to see if there was any film. Yes. There were twenty-six pictures left on a roll of thirty-six. But I couldn't remember the last time I'd taken any photos. Had it been this summer? Or even before that? The last time I could actually recall was Christmas at Ben's house, and then my mom's apartment after that. But I'd already developed those. So when had I taken ten pictures and, more importantly, what had I taken them of?

The only way to find out was to finish the roll and get it developed. I headed outside and walked through Lincoln Park up to Fullerton Avenue until I reached the botanical gardens. It used to be a favorite practice site of mine, the huge greenhouse, its glass bleary with humidity and the oval ring of flowering bushes outside. I started shooting one frame after another, loving the satisfying click of the shutter. I tried out some of Cole's techniques—using a long lens to shoot a single bloom and fuzz out the background, taking the shot a little off center to bring some other element into the picture.

When I was finished with the roll, I walked back to my place, feeling pleased, centered. Taking pictures always did that to me. As I neared my apartment, the sky was hanging low and purple, the way dusk falls in Chicago. The encroaching darkness brought a chill with it, but I was warm inside. Things were finally falling into place. I had a decent job, I was getting over Ben. No, I *was* over Ben. I marched on happily toward my building, crossing the street and walking up my circular drive.

And there he was, as if he'd heard my thoughts, sitting right in front of my building on the rim of the fountain.

15

Ben stood when he saw me. "What did you get?" he said, gesturing to my camera bag.

It was such a familiar question, the one he'd ask whenever I came inside from taking pictures, that I immediately began to answer it, telling him about the botanical gardens and the flowers I'd shot. For a second, I could see us in my town house, Ben sitting at the kitchen table while pasta boiled on the stove, me rambling on about the shots I'd taken.

Ben nodded as I talked, and asked other questions, and before long it began to feel comfortable. Too comfortable.

"Why are you here?" I said suddenly.

He blinked a few times, as if he hadn't expected me to say that. "I, um, forgot to ask you something on Saturday."

"Yeah, me, too." *Why didn't you want to marry me?*

"Okay, well, should I go first?" he asked.

"Sure." I set my camera bag down and pulled my jacket tighter around me.

"Should we go inside?"

"No." I answered quickly. I didn't want him to see my bland apartment, which was such a step down from the town house.

"Okay. It's just that I forgot to ask you about this memory thing." He waved a vague hand toward my head. "I mean, are you still having problems?"

"It's *not* a problem."

"Oh. Great. So you can remember everything again?"

"I didn't say that."

More blinking. "So you still have this memory gap, or whatever you're calling it."

"I'm not calling it anything, and it's not a problem. It's just…there."

"Kell, that's not good. I really think you should go to the doctor."

"Well, you don't get to have an opinion anymore, do you?"

He shook his head, as if refusing to get pulled in by my childish taunt. "It's not healthy, not remembering like that. You need to see someone about it."

I squirmed. My body was agitated and itchy with the introduction of this issue that I didn't want to think about from someone I didn't want to care about. "I'm not kidding, Ben. You don't get an opinion on this. You wanted out. You're out. So don't come around here telling me what to do."

A car drove into the circular drive and parked near us. Ben glanced up, then back at me. I could tell he was reining in something else he wanted to say. "Fair enough," he said finally. "So what was the thing you forgot to ask me this weekend?"

I squirmed again. Why now? Why was this happening now, when I was just starting to feel like I was getting my act together?

"It was nothing," I said.

"Well, it was *something*."

"No, it's nothing."

"You said you forgot to ask me something, so just ask."

"Why didn't you want to marry me?" I blurted it out, right in the middle of his question, right there in the middle of the driveway.

His mouth hung open a little, and a heavy silence weighed on us, despite the buzz of the city and the cars speeding by on Lake Shore Drive. His face was turning a little pink from the chilly night air, and old instincts made me want to hurry him inside and fix him a cup of coffee.

"I told you," he said after a few long seconds. "You made it clear that you wanted a ring by your birthday, and I couldn't give you what you wanted."

"I know that, but you didn't tell me *why*. Why couldn't you give me what I wanted? Why didn't you want to marry me?" I fought back a few tears that seemed to pop into the corners of my eyes. Okay, maybe I wasn't totally over him.

Ben's own eyes looked so sad. "Here's the thing, Kell. I'm not so sure about that anymore."

"What? What do you mean?"

"I think I made a mistake."

I walked Ben around the corner to a little Italian restaurant called Angelina's that I'd spotted recently. I still wouldn't invite him into my new apartment, but we couldn't have this talk in the driveway, either. The dinner rush wasn't on yet and so we were soon seated in a front table by the window with two glasses of Chianti in front of us. To someone on the street who happened to glance inside, we probably looked incredibly romantic, a couple who'd clearly known each other for a long time, tucked into a cozy table, our heads pushed close together as we talked.

In reality, I was feeling about every emotion imaginable

except cozy and romantic—love, hate, anguish, regret, anger, confusion, you name it.

"Let me start over," Ben was saying. He put his hands flat on the table for emphasis. I'd seen him do that a million times at Bartley Brothers when he was trying to make a point. "You know I don't like being told what to do."

I huffed but didn't say anything. It was one of my pet peeves about Ben. If he thought you were ordering him to wash up the kitchen or pick up the dry cleaning, then he would act out like a kid—delaying, pouting, stomping around.

"Look, I know it's not a good trait, but I can't help it sometimes," he continued. "And when you said that you had to be engaged by your birthday, I felt like you were telling me what to do instead of us making a joint decision."

"So why didn't you make it into a joint decision? Why didn't you talk to me about it?"

"Kell, you know how you are when you want something, and you made it perfectly clear you wanted a ring or we were done."

"Fine," I said, practically spitting the word, because he was right. "What I've been asking you, though, is why you didn't want to marry me. Even if you did feel like I was telling you what to do, *why* couldn't you do it eventually?"

"That's the thing. I felt I did want to marry you. Eventually. But I didn't like that ultimatum you were giving me. I didn't want to be pushed into it, so I finally decided that if I couldn't do it in your time frame, maybe I shouldn't do it at all."

Was he actually telling me anything new? It didn't feel like it.

"That night of your birthday was one of the worst days of my life," Ben continued.

"Join the club." I said it sarcastically before I realized that I couldn't technically remember that night. It angered me all of a sudden, this memory thing, because although it had delivered me from depression and given me a shot at a new life, it had also stolen from me the right to remember, to revive how fucking pissed off I was at Ben that night.

"I know it wasn't a good day for you, either, and I'm sorry about that, about breaking up with you on that day." He rubbed a hand over his eyes. "I was a mess after we broke up. I couldn't stop thinking about you and what an ass I'd been, because by breaking up with you, I was actually coming to terms with the fact that I *did* want to marry you someday, and then all of a sudden, I didn't have you at all. It was killing me. But right when I was about to come talk to you about all this, to tell you that I'd made a huge mistake, you started calling me at all hours and stopping by work or my apartment. You didn't seem like yourself anymore."

"Why? What did I seem like?" Half of me didn't want to know, but I was too curious. I needed to hear Ben's take on what I'd been like during that time.

"You were down. *Very* down. It was almost spooky the way you acted. Kind of like you were on the edge, and if we didn't get back together you were going to lose it. It got pretty creepy for a while, and I called Laney to ask her what in the hell was going on, but she didn't know, either." He shook his head. "The thing was, once *you* started acting so strange, *I* started feeling better. I know that sounds shitty, but it was like you were reinforcing my decision. Every time I found you sitting on my doorstep or waiting for me by the El after work, it was like a confirmation that we weren't supposed to be together."

He paused and looked at me for a response. I wanted to scream at him, to call him selfish and shallow and reactionary and shortsighted, but the thing was that I might have acted the same, felt the same, if the person I thought I loved had forced me into a corner. "What did you mean tonight when you said you thought you'd made a mistake?"

He gave a short, embarrassed laugh. "Well, it's all different now, isn't it?"

"What's different?"

"You, for one thing. You're totally different now than you were this summer."

"How?" I thought I knew what he meant, but some needy part of myself wanted to hear it.

"You're like you used to be before we got so caught up at Bartley and before all this marriage talk. You're confident again and funny and laid-back—and let's face it, you look gorgeous. Every time I see you like this, I realize that I might have made a really, really grave mistake. I miss you, Kell."

I pulled my glass of Chianti toward me and took a glug of it, my head swirling. On one hand, I hated him for deciding this *now*, for being such an asshole that he couldn't have realized before how awesome I was. On the other hand, I felt fluffed up and proud at his praise, his second thoughts.

"I don't know what to say, Ben. I mean, what do you want from me?"

"Didn't get that far." He laughed. His nervous laugh. "I guess I just want us to be able to keep talking about this."

"What about Therese?"

He looked at the table, then back up at me. "I just want to talk to you, Kell, that's all. Maybe in a few days, maybe on the phone, whatever you want. Can we do that?"

I wanted to tell him to fuck off, that he'd already made his one mistake. But I'd made mistakes, too, mistakes that might have been even bigger than his, and sitting across from him like this, our hands almost touching on the table, I missed what we used to have.

"Yeah," I said, "we can do that."

16

Ben called the next morning before I left for Cole's. "Hey, I forgot to tell you something last night," he said, as if we talked on the phone all the time. "Tony Poppin came out of the closet."

"No!" I yelped, so surprised that I couldn't even be annoyed at Ben's casual tone.

Tony Poppin was another analyst at Bartley Brothers who had long been suspected of being gay. Not that anyone would have been upset or particularly put out by this, but because he rarely dated, was always dressed impeccably and had season's tickets to the opera, he was forever a source of office speculation. Was he or wasn't he? I'd never chimed in on this topic, of course, given my gaydar history, but everyone else liked to give their best guess. He did talk on the phone *all* the time, some people said, and he was forever taking classes on cooking with truffles and flower arranging. But others pointed out that he always showed up at the Christmas party with a gorgeous female date, and so the questions would start again. It's sad, really, that this was such a topic of conversation at Bartley, but let's face it, most corporations are simply big high schools.

After that conversation about Tony, Ben started calling nearly every day, sometimes a few times a day, and our chats were always just that—chats. We gossiped about people at Bartley, told stupid little stories from our day (Ben being mistaken for the Bears quarterback while on the El; me getting a heel stuck in a street grate outside Cole's building) and reminisced about some of the great times we'd had together (the Halloween party we had two years ago; the time we got upgraded to first class flying home from Paris).

I didn't tell Laney how often Ben and I were talking. I'd told her about that night at Angelina's, of course. I'd called her as soon as I walked in the door, and we analyzed that encounter for a solid two hours. But I was embarrassed about how easily I'd let Ben slip back into my life after he'd dumped me on my birthday and helped to send me into a depression. Actually, I now considered it a bit of a bonus that I couldn't remember the breakup or the depression, because how upset about something can you be when you have absolutely no memory of it? But I knew Laney remembered for me, and although I loved her for it, I couldn't betray her by telling her that I was talking to the enemy all the time now. And enjoying it.

And so it became weirder and weirder. A few weeks went by during which I told Laney very little about my days or how I was filling them. Since we'd met, I'd rarely kept anything from her, and although I didn't think she suspected anything now, our time together became strained. I felt awkward for hiding something from her, and over and over, maybe in response to my holding back, she insisted that this memory gap had gone on long enough and I needed to do something about it.

"I'm serious, Kell," she said on the phone one day, "you've got to see a doctor."

She'd called me at Cole's. I had a booker on hold on the other line, and Cole gesturing to me to help him with something.

"I can't talk about this right now," I said, glad I hadn't told her much about my pesky headaches. In fact, I had another one right then, and I didn't relish a lecture from Laney.

"You're going to have to face this."

"Yes, I know. You've told me."

"At least go see Ellen Geiger again."

"Why? So I can pay her over a hundred dollars to tell me nothing?"

"You haven't given her a chance."

"I gave her a chance all summer, and I'm doing better now without her. I'm fine!" I looked over to see Cole making a face at me.

"I've got to go, Lane." I clicked over to the booker before she could say anything else.

Meanwhile, it was so much more enjoyable to talk to Ben or meet him for coffee (that's all we'd done; no physical contact), and I actually began feeling closer to him than Laney.

My life began to take on a surreal slant. Here I was living in my new apartment, as I still called it in my head, having coffee and marathon phone calls with my ex-boyfriend, and, at the same time, avoiding contact with my best friend who'd just nursed me out of a five-month downward spiral. I felt guilty. So guilty. But I just wanted to have a good time. I didn't want to worry about those five months or why I couldn't remember them, or anything else, for that matter. The fact was, Ben was simply more fun to be with.

Strangely, even Cole had become more fun than Laney. During the lingerie shoot, he let me take the test shots and then a few frames every hour or so. He hovered behind me, offering encouragement and whispering instructions about what I should be seeing, how the photo should look. I brought coffee in the mornings from Katie's, and we talked about what *we* would be working on that day.

I knew that I was really hitting some kind of stride in my life during the two days when the studio was filled with lingerie models dressed in a few strips of lace. You'd think I would have been insecure, maybe going to the bathroom to check the size of my gut and comparing it to the concave abdomens of the models, but I didn't. I ate fat-ridden muffins while watching them lie in sexy poses over a black-velvet-covered box. I chatted with them while they were naked in the dressing room. Not once did I consider myself deficient compared to them. That's the whole point, I guess—I didn't compare myself to them at all.

It probably had something to do with the fact that I'd lost weight, but it was more than that, more than just body image. There was some sense of contentedness about the way my life was going. For the first time in a long time I was excited to go to work in the morning. I could hardly wait. It seemed that so many parts of my new life were falling into place, a good place.

Except for the Laney part.

Well, to be honest, there was one other piece of my life that wasn't so spectacular, either—my evenings. My nights were a little lonely. It wasn't as if I had no options. Laney called every day, and almost every time, she offered to "take" me to a movie that night or to come over with some Chinese food. The strange thing was that the more she offered, the more I backed away. I had to work late, I told her. Cole was such a slave driver, he was keeping me overtime. But the truth was that things had grown so awkward between Laney and me that I actually preferred my lonely apartment.

I had the occasional cup of coffee with Ben after work, but I was always sure to end it after an hour or so, no matter how hard we were laughing, no matter how many times he flashed his bedroom eyes. As much as I wanted to have sex with him (and I really, *really* wanted to), I didn't want it to progress to the point where I had to make a decision about our relationship. Also, I found myself overly conflicted about the subject of Therese. On one hand, I felt strangely ashamed. What was she doing while we had coffee and yammered on the phone? Did she even know? It was technically Ben's problem, not mine, but I couldn't help but have a little sympathy for the girl. And yet on the other hand, if he really had made a mistake by breaking up with me, shouldn't he break up with *her* now? I didn't ask Ben these questions, because I guess I didn't want to know. I didn't want to be culpable for keeping him away or breaking them up when I wasn't sure if I was ready to recommit to him. I didn't want to think about what a shit he was for seeing someone other than his current girlfriend. I just wanted to keep laughing, to keep having fun with him for an hour or so at Katie's Coffee. So I kept it short and was always back at my apartment by seven or eight o'clock, the rest of the evening stretching out ahead of me.

Jess and Steve were barely back from their honeymoon and busy moving into their new place, so I couldn't go out with them. I did call a few analysts that I used to work with at Bartley Brothers, but they were all at a conference in Tahoe, one that I would have attended if I still worked there. Not even my two-freckled guy had visited me again.

On one Thursday night, when I could have been out with Laney at a trendy new wine bar she wanted to try, I decided to take a bath. The tub in my new apartment was rather large, with two armrests cut into it. I started the water and rooted around under my sink until I found some paper packages of aloe vera bath salts. I didn't remember buying them. Probably a gift from Laney when she'd stopped by over the summer. I poured a whole package into the bath, making it a milky, foaming green. Lighting a few candles, I set them on the countertop. I dragged a boom box out of my bedroom closet and put on an Eric Clapton CD. Then I turned out the lights, stripped and slid into the steaming bath.

It was perfect and soothing. For about five minutes. But then I started to feel sweaty and red-faced, and Eric's guitar sounded screechy rather than melodic. I took a sip of the wine I'd brought in with me. I slid deeper into the tub. *Deep breaths,* I told myself. *Just relax.* All I could think about, though, was what I would do with the rest of the night. It would be, what, maybe eight-thirty by the time I got out of the tub? There'd be hours and hours with nothing to do, since I rarely went to bed before eleven. Maybe I should call Ben and see what he was doing tonight. But if I did that, wouldn't I be looking for Ben to save me from myself, the same thing I'd done when I'd ordered him to give me a ring or else?

I squirmed around in the tub, willing myself to just calm down and enjoy the heat. What was wrong with me? Why couldn't I loosen up for two frickin' seconds?

Even though it never worked, I tried the meditation breathing again. I hadn't listened to those tapes in God knows how long, but I could hear the instructor's voice— *Breathe in, breathe out, focus on your breath.* I made myself do it. I made myself stay in the bath, in the heat, in the foamy water. And pretty soon, I started to relax. A little. Actually, my body still felt like leaping out of the tub, but my mind was slowing down, and so I made myself stick with it. *Breathe in, breathe out, focus on your breath. Let all other thoughts slide away.* It started to work. The image of Ben faded. The thought of Laney's overly concerned face took a back seat. I pushed away any inklings about Cole or his many secretive talks on the phone as of late. Dee popped into my head once, but I wouldn't let myself get hooked in. I let her float away.

And pretty soon there was just me. Finally. Just me in the tub, surrounded by suds. I could actually see myself, even though I had my eyes closed. This must be good. Possibly I'd tapped into some Zenlike avenue of introspection. I might be the first Westerner to master this technique. I'd probably be invited to give self-help seminars around the world.

I stayed with it, breathing deeply, seeing myself in the tub. But as I did so, I started to notice something. Something off. It had to do with my hair. I concentrated, and I could see that my hair was not the shiny caramel color with the cute style that Lino had given it, and it was not in a twist on top of my head, the way I'd done it before I'd gotten in the bath. Instead, it was dull and lifeless and long, the ends floating in the green foam. I looked closer and saw that my face looked different, too. Almost gray, my cheekbones too sharp in my face. And my eyes were open. Dull and staring straight ahead, as if there was no thought behind them, no hope or happiness or optimism.

My face, the one I was seeing now, scared me. I tried to sit up in the tub. I tried to stop my Zenlike breathing. I didn't need to give self-help seminars, I just needed to get out of this bath. But the image stayed there—strong now— and I couldn't seem to move. It was as if the bath were a tomb from which I couldn't escape. The coffee in my stomach made me feel nauseous. I needed to take some Tums, some Advil, *something*. Strangely, I could feel my legs twitching under the water, but I still couldn't get them into any kind of concerted motion that would get me out of the tub. I couldn't stop seeing myself. What was wrong with me? Why was I just staring ahead like that, at nothing? I tried to stay calm and think of something else. Maybe if I could replace the image of myself, I could get out of this state. I tried to instill new topics in my head—my new job, Ben, my mother in L.A.—but my face, that sad, dull face, stayed right there, and something about it was drawing me in.

It was me sometime over the summer, I realized. Sometime during those horrible months. And I was thinking how there was no hope. No hope for what? What was I so distraught about? It was partly about Ben—I could feel that now. And it was partly about getting fired from my job. And of course, there was Dee. But there was something more, too. What was it? The two-freckled man, the one with the dark hair. It had something to do with him.

I finally wrenched myself away from the image and sat up so violently in the bath that lime-green water surged over the edge and splashed on the bathroom floor. I shook my head and blinked like crazy. I was here. What the hell was that? What had happened? It was like the flash I'd had of the two-freckled man, but this one had been about me. The me I didn't want to be anymore. The me I was running from.

17

That image stayed with me all night and all the next morning. Over and over, I saw my drawn face just above the bathwater, my vacant eyes, my lifeless hair snarling and floating around my head like Medusa's snakes. It was Friday, a day I used to long for when I worked at Bartley Brothers, but now I worried about what I would do with my weekend, whether that woman in the bath would come back to me.

That day, Cole was taking portfolio shots for a few models sent over by a local agency. The idea was to build up the books of these models, make it appear as if they had more experience than they actually did, and so we worked hard to change the set, the models' looks, the lighting, anything to make it seem as if the photos weren't taken at the same time. Luckily, all the activity took me out of my head, and by noon I'd exorcised that awful image of myself.

"Kelly," Cole said to me after lunch. "Why don't you take a few here? You might bring a different look to the shot."

"Sure. Great. Just one second." I had my arms full with a huge fan that we'd used with the last model.

"Hurry up, Kelly. I want this done."

I glanced over at Cole. He hadn't snapped at me like that since before the William shoot, but all day he'd been tense.

I stepped behind the tripod and smiled at Tracy, the model. She had stunning ebony skin and wore a khaki dress unbuttoned almost to the waist, with stiletto heels. Her hair was pulled back in a bun, her eye makeup dramatic—a sexy working-woman look. The fact that she was fifteen wouldn't show up on camera, but it kept freaking me out, the age of these girls. I'd always envisioned models as sophisticated women drinking cosmos in Manhattan, but the Snapple-slurping fifteen- and sixteen-year-olds in the studio that day were actually the norm. Most of them hadn't even gone to a prom yet, and they were all making more money than me.

"Tracy, can you turn around and look at me over your shoulder?" I said.

Cole had been shooting her in some stern, businesslike poses, but she had a playful side that came out between shots—a cute smile, a girlish giggle—and I thought we might use some of that personality to even out the austere outfit and makeup.

She turned her body to face the back wall and swung her head around.

"Chin down," I instructed her. "Small smile. A little bigger. There you go."

Tracy responded well to me, and it took only five minutes to shoot off a roll of twenty-four.

"Good work, Kelly," Cole said when I was done. His face was serious, though, different than his goofiness of the last week, and I wondered if he'd lost that assignment he'd been hoping for.

The studio phone rang then. I dashed across the room to answer it.

"Hey, hon." It was Laney. "How's that boss of yours? Still cute?"

I glanced at Cole across the room. He was talking to the head of the agency, looking nervous. "He's okay."

"Say hi for me. Anyway, I wanted to tell you about this memory-loss Web site I found on the Internet. You really need to check it out. From your symptoms, you could have a medical problem, or it could even be psychiatric."

"Well, I'm definitely crazy right now," I said, trying to ignore her ominous tone and hold on to the good feeling I'd gotten from taking the shots of Tracy.

"You know, it's nothing to ignore. We've really got to figure this thing out."

"Mmm-hmm," I said, doing my best Ellen Geiger imitation. "Well, now's not the time."

"You can't keep putting this off, Kell."

"Yes, I can!" My voice was raised. One of the moms who was passing by looked at me in alarm, but I couldn't stop. "I can do what I want with my life, and right now I want to enjoy it. I'm an adult for Christ's sake!"

Silence on the other end.

"I'm sorry." I sighed. "I'm working here, and there's a lot to do."

"I'm just trying to help, you know."

"I know, and I'm sorry. Like I said, it's just crazy around here. That's all." That wasn't all, of course. There was much more—something else that was going on with Laney and me—but now wasn't the time to talk about it.

After another silence, Laney said in a small voice, "Well, do you want to come to Gear's gig tonight?"

I was meeting Ben for a drink after work, and I really didn't need a whole night of Laney mothering me, but I felt so bad for snapping at her. "Sure. Where is it?"

"The Metro. They're the opening band."

"Meet you there at nine?"

She paused. "You don't want to get dinner first?"

"I'm actually having drinks with some people from Bartley Brothers." That was true. Sort of.

"Okay," Laney said. "See you at nine."

Cole wrapped up around four. He asked me to run to the photo shop to drop off the day's film and pick up the rolls from the lingerie shoot. The shop was about ten blocks away in the Loop, and I decided to walk, since it was one of those Indian summer days in late October, at least sixty degrees. The trees in the city were practically bare now, but I liked them better that way because I could see the sky through the branches—royal-blue and growing darker. The city had that buzzy Friday afternoon feel to it, like everyone was on the verge of something wonderful. I hadn't been plagued by a headache for a few days, and I felt light on my feet, happy.

Cars streamed by me as I crossed Michigan Avenue, shouts of laughter as the doors to the bars opened and closed. I took my time walking to the shop, glad that I wasn't working at Bartley Brothers right now, where leaving the office before seven at night was frowned upon.

"Hey, Nate," I said, greeting the balding store owner as I walked into the photo shop.

"Happy Friday," he said. "I've got your stuff in the back."

He disappeared through the rear door of the shop, and I busied myself by playing with point-and-shoot cameras on display.

"Here you go." Nate swung through the back door again. "Fifteen rolls."

I glanced down at the sheet where Cole made me record every film delivery. "Lingerie shoot—fourteen," it said.

"I think that's one too many," I told Nate.

He counted through them again, looking at the labels

with Cole's name on it. "I've got fifteen. Why don't you go through them?"

This was what Cole required me to do, anyway—briefly review each roll to see if any photos needed obvious redeveloping. I peeled back the flap on the first envelope, flipping through the shots, then moving on to the next and the next. Lots of women in very little undies looking mostly gorgeous and ridiculously thin.

When I'd gotten to the eighth roll, another from the lingerie shoot, I suddenly remembered why there was an extra one. My roll was in this bunch—the roll I'd finished at the park that day that Ben had shown up, the one that held ten mystery pictures. I'd brought it in with Cole's film, and somehow I'd forgotten. Maybe because of Ben and Laney and everything that'd been going on lately, or maybe I just wanted to forget.

I paid Nate, pocketed the receipt for Cole and was out the door and back on the street. Now the crowd on the sidewalk seemed pushy and rude instead of giddy and fun. The cars honked over and over, exhaust hanging thick in the air.

What was in my roll of film? What was on those pictures? I kept my feet pounding, heading back toward Cole's. In my hands I had a glimpse of the last few months, but I wasn't sure I wanted to see it.

Yet I knew I had to look. I stopped and sat on a concrete bench. A woman sitting there with a host of stuffed plastic bags sniffed as if I was really putting her out, then finally scooted over to give me more room. I had to flip through a few more rolls of broads-in-thongs before I came to the one that was mine. I could tell before I even opened it because it was thicker than Cole's. I always got doubles.

I tapped the unopened packet of photos on my leg. A bus pulled up, brakes squealing, and the plastic-bag lady heaved herself up and onto the bus, leaving me alone.

I finally turned the envelope over and slowly slid the flap

open, watching the glue stretch into thin threads before snapping. I lifted the smaller envelope from inside. Another second went by before I removed the stack of photos.

I breathed out, quick and heavy, when I saw the top one. It was me, just me by myself. I raised it closer to my face, recognizing the Van Gogh print behind my head and the mustard-yellow of the walls. It was my town house, and I stood in the same spot I always did when I took an automatic shot of myself. I believed in taking photos for posterity, even if they were of me, alone. In this particular photo, my hair was like it used to be—longer, light brown, pulled back in a shiny ponytail with short bangs in front. I had on a big smile, full makeup and a V-neck black dress. When had this been taken?

I looked at the bottom righthand corner, and sure enough, I'd turned on the date function of my camera. May 3. My birthday. I could tell from the light in the room that it was early evening, which meant I'd taken this photo after I got fired but before Ben and I went out for dinner.

I flipped to the next picture. It was a shot of the living room and dining area of my town house, and the date was the same. I'd bought flowers and placed them on the polished dining room table. The place was spotless and gleaming. I'd probably cleaned, waiting for Ben to come over, wondering whether he would propose there, at our future home, or if we would go out to dinner. I couldn't remember taking the picture, and yet seeing it was as depressing as watching an alcoholic stand outside a closed liquor store.

I quickly moved to the next one and then the next and the next. What the hell?

They were all similar in a way. They were all of Ben. But he hadn't posed for these shots. They looked like surveillance photos—an out-of-focus shot of him leaving his apartment; Ben kissing Therese on the street; Ben pushing through the doors of the Bartley Brothers building on Madison; Ben buying something at an outdoor fruit market in the

Loop. I could tell that I'd used my 200 mm lens for most of them, that I'd been rather far away when I'd taken these. I'd been following Ben around, stalking him in a sense, just as he'd told Laney. Damn.

When I got back, I heard the low rumble of male voices as I took the elevator up to Cole's studio. I wondered about the type of people he hung out with, eager to forget what I'd seen in those photos. The elevator opened, and I stepped into the room, the voices clearer—and both familiar.

"She's brilliant," Cole said, "really brilliant."

"I know that," the other man said. "I'm sure I know better than you."

I froze. Oh, God. I did know that voice. It was Ben.

I hurried down the steps and looked to the right, and there, standing over Cole's butcher-block table, were Ben and Cole. Ben's arms were crossed—his defensive pose. Cole looked a little more loose, a little more amused.

"Hello, Kelly Kelly," Cole said, and I saw Ben's eyes narrow at his use of the nickname.

"Ben," I said, wrapping the plastic bag tight around the photos as if he could see through it to those surveillance pictures of him. I stuffed the bag deep into Cole's beanbag chair and walked toward them. "What are you doing here? I thought we were meeting at the bar."

"Yeah, well, I thought I'd come pick you up, see what you've got going on over here." He cast a disdainful glance around Cole's studio and raised his eyebrows as if to say, *You could do better.*

"Look, mate," Cole said. "We're working, so we'll see you later, okay?"

"I'll just hang out and wait."

"Sorry, doesn't work like that," Cole said. "This is a private studio."

"Yeah, thank God it's not open to the public," Ben said.

It was Cole who looked pissed off and defensive now.

"Okay," I said in a loud voice. I grabbed Ben by the arm and propelled him toward the elevator. "I'll meet you at the bar in half an hour, all right?"

"Sure, sure," he said. He leaned down, as if to kiss me, but I turned it into a quick hug and practically pushed him into the elevator.

"What a prat," Cole said when the doors closed. "You're not serious about that guy, are you?"

Ben and I sat on stools in the dim light of Trattoria No. 10, or "T-10" as it was called by the Bartley Brothers employees. It was an Italian restaurant and bar, housed in the belly of a building on Dearborn Street, a place I'd been with Ben a million times. Ben hadn't mentioned his visit to Cole's studio, and aside from telling him to call next time before he stopped by, I had let it go. I just wanted to enjoy myself.

"Another one?" Ben said, pointing to my nearly empty wineglass.

"You bet." What the hell? I'd been drinking merlot, the heavy red sinking through my stomach and into my limbs.

Ben lifted himself off the stool and walked a few feet away to catch the bartender's attention. I started to think again about those photos I'd taken of him. Did he know? Was that why he'd told Laney I was stalking him? Or was it just my constant appearance on his doorstep in my pajamas? Whatever the answer, I wasn't going to tell him now. No way. It made me feel guilty knowing about those photos if he didn't, but to admit that I'd been following and photographing him would change the tenor of our time together. I'd revert to psycho status in an instant.

I watched him talk to the bartender, noticing how different it was to be here with him, in a dark, crowded bar drinking too much wine. So different from the steaming mugs and the cozy comfort of Katie's Coffee. It seemed more adult now. Closer to sex—a possibility that was eating away at my mellow buzz. I mean, let's face it, I hadn't had sex in God knows how long, and human beings simply weren't made to abstain forever. There was also the fact that I was feeling physically fantastic, lean and mean in my new clothes and my new body, all of which had been bringing sex to the forefront of my brain lately.

"Here you go," Ben said, placing another fat glass of red in front of me and hitching himself back onto his bar stool. He wore a dark gray sweater that I'd never seen before. Cashmere, I could tell. Something from Therese? Or maybe a gift to himself after he'd made partner?

"Thanks," I said, giving him a flirty smile. I couldn't help it. I couldn't help thinking about sex with him because I knew how it would be. How *good*.

"So, tell me more about this Cole guy. What's with the attitude?"

"Ben, don't."

"Don't what?"

"You know. Don't slam him. He's my boss, and I like him."

"Fine, then tell me what you've been working on over there."

I told him about the models, about my shots of Tracy. Yet as the words came out of my mouth, my head was a little detached, because I kept seeing Ben naked. I kept seeing the barely there hair on his chest, the mole on his left hipbone. Each time I let my mind's eye wander lower, I'd blink madly to scare away the image, and focus again on what I was saying, what Ben was asking me. Thank God I'd agreed to meet Laney so that I wouldn't have to make any kind of decision about sex with him. He hadn't made any advances toward me, except for that near kiss today at Cole's, and I didn't even know where we'd go if we wanted to do it. Hell, I wasn't even sure if he lived with Therese or if she'd just been at his place that day. We didn't talk about stuff like that.

Ben was beaming at my success with Tracy, his eyes clear and happy, like they used to be in our first few years together, before we both got bogged down with climbing the ladder at Bartley. "Bogged down" was how I used to think about it, because Ben and I had gone the way that so many couples do—we'd gotten inordinately busy and inordinately used to one another, and as a result, we didn't treat each other quite as well as before. Aside from sex, which was always wonderful, we just weren't as close as we had been in the early days. I assume that there are couples who actually grow closer as they grow older, but I haven't met them yet. Jess and Steve might qualify someday, yet they've only been together two years, so it's hard to say.

"You're loving this, aren't you?" Ben was smiling at me, sort of an indulgent, proud smile, like the one he'd given me at Jess's wedding when I was singing the bawdy love songs.

"What?"

"This whole photography thing."

I shrugged, trying for nonchalance, but I couldn't stop myself from smiling, too.

"You do. You love it," Ben said.

"Yeah. I mean, of course."

"It's like having a hobby for a job."

"I guess that's true." God, *was* it true? Ben's statement seemed insulting but with an underlying layer of truth.

"You don't make much, right?"

"In terms of money? No." Why did I feel so defensive? He was right. My hourly wage would barely support a teenager's Mountain Dew habit.

"You know…" Ben's words drifted off as he took a swallow of his beer. He looked at me. "I could support both of us now that I've made partner."

My own glass was halfway to my mouth by the time I processed his words. I quickly lowered it back to the shiny wooden bar. "What are you talking about?"

He was nervous. I could tell from the way his face colored a little. "I'm just saying that if we, you know, got back together, you could get a job with some other photographer, someone better, or if you really wanted you could keep your job with Cole."

"I can already keep my job with Cole. I'm supporting myself." Sort of. I didn't mention the severance or the money from my town house.

"Hey, Kell." Ben's tone was soft. "Don't get like that. I'm just saying that long-term, down the road, if we're together, you can keep this job as long as you want or take any kind of job or even just do photography on your own, because I can afford it."

His words scared and thrilled me at the same time. Did he really want to get back together? And if he did, was he talking about today or "down the road"? Why was he *now* able to make plans that sounded decidedly long-term? And what was this about supporting me? It seemed a nice gesture, but it rubbed me wrong, too. An even better question— did I want to officially get back together?

"No pressure," Ben said. "But think about it. We can travel to amazing places, go out to the best restaurants, you can do your photography, whatever you want. We can have a blast together, and still have enough money to live in style. You know what I mean?"

"I guess." It was true that the money from my town house and the funds from my severance package, combined with my meager salary from Cole, wouldn't last forever. I'd have to make some major changes if I wanted to keep my job with him.

"Look, I'm just throwing it out there," Ben said. "I've been having so much fun with you, and I think we can keep doing that for a long time. But we don't have to worry about this now, okay?"

I nodded.

"In fact," Ben said, lifting his beer glass, "let's have a toast to good times."

"Good times," I said, clinking my glass to his, my head bustling with everything he'd said.

"Want an Attila story?"

"Sure."

Ben started cracking up before he could even tell me the tale about my ex-boss, and soon I was laughing along with him. I let his words about the future drift away in a merlot haze. I wouldn't worry about it now. I wouldn't worry about anything, just like Ben had said.

Thirty minutes later, I glanced down at my watch. "Shit! I'm supposed to meet Laney in half an hour."

"Where?" Ben said.

"The Metro."

"Well, c'mon. It's only a few blocks from my place. We'll share a cab."

We slipped into our coats and climbed the stairs to the street. The Loop was mostly deserted now, only a few random squares of golden light glowing from the office buildings.

We tucked ourselves into a taxi. The back seat was ripped and dirty, but the driver had the heat cranked up and jazz blaring from his CD player.

The cab got onto Lake Shore and the glittering lights of the city flew past us as we sped north. By the time we got to the Metro, I was laughing again, this time at Ben's imitation of his younger brother's drunken speech at a family dinner a few weeks ago. We stayed in the cab, sitting just outside the Metro, while Ben finished his story.

"I should go," I said after a few minutes. "Thanks for the drinks."

"No problem. Highlight of my week."

We sat there for a moment, which started to grow awkward. "Can I give you a hug?" Ben said, sounding a little shy. It was sexy, somehow, and I had an urge to say, *You can give me more than that.*

Instead I nodded, and he tugged me into his arms, pulling me across the cab seat and into his body. I closed my eyes tight, feeling the weight and warmth of him, letting it lull me.

I heard a terse tap on the window. Without letting Ben go, I opened my eyes, and saw it was Laney.

18

"Laney!" I chased her down Clark Street. "C'mon, just wait!"

The minute she'd seen us, Laney had stormed off, and I'd said a quick goodbye to Ben.

The tiny black heels of her boots clicked on the sidewalk now as she hurried away from me, her dark hair flying behind her.

"Lane! Talk to me!"

I broke into a jog. She spun around right as I reached her, and we nearly crashed into each other.

"Sorry—" I started to say, but Laney's words rolled over my own.

"I can't believe you. I can't *fucking* believe you!"

I noticed that her eyes were a little teary, which surprised me. I assumed she'd be annoyed—disgusted even—if she knew I'd been seeing Ben again, but why the tears?

"Lane, I..."

"This is what you've been doing while you've been avoiding me, right? Sleeping with Ben? Just jumping right back where you left off?"

"What? No!"

"You've been sleeping with him!"

Three guys dressed in baggy jeans and baseball hats walked past us, snickering. "Take it easy, honey," one of them said. "I'm sure she'll come back to you."

Laney turned to him with a murderous look. Usually it was me who had the temper, but she seemed pushed to the very edge right now. I grabbed her arm before she could think about punching him, and pulled her down the street until we were behind the Cubby Bear Lounge. Laney leaned back against the blackened brick wall and gave me a stony stare, shaking her head over and over. Music thumped from inside.

"Look, I'm so sorry I didn't tell you about it," I said, "but it's no big deal. We've talked on the phone, we've had coffee a few times and that's it."

She scoffed and kept shaking her head, her eyes growing watery again. She stayed quiet. I would rather she screamed at me than give me the silent treatment, especially when she looked so sad.

"Please talk to me," I said.

"Gear didn't even put me on the fucking guest list tonight, and now this." She bit her bottom lip, chewing off her peachy gloss.

"Oh, honey, I'm sorry about Gear."

"It's the same old shit I always take from these guys. But that's not what I'm pissed about. I can't believe you!"

"I know he dumped me, Lane, but I made some mistakes, too. I pushed him into a corner and tried to make him do things on my time. We're just talking now, that's it. We haven't slept together. It's just been a few cups of coffee."

I remembered the wine tonight and so I added, "And a few drinks. But that's it."

"Are you getting back together?"

"No!" I said defensively, but then I thought of Ben's words about the future. "Well, he mentioned something, but we haven't really talked about it."

Her eyes narrowed. "What did he say?"

"Just that he could take care of us now that he's made partner. He said I could keep my job with Cole, and we could still live in style and have a lot of fun together."

"Right. Fun. You and Ben can have all sorts of fun." Her voice was heavy with sarcasm, and it pissed me off. I still wasn't even sure what she was so upset about, and now it seemed as if she was insulting me.

"What in the hell is that supposed to mean?" I said. "He's been a hell of a lot more fun than you lately." I regretted it as soon as I said it.

She reared her head back as if I'd raised a hand to her. The tears crept back into her eyes. "You know what? *I'm* the one who took care of you all summer. *I'm* the one who brought you food and tried to get you out of the house. Not your mom, not fucking Ben. *Me.* And now, all of a sudden, I'm not fun enough for you? I'm a drag? And so you just flit back to Ben like nothing happened, because you can have *fun* with him? Guess what, Kell? He's only crawling around again because Therese gave him an ultimatum. Just like you did."

It was my turn to flinch. Was it true? Was that the only reason he'd been coming around?

"Yep, that's it, Kell. The commitment-phobe is on the run again, this time back to you."

I hated that she could read me so well. "How do you know this?"

"Steve talked to Ben, and Jess told me."

"Oh." That was the only response I could muster. I felt so

miserably second-rate. But it couldn't be true. I wouldn't believe that Ben was just running from one woman to another. He'd known he'd made a mistake about not marrying me right after my birthday, and it was only my strange behavior that had driven him away. He was realizing that now, especially since I'd turned over a new leaf.

"He'll just balk when you get close again," Laney said. "He'll take off on you, too."

"I don't think that's true. He wants us to have a future together. He went on and on about it tonight."

"Really? Well, you'd better take a close look at what that future will entail." She shook her head as if in disgust. "Call me when you get your shit together. I'm done saving you."

She turned and walked back toward Clark Street, her heels making sharp, angry clicks on the sidewalk.

I looked up at my town house—my *old* town house. I'd taken a cab here after my fight with Laney. I wanted to go somewhere that would soothe me, and this was the only place I could think of.

The street was dark, except for the golden globes of the old-fashioned streetlamps. In my town house, there was only one small light on—in the master bedroom. Probably Beth Maninsky reading a book next to her husband, while her baby slept in the other room. I was so jealous of Beth Maninsky right then.

Ever since that horrible day about a month ago now, when my key wouldn't fit in the lock, when I'd realized that I couldn't remember a chunk of my life, I'd sworn to myself that I would appreciate every day. I wouldn't think about what I wanted to happen in the future or what was missing from my life. And I'd done that pretty well. I'd been proud of my new job, my new look, my new ability to get along in the world even without Ben or Dee or my mom.

But now, on a chilly night outside my old home, I lost

my ability to appreciate what I had, because it seemed that I didn't have much at all. Dee—gone. My job at Bartley Brothers—gone. My mom—across the country, probably digging up dirt on Britney's favorite new thong. My town house—still there, right in front of me, but actually owned by someone else. Laney—pissed off at me, and rightly so I supposed, although I still didn't understand the force of her anger. My new job, the one I'd been so proud of as of late—only a hobby, just like Ben said. And Ben—a big question mark.

Another light went on on the second floor. The kitchen. I wondered if they'd kept the walls the same rust color that Ben and I had painted them. It'd been hell painting those walls, all that taping and trying to maneuver around the appliances. At first we'd tried to make it fun. We'd made a pitcher of gin and tonics and cranked up the stereo, but Ben became more and more annoyed the longer it took. We thought we could finish the whole room in an hour or two, but it stretched into four. Ben grew crabby with each passing minute, snapping at me when I tried to tell him he'd gotten paint on the trim.

Now that I thought about that time, I realized there'd been others like it. Ben often grew cranky and irritated with a house project or even a discussion about other work around the place.

"Can't we just pay someone to do it?" he'd said one time when I told him how I wanted to rip off the wallpaper in a bathroom.

"It'll be fun," I said, and I believed it. I *loved* doing projects around that place. I loved putzing around when I came home from work—arranging flowers in a vase, cleaning up the kitchen, throwing some towels in the dryer. I adored all that because it was my place, and the place where Ben and I would live when we got married. I felt as if I was preparing a little spot for our future. And I couldn't blame Ben for not wanting to spend his weekends hanging wallpaper. It wasn't his place, at least not yet.

But as I stood there now on a lonely Friday night, it occurred to me that it was something more than that. Those things weren't fun for Ben because they meant growing up a little, spending less time at the bars and on his races, and he didn't want that.

He still doesn't want it, Laney's voice said inside my head.

I thought back over the times we'd spent together the last few weeks. Light, easy times. I thought about the words he'd used tonight when he'd talked about our life together "down the road." He'd spoken about traveling and great restaurants and allowing me to keep my hobby of a job. He hadn't mentioned a home or children or growing old together, things I'd always told him I wanted. Maybe he hoped that I didn't want those things anymore. Maybe he was having thoughts about restarting our relationship because he wanted something simple, something *fun.* He hadn't been around when I was so depressed this summer, and now that that time had passed, Ben was, conveniently, back.

I stared up at the town house, my body motionless. The kitchen light went off. A few seconds later, the master bedroom went dark, too.

Standing in the dark on Bissell Street, I dialed Ben's number on my cell phone.

"Hello?" It was Therese. I shouldn't have felt hurt or surprised, but I was both.

Then I felt guilty. Therese had never been particularly nice to me, but I'd been just as bitchy. And why? Because of Ben, because of some guy. Wasn't that what usually kept women apart?

I felt so guilt-ridden that I couldn't bring myself to ask for him.

"Hello?" Therese said, in a caustic, angry tone, and I knew that she knew.

I still didn't say anything. She slammed down the phone.

I waited a minute, then called back.

Ben answered this time.

"I'm sorry," I said, "but I need to talk to you."

"Yeah. Sure." He sounded nonchalant—like Therese wasn't next to him. How easily he ran back and forth between us.

"Can you meet me at Chuck's?"

"When?"

"Fifteen minutes?" I said.

"No problem."

I grabbed a cab and was at the bar before Ben. I don't know why I'd picked Chuck's. It was close to his apartment, sure, but it was also the place I'd come that day when I realized that Ben had broken up with me and I couldn't remember a part of my life. Maybe I wanted, inadvertently, to remind myself of that day.

Inside, the place was smoky and loud. Luckily, there was an empty table by the front and I slid into it, ordering a glass of water from the annoyed waitress.

Ben was there a minute later, running his hand through his light hair as he stepped in the doorway, his cheeks tinged pink from the cool air. He saw me and broke into a smile.

"Sorry about calling you like that," I said as he slid into the chair across from me.

"No problem." He smiled again as if Therese wasn't waiting at his place, in his bed. Or maybe she wasn't. Maybe she'd stormed out after I called. My stomach churned.

"How's Therese?"

His eyebrows shot up. We never mentioned her. "She's, uh, she's okay."

"She wants to marry you, I hear."

He paused. "Where'd you hear that?"

"Around," I said. "Good news travels fast."

"What do you want me to say?"

"I don't want you to say anything. I want you to be honest with me."

He sat back, away from me. I could see him growing annoyed. "I *have* been honest, Kell. I told you tonight that I want to be with you. I want to have a good life and—"

"I know. You want to travel and have fun."

"Hell, yeah. Don't you?"

"I want more than that," I said. "And so does Therese, evidently."

"I don't want to talk about her."

"How can we not? How can we keep ignoring her, like you aren't cheating on her with me?"

"Hey! We haven't even slept together." He sounded like I did talking to Laney, spouting mere technicalities.

The waitress delivered my water then, and I gave her a few bucks for the trouble. Ben ordered a gin and tonic.

I leaned in, moving the water aside. "What did you tell Therese when you left tonight?"

"I told her I had to meet a friend."

"And she just let you go?"

"Uh-huh."

"Because she wants to marry you," I said.

"What do you want me to say?"

I couldn't stop thinking about Therese then, probably crying in Ben's bed, wondering if she'd pushed too hard.

"Have you told her you don't want to get married?"

"Not yet. Look, what's this about? What are you getting at, Kell?" The pink had crept back into his cheeks, and it wasn't from the temperature. He was getting angry at me, at the conversation growing heavy. Exactly what he wanted to avoid. Exactly what he thought I wouldn't do anymore because I was the new Kelly.

I lifted my shoulder bag from the floor and plunked it onto

my lap, digging inside for the photos I'd picked up that day. The ones of Ben. When I found them, I slid the packet across the table to him.

He looked at me, then down at the packet of photos as if they were an explosive device. "What? What am I supposed to do here?"

"Look at them."

Ben opened the flap slowly, removing the stack of pictures, flipping through one, then another and another. "They're nice. I like the flower in this one."

"Not *those*." Irritated, I took the pictures from his hand and skipped through the ones I'd taken at the botanical gardens until I came to the surveillancelike photos of him.

I'm not sure why I showed them to him. They were mortifying, the work of a depressed person. But I guess that was it—that depressed person had been me, was me. Even though I had been running from her. Ben's obvious attraction to the new me made me feel sorry for the old, unable to leave her behind. Because I was the same person. Or at least I was a composite of all the past Kellys—the Kelly I'd been before my thirtieth birthday, the sad person who'd spent five months in a fog and the new woman I'd become since that one strange Saturday.

Ben's mouth grew tight, his eyes troubled as he looked at the photos. "What the hell are these?"

"I found some film in my camera and got them developed. I must have taken them this summer."

"Why?"

"I guess I didn't want to let you go, even though you'd already gone."

"So why do you want me to see them?" he asked.

"I suppose because I want to be honest with you, just like I want you to be honest with me. And I need to remind you what kind of person I am."

Ben grabbed the envelope and stuck the photos back inside, not bothering to flip through the entire bunch. "But you're not that person anymore, Kell. Look at you! You're back on top. You've got your shit together again. You can't even remember being that way."

It was true. I'd lost a bit of myself, a bit of my life, but my parts were all still there at the core. And now that I'd recognized that, I couldn't act like I had all the time in the world to achieve what I wanted—a stable career, a husband, kids. I didn't. All I had right now was a "hobby of a job," one that wouldn't pay the bills for long. I'd been in a fantasy world, thinking I could live like this. I needed to get on with my life, the way I'd originally designed it, and obviously Ben wouldn't be able to give me that. He still didn't want those things, not from me. Not from Therese, apparently, either.

"You know this isn't going to work," I said.

The waitress dropped off his drink then, but he pushed it aside. Some of the alcohol sloshed over the side and puddled on the table.

"Kell, don't get all crazy about this."

"I'm not in the slightest bit crazy."

"That's not what I mean. I'm just saying don't get worked up about this thing with Therese."

"This *thing?*" I said. "Is that how you think of it? That poor girl."

He looked confused when I took her side.

I stood up. "Go home and talk to her. Tell her the truth. Tell her how you really feel."

The confusion stayed on his features. "Yeah. Sure." He nodded a few times. "I'll call you tomorrow."

"No. Don't call me anymore, okay?"

Ben opened his mouth, then closed it. He started to stand, but I pushed him back down by the shoulder, then kissed his forehead, just like I used to before we went to sleep at night.

I turned then and walked through the bar, back toward the

bathroom, toward the pay phone where I'd called Laney that Saturday.

As she had that day, she answered after a few rings.

"Can I come over?" I said.

19

Exhausted, I trudged up the two flights of stairs to Laney's apartment. I mentally practiced how I would explain everything to her, but in the back of my head I knew everything would be okay, because that's how we worked.

It was Laney who'd taught me how to fight. My mom, Dee and I were three girls all growing up together, all in our different stages, and so we orbited each other in whatever apartment we were living in, rarely getting into any tussles. But Laney's family fought about everything, often letting fly phrases like "fuck you" and "go to hell, freak." The first time Laney was mad at me—something to do with a shirt I'd borrowed and spilled ketchup on—I had thought our friendship was over. No one had ever really been upset with me before, and I had no concept of how to argue and move on. I'd watched her mouth move as she let me have it about the shirt, telling me how she'd saved her baby-sitting money for that damned thing, and when she was done, I nodded and walked away.

"Where the hell are you going?" she'd said, chasing after me.

"Calculus."

She'd laughed. "Wait. You have to tell me not to be so picky, that it's just a stupid shirt, after all."

I hesitated, then said, "Don't be so picky? It's just a stupid shirt?"

She shrugged. "You're right. Let's go to class." She linked her arm in mine and led me down the hallway.

We'd had a bunch of spats since then—there were numerous arguments over directions when we drove to Padre Island for spring break, and we'd had a couple of run-ins over Laney's propensity to be fifteen minutes late and the way I spent too much time with my current boyfriend. But we always made up. Always.

So now, as I rounded the last landing, I worked myself up to an apology, but was already thinking about my epiphany of the night—how I'd decided that I had to get my life back on the track I'd originally set for myself.

I tried the doorknob, but it was frozen. Usually Laney unlocked the door after she'd buzzed me in. I rapped a few times.

It seemed to take her forever. I was just raising my hand to knock again when it opened a few inches and Laney appeared in the doorway.

"Hey," I said.

"Hey." She didn't move away from the door, didn't open it.

"I'm really sorry. I should have told you I was hanging out with Ben. I just meant to see him once, but somehow it picked up steam. We weren't sleeping together, honest. It was just—"

"Kell," Laney interrupted.

I stopped, waiting for her to say something, but she just

stared at me, then down at the floor. "Can I come in?" I said finally.

"I need a little time."

"Oh." This was new—Laney asking for time to get over something—but of course I'd give her whatever she wanted. "Want to meet for breakfast tomorrow?"

"No, I mean more time than that."

"Like how much?"

She looked over her shoulder as if searching for the answer in her apartment. She faced me again. "I'm not sure. I'll call you, okay?"

"When? What's going on?"

"I don't know. Just give me some time to figure it out."

"Figure what out?" I felt panicked suddenly. What was she talking about?

"I'll call you," Laney said, the same thing guys often say when they're talking to you for the last time.

The rest of the weekend was hell. I rattled around my apartment with nothing to distract me. I picked up the phone to call Laney every hour or so, but after dialing the first couple of numbers, I'd remember her words *I need some time,* and I would softly place the receiver back on the phone, wondering if my horrible summer had pushed her away, if I'd relied on her too much. It was exactly what I'd been trying to avoid lately by not spending as much time with her. I'd tried not to call her with every neurotic thought in my head, and when she kept bringing up my memory loss, suggesting doctors and Internet research, I'd stayed away even more. It was killing me not to know what she was doing, whether she was hurting or just angry, whether she ever wanted to be friends with me again.

And the thing with Ben nagged at me, too. Most of the time, I was sure that I'd done the right thing by breaking it off with him. The life I'd always wanted wouldn't just fall into my lap. You had to plan for these things, and Ben had made it clear he wasn't up for that plan. But for some crazy reason, I still missed him.

On Sunday morning, I spent a few hours at Katie's Coffee, reading through every section of the paper. I spent a considerable amount of time on the real estate section, trying to gauge the cost of a house somewhere outside the city, like the one I'd always planned to have. The prices gave me sticker shock, and the realization kept coming to me that the pathetic hourly wage Cole gave me would never, ever get me a down payment on a four-bedroom-three-and-a-half-bath-with-attached-garage-and-one-acre.

And so Cole was on my mind when I got home that afternoon and found a message from him on my machine.

"Kelly Kelly. Cole here," he said, sounding faintly out of breath. "Call me back, yeah? Tonight. Whenever you get in."

I picked up the phone, a little alarmed that maybe there was some kind of bad news, like we had to do a reshoot with William or maybe I'd lost a roll of film on the way to the shop.

He answered on the first ring. I barely got my name out before he started talking. Fast. "Hey, remember how I told you about that assignment I might be getting?"

"The ad for the children's cold tablets?"

He made an exasperated sound. "No. A rather *big* assignment. I was waiting to see if I'd got it."

"The one you didn't want to talk about because you didn't want to jinx it?"

"Yes. Right. Good." He was all pleased again, now that I was back on his page. "Well, it came in, so to speak."

A pause. I realized that he needed me to ask. "So tell, tell," I said.

"You're familiar with *U Chic?*"

"Sure." *U Chic* was a lifestyle magazine similar to *In Style.* It featured gorgeous photography and lots of celebrity names to make you feel like a podunk farmer unless you acquired Julia Roberts's Navajo rug or Whitney Houston's moisturizing eye pads.

"Well," he said, followed by another dramatic pause. "I have a friend who's an editor there and he's been trying to get me work, but so far nothing, okay? *But* another photographer just cancelled for a shoot this week, and they couldn't cancel all the models and the site and such, and so *U Chic* has asked me to go to the British Virgin Islands for a beach fashion layout."

I'd never heard him so effusive, so puffed up with pride. It made me a little sad, to tell the truth. It was a great assignment, but I was pretty sure that something like this would have been relatively routine for the Coley Beckett of old. He'd gotten so used to being on the outside, though, that he was like a teenager with his first date.

"I'm really happy for you," I said, and I was, although it struck me then that he'd be gone for a week or so and I'd have no work. It was probably just as well. I'd been unable to stop thinking about Ben's words—*hobby of a job*—and that, combined with my foray into the real estate pages, had made me think that maybe I should start calling headhunters. Maybe I should think about getting another analyst position. But the thought of giving up the job with Cole when I'd just given up Ben, and maybe Laney, was too much. I wouldn't decide now.

"I could do some projects at your studio while you're gone," I said. "You could even pay me part-time or something."

"While I'm gone? Kelly Kelly, you don't understand. *You're* going with me, right? We're leaving Wednesday."

The next few days flew by, in direct contrast to the crawling pace of my weekend. I was on the phone with *U Chic* nearly all day Monday, getting the details of the trip and working with their travel agent to make arrangements for Cole and me to fly to Tortola. And then there was the packing. When I used to flip through *Vogue* or *Vanity Fair,* I'd never given a thought to what was brought along to those tropical locations in order to get an apparently simple shot of a girl on a beach. But now I was the one who was packing it all—the lights, the seamless, the stands, the cameras, the film, the batteries, the backup cameras, the reflectors. Some of it had to be shipped, the rest we would bring with us.

Then there was my own packing. Since I couldn't remember what I'd worn this summer, it seemed even more difficult to determine what I should bring along for the hot weather. On Monday night, I tried on a host of shorts and bathing suits and summer dresses that I'd found in my bedroom, but none of them fit properly. Now that I was eating more normally, I had gained a little weight, but I was still smaller than I used to be and as a result, the capri pants hung too low on my hips, the shorts sagged in the butt and the bikini tops gaped. The fact that my clothes were too large would have made me gleefully happy a year ago, but it was an annoyance now. I didn't have time to look for new outfits.

In a panic, I called Melanie at Saks and asked her to pull any leftover summer clothes and a few pieces of their resort wear. And so on Tuesday, when Cole thought I was running around town doing a host of his errands, I was actually back in the yellow, silk-lined personal shopping department of Saks.

"Hello, hello!" Melanie said, wafting into the room. Two assistants followed her, pushing carts piled high with clothes. Melanie's eyes fairly glittered, and I could see that I should have warned her that I wasn't in the same kind of buying mood as I was last time.

"Champagne?" Melanie said, already making an uncorking gesture to one of her assistants.

"No, thank you. I'm in a rush, actually. I just need a few things for a trip, and then I have to get back to work."

"Fine. So where are you going?"

"The Caribbean."

"Ooh. A few weeks at Cap Juluca? Nevis, maybe?"

I felt an unexpected pang in my gut. Cap Juluca was the resort on Anguilla where Ben and I had always talked about spending our honeymoon. Come to think of it, I had done most of that talking, Ben merely nodding along, but still the thought turned my insides.

"No," I said to Melanie. "I'm going to Tortola, actually. It's for work."

"Work in the Caribbean. Lucky you."

Hearing her say that gave me a little boost. Melanie was right. I was getting a free trip to the British Virgin Islands for my job. I should enjoy this time, particularly when I might have to leave it shortly and find another analyst position.

I took the armload of clothes that Melanie offered and headed into the curtained dressing area. I was just pulling up the bottoms of a blue bathing suit when I heard Melanie say, "Where's your friend today?"

I stopped moving, the bikini bottoms in a twist around my thighs. "What's that?" I said, although I'd heard her perfectly.

"Your friend. Laney, was it? How is she?"

I absently tugged the bathing suit up, slipping the tank-style top over my head. "She's okay."

I'd been itching to call Laney ever since Cole had told me about the shoot. What was a free trip to the Caribbean if you couldn't brag about it to someone? But I wanted to respect her need for time, even though I didn't understand it, and so I'd stayed away. And she hadn't called.

"You two seem very tight," Melanie said. "Have you been friends long?"

"Yeah. High school." My voice was flat. I wondered if Laney and I would be friends for much longer.

20

After two delays, one change of planes in San Juan, and middle seats that were ten rows apart (the only ones the magazine could book us on), Cole and I arrived on the island of Tortola well past midnight. I was so exhausted that I barely had time to notice the rusty-red print of the cotton bedding before I crashed on top of it. Cole had given me the green light to book my own little bungalow instead of a room in the main building, which made me want to hug him. I didn't, of course. Cole and I never touched each other. But I was even more grateful the next morning when I opened my very own door leading onto my very own little wooden deck and saw the luminous teal of the ocean below me.

There were two wooden rocking chairs on the deck—one painted peach, the other a mauvey purple. I immediately took up residence in the peach one and rocked for half an hour, just staring out at the line of boulders that formed a breakwater around the resort, and the splotchy patterns of the coral on the ocean floor.

I glanced at my watch, wondering when Cole wanted to begin our search for sites. His friend Sam, the travel editor at *U Chic* who'd gotten Cole this gig, was supposed to be here already to help us, but because of some problem in New York he wouldn't arrive until tomorrow. Since he planned on being there for the whole shoot, Sam hadn't hired an art director, and now Cole and I would have to decide on the locations—very big decisions, I knew, since Cole was counting on this job to reestablish his reputation.

For now, though, I just wanted to sit on my private deck and stare at my private slice of ocean and feel my private soft breeze. There was something intensely wonderful about being all by myself at that moment. I'd forgotten how to be alone during the many years with Ben. Once we started dating, I was rarely by myself, something I was grateful for at the time but saw as problematic now.

Cole called a few minutes later, and forty-five minutes after that, he and I were on a chartered powerboat, bouncing across the water. I held one hand to my head, trying to secure the wide-brimmed straw hat I'd bought from Melanie, trying to ignore the way the jolt of the boat made the throb in my temples stronger. My headaches were back. I squinted through my sunglasses at the islands in the distance—mounds of green and brown dotting the sky-blue sea. It was sunny and blisteringly hot already, even though it was only ten o'clock, and I wished I'd brought extra sunscreen. Cole, standing near the front by the driver, looked entirely out of place, still wearing black pants and big black leather boots. His only concession to the weather was the white T-shirt he wore, making his pale skin look even more ghostlike beneath his black, choppy hair. Still, there was no denying his good mood. He asked rapid-fire questions of the driver, a black man in his fifties. Would we have to get permits to shoot on the different islands? Could the weather change drastically? What time was the sunset? Did he know other drivers who could haul our stuff every morning?

We stopped at a number of private islands that day. Each had stunning white sand beaches and friendly hotel proprietors eager to have a photo shoot on their property. But it was the Baths at Virgin Gorda that caught our imagination. Giant boulders were strewn across the sandy beach, forming exotic pools and caves.

"It's perfect, right, Kelly Kelly?" Cole plowed around in the wet sand, his combat boots making sucking sounds as the surging surf tried to pull him into the sea. He barely seemed to notice, too busy taking a few shots on his ancient Polaroid and mumbling to himself.

By the time we got back to our place on Tortola, it was six o'clock. A whole evening stretched ahead of us, our work done for the day. None of the models or the rest of the crew would arrive until tomorrow.

"So, how about getting a bite to eat?" I said, after our taxi had rumbled away. We were standing in the tiny lobby, Bob Marley music booming from the bar on the other side of the hut. I felt odd, making that social gesture toward Cole, almost like I was asking him out, but he was still too charged from the day to notice.

"Sure," he said. "I've got to make a few calls to *U Chic,* and I'll meet you at the bar in half an hour, yeah?"

I went back to my own bungalow, checking the phone on the off chance that anyone had called. The problem was that no one knew I was here. Laney, the person I usually checked in with before I went out of town, was off-limits to me. I'd removed myself from Ben's life, and my mom, well, I didn't want her to worry about hurricanes or other natural disasters. I'd call her when I got home. Naturally, I had zero messages.

I changed into one of the sundresses I'd bought at Saks,

pulled my hair back in a short ponytail and was at the bar in twenty minutes. It was a small space with a few white tables and a plank wall covered with pale seashells and fishnets. The stereo pumped out steel drum music. A group of stragglers from the beach had pushed two of the tables together and sat drinking beer, looking sandy and drunk and happy. I ordered a rum punch for myself, something that seemed tropical and refreshing, something that might erase the persistent pounding in my head, if only for a few hours until I could go to bed.

The sugary-sweet drink couldn't hide the one-two punch of the rum, but it went down smoothly. I was almost finished with the first one by the time Cole joined me at the bar, his hair wet from a shower, a purple Hawaiian shirt hanging over his black pants. I nearly spat out my drink at the sight of his shirt.

"What is it?" he said, glancing down at himself, then back at my surprised face. "Right. It's the shirt. I thought this was how people dressed here." He glanced at the bartender, who wore a golf shirt, then at the beach group in bathing suits. "Maybe I should change. It's rather embarrassing, isn't it?"

"It's fine." I pushed down my laughter and ordered him a rum punch.

He took a stool next to me. "I wasn't sure what to pack. I haven't been to the Caribbean for a while, and to be honest, I can't really remember those times."

"Sure," I said, trying to be helpful. Many men could have gotten away with vacation gear like that, but Cole wasn't one of them. He'd have looked more at home in S&M leather.

"I suppose it hasn't been that long," he said, "but I, uh…I used to have some rather bad habits."

"You mean clothingwise?"

He shot me a look. "I mean drugwise."

"Ah."

I slurped up the last of my drink and ordered another. I felt strangely giddy and slightly fuzzy from a combination of the punch, my headache and the fact that I was here with Cole, thousands of miles away from Chicago, just the two of us, with the sky outside turning a pinkish-orange. Maybe it was the drink or the odd intimacy that made me blurt out the question I'd wanted to ask for so long. "Is that why you had to leave New York?"

His face muscles seemed to sag, just as they had that one time I'd asked him a similar question at his studio. But he didn't snap at me now. In fact, he didn't say anything for a long moment.

Then he sighed, sipped his drink and finally shifted on the stool until he faced me. "Shall I tell you the whole story then, Kelly Kelly?"

I wanted to say *Yes, yes, I'm dying to know,* but his resigned expression made me ashamed of my prurient curiosity. "I'm sorry, I shouldn't have asked."

"No, I ought to tell someone. Only a few people know, and none of them lives in Chicago. I'm getting a bit sick of carrying it around by myself."

I nodded, not wanting to break the spell.

"You don't write for the *Enquirer* on the side, do you?" Cole said with a small smile. "No family members at the *Post* or some such?"

My stomach churned a little. "Actually, my mom works for *The Biz.*"

"That crap television show?"

"Yes, but I swear I never tell her anything, and I won't tell her about this."

His eyes squinted a little, and he stared at me as if he could see inside my head and discover my true intentions.

"Look, Cole," I said, sorry that he had to be so wary about some incident that had obviously changed his life. "You don't have to tell me. It's really none of my business."

"No, it's not, but as I said, I need to tell someone." He drank from his rum punch. "Okay, here it is. It's not really so big a deal, at least it wasn't at the time, until I found out about her."

"Her who?"

"I'm getting to that."

"Sorry." I clamped my mouth shut and pulled my drink closer.

"I don't know what you've heard about me or if you know anything about what I was like in those days, but it's all true, whatever you've heard. It's the usual sad tale—I got too big too fast, and I never thought I deserved it. At the same time, I never thought that it would go away. It was as if my life was one big toy—a toy that wouldn't break, and I could play with it as much as I liked. And so I did quite a bit of drugs." He shot a sidelong glance at me, as if searching for signs of disapproval.

I nodded silently.

"And I drank too much, of course. Still do, really, but it was the drugs that fucked me up. I actually thought that I could shoot better when I was high. I suppose that might have been true for a while. It gave me a lot of ideas about how to approach a picture that I might never have had sober, but it began affecting my judgment. Ah, it's pathetic, really. I started thinking I could do no wrong, not with photography, or with anything else for that matter. One day, I had a shoot with a model. Britania. Just that one name, like Madonna." He rolled his eyes.

"I remember hearing about her," I said, "but she dropped out of sight, didn't she?"

He looked at me for a beat, but didn't answer my question. "She was getting a lot of work back then, but that day was the first time we'd had a shoot together. It went late and everyone left, and well… How shall I put this? She stayed."

"Sure." I thought I saw where this was going. They'd

slept together, right? Probably like he had with many models? So what was the big secret?

Cole sighed. "And then we had a drink, and then we had some other…things. And she just never left. We had sort of a lost weekend. Sex and drugs and all that crap."

He shot me another glance, as if to check my reaction. I made sure to keep my expression flat.

"And so," he continued, "that was it, you see? Or at least I thought so. Monday morning came, and she was gone, and I cleaned myself up and got back to work. But here's the thing. Britania, who I thought was twenty-something, was actually not so old. She was—" he took a swallow of his drink "—fifteen, and her father was Morton Lankton."

I gasped. I couldn't help it. Morton Lankton was a publishing magnate who owned a large number of glossy magazines, and I was sure it was precisely those magazines that had given Cole most of his work, and, therefore, his rise to fame in the industry.

"Ah. I see you know who he was."

"Was?"

"He died last year."

"Oh. And you didn't know Britania was his daughter?"

He shook his head. "Hardly anyone did. She was one of those kids who wanted to make it on her own."

"So what happened?"

"I was served with a summons and complaint for a civil suit from Lankton's lawyers. I was told, in no uncertain terms, that if I left town the case would go away. If not, I could expect a criminal action, as well."

"And you left."

"Of course I did. I was embarrassed about what I'd done. Sickened actually, even though I had no idea of her age. And I knew my career couldn't survive something like that, not with Lankton owning half the town. He could easily dry up all my work, so it was either leave without anyone knowing that I'd sexed and drugged a fifteen-year-old, or let everyone find out and lose my work, anyway."

"But if he's dead now, doesn't that change things? I mean, I hate to say it like that, but now that he's gone, can't you get back into that scene?"

"I've been trying, Kelly Kelly, but there've been so many bloody rumors about why I left that everyone has been afraid of me. Until now. My mate Sam has been trying to get me a shoot like this for ages, and he finally came through."

"And what about Britania? What happened to her?"

Cole's head dropped. "She was shipped off to some detox hospital for a few months. Last I heard, she'd gone on to college."

"So that's why you don't date models."

He stared into his drink. "That's why I don't date at all."

"But you didn't know. You can't let that incident keep you away from the entire female population."

"Kelly Kelly, that incident nearly ruined my entire career."

"I understand, but you can't stay single your whole life because of it." I wondered why I was arguing that particular point. It wasn't as if I wanted to date Cole. He seemed more like a pain-in-the-ass-yet-lovable older brother than a potential boyfriend. But I guess I was starting to think of Cole as a friend, and the fact that he'd confided in me made me want to help him somehow.

"Perhaps I'll stay single forever. The women that used to appeal to me simply don't anymore, and I don't make much of an effort to find any others. I did meet this woman once or twice—very briefly, you understand—but there seemed to be something special about her, a connection between us."

"Well, there you go! Call her!"

"Kelly Kelly, enough about me. Since you're such the dating expert, tell me about your love life."

* * *

Sitting there, elbow to elbow with Cole (a guy I couldn't stand a short while ago), I told him the whole story about Ben and me. I told him about the way we'd met at work and the fun of those first few years. About the town house and the wedding plans, the ones I'd made and thought Ben had wanted as well. I faltered a bit when I got to my birthday and the way Ben had broken up with me. Should I admit that I couldn't remember, or act as if I had no memory problems? Cole would never know the difference. I'd gotten the elongated version of the breakup from Laney, the one I'd told her myself, so I could have easily faked it.

But there was something about the earnestness in Cole's eyes, and the fact that he'd confided a major part of his own life, that was getting to me, particularly when he sputtered, "The bastard broke off with you on your birthday? I knew I hated that fucker!" I could see that he was honestly outraged, that he honestly felt sorry for me. The fact that he felt anything for me at all was touching. Cole and I seemed to have stumbled into some sort of unplanned, oddball friendship.

"What did you do?" he asked. "Did you punch the rat bastard?"

I laughed. "Well, since we're telling secrets…"

"You set his house on fire?"

"No, no. Nothing like that. Just listen."

Cole pulled at an imaginary beard and crossed one leg over the other, looking like a talk show host.

"The thing is…" Cole hadn't cut me off this time, but I found it hard to find the right words, words that wouldn't make me sound crazy.

"What is it?"

"What it is…is that I can't remember Ben breaking up with me."

"Oh. It's not problems like I had, is it? Coke, speed, maybe something harder, eh?"

"Nothing like that. I don't think so, anyway. The problem is I can't remember five whole months of my life."

Cole's eyes grew wide, concerned again.

I told him *that* story then, from the episode with Beth Maninsky, to Laney's saving me, to getting the job with him, to Ben and me hanging out again, and finally the fight with Laney. Getting it out felt like releasing the steam from a pressure cooker. And Cole, for his part, didn't run screaming to phone a physician or intimate that I might be losing my mind.

In fact, when I'd finished my story, he leaned back, looked me up and down and said, "Well, it doesn't seem to have hurt you at all."

"No injuries that I know of," I said, although that wasn't entirely true. There were the headaches, the weird flashes of the two-freckled man, and that scary night in the bathtub when I couldn't move my legs. And I needed to do something more for those headaches than just attack them with Advil and alcohol. Since the day Laney had brought me back to my Lake Shore Drive apartment, I'd avoided that cabinet in my kitchen, the one that held the prescription bottles of antidepressants and pain relievers. But when I got home from this trip, I might have to give the pain relievers a try.

"I mean all around," Cole continued. "Seems to me that you're in a better position now than before your birthday. This Ben chap certainly wasn't going to win any prizes, if you want my opinion. And that financial job wasn't for you, was it? You've got real talent with the camera. You're in the right field now."

I felt a wave of satisfaction at his words, then remorse hit. I didn't know if I could afford this job much longer.

I made a noncommittal sound, then tried to deflect his attention from my assistantship with him. "But Laney still won't talk to me."

"Yes." Cole waved at the bartender and ordered another

round of drinks. "Speaking of Laney—your official friend— you'll patch things up, eh?"

I shrugged, afraid to say out loud that I truly didn't know the answer to that question.

"Well, say you do. Say everything is just fine. What would you think of me asking her out?"

A piece of mango from the punch lodged in my throat. I coughed until it went down, grabbing for my glass of water. "You want to take Laney on a date?"

"Possibly." He looked like a kid caught stealing. "I mean, yes. But only if you think…I mean—"

"Was that the woman you were talking about? The one you met once or twice but thought she was something special?"

He gave a short nod, his eyes wary.

"It's fine with me." I wished I could run to the phone right now. I'd call Laney and tell her that a boy she thought was cute liked her. Shades of high school, shades of a time when everything was perfect between us.

"Yeah?" He sat up straighter.

"Of course. You'd be a great date, I'm sure. And it really doesn't matter what I think anyway, because I honestly don't know what's going to happen with us—if she wants to be friends anymore or not. It would break my heart if that happened, but I have to be prepared, I suppose. It's just that life wouldn't be much fun without Laney around. I can't even imagine…"

In the middle of my rambling, Cole put a rough hand on my shoulder. I looked at him, surprised.

"It'll be okay, Kelly Kelly," he said, his voice soft. And then he pulled me off the bar stool and gave me a hug.

21

We'd rented a car, and it was my duty to collect everyone from the airport. The rental was a tiny Honda with a barely breathing air conditioner. I opened the sunroof and found some island music on the radio, turning up the volume as I made my first run to the airport on dusty, winding roads along the water. Everyone else drove a hell of a lot faster than me, and I drew a number of bleating honks from other cars. It was then I realized that I was on the wrong side of the road.

"Left, left, left," I chanted to myself but it seemed so wrong, so distracting, so dangerous.

After the drinks with Cole the night before, I'd gone back to my bungalow and sat out on my deck, staring at the moon, the sea as dark as the sky. I was buzzed from the rum, but instead of feeling drunk, I felt introspective. And so, after thinking about my talk with Cole and everything that had happened since that day at the dry cleaners, I decided to view this trip as my last hurrah. I had to be an adult. I had to get my life back on track, financially and otherwise, and hopefully, I'd soon meet the perfect guy who wanted to have the perfect family with me. But since none of that was going to happen in the Caribbean, and God knew what would happen with Laney when I returned, I was going to treat this trip like spring break. It would be my last fling before I got serious again.

And so now I waved at the angry drivers, mouthing "Sorry" but refusing to rush. I turned the music up even louder, singing along when I could pick up some of the lyrics.

The airport was basically a landing strip with a squat little building beside it. The terminal was even stuffier inside than my car. The crew that Cole had hired from Chicago came through the doorway marked Customs. There was a Filipino hairstylist, Robbie, who wore a yellow rugby shirt over his broad shoulders and carried three large black cases of equipment. Francie, the makeup artist, was there, too, a petite woman whose tiny face was, of course, perfectly made up even after a six-hour journey from Chicago. Lastly, a stylist by the name of Chad came though the doorway, carrying duffel bags stuffed with what I assumed to be scarves and hats and beach balls and other props.

I greeted everyone, gave them the schedules I'd typed out on the hotel's computer and squeezed them all into the car, along with their luggage.

Chad complained the entire trip back to the hotel. "Jesus, couldn't they have hired us a limo?" he said from under the mound of duffel bags on his lap.

"It's a little island in the Caribbean, you idiot," Francie said. "There are no limos here."

They must have worked together in the past, because after a few pointed comments from Francie about his snobbery, Chad stopped his grumbling. A half hour later, I dropped them off at the hotel with directions to call Cole, who would brief them on the shoot.

I was a little more nervous for my next airport run, because even though I was starting to get the hang of the left lane, I was picking up the models, including Mella, who my mother had been writing that piece on about her alleged weight gain. As a celebrity, Mella had achieved mythical status lately and could be seen on everything from Victoria's Secret spreads to the *David Letterman Show*.

When she stepped through the doorway and into the main part of the terminal, everyone stopped to stare. It's possible that many people didn't even know who she was, but when a gorgeous, six-foot blonde dressed in gauzy white linen walks into a tiny room that smells like an armpit, people tend to stare. Behind her, another model who looked surprising similar to Mella—tall, blond, et cetera—came through the doorway. I remembered Cole's words about how *U Chic* liked to have models that resembled each other at some of these shoots.

I hurried toward them, having to crane my neck upward to shake hands and introduce myself.

"Phew! It's hot," Mella said, giving me a smile. She was apparently oblivious of her audience.

The other woman introduced herself as Corrine and didn't say much else.

They were entirely too tall for the car. It was actually embarrassing to watch Corrine trying to fold herself into the back seat.

"Can I stop and get you anything before we get to the hotel?" I asked as I cruised along the sandy road, the waves crashing only a few feet from the car.

"I'd love a Reuben," Mella said. "Do you think I can get one around here? Or maybe a cheeseburger?" She was leaning forward, swiveling her neck to check out the island. I'd heard that she was Swedish, but she sounded as American as I did.

I remembered my mother's story about her weight gain. She certainly didn't look overweight in the slightest. She was emaciated, if anything. "We can look for someplace," I said. "What about you, Corrine? Are you hungry?"

She scoffed, then stayed silent.

"She's just pissed off because I can eat whatever I want," Mella said.

"Is that true?" I asked. "You don't have to watch your weight?"

"You've heard those stories, right? About me pigging out and getting fat?"

I nodded, failing to mention that my mother had crafted one of them.

"Well, they're partly right. I do eat like a pig, as long as it's before four in the afternoon." She glanced at a delicate platinum watch on her wrist. "If I eat before four, I can chow down on whatever the hell I want and not gain weight. Reporters like to write those stories after they see me load up on pasta or something." She looked at her wrist again. "I've got one hour to go. Can we find a restaurant before then?"

And so that's how I found myself eating cheeseburgers with Mella, sitting at a red picnic table by the harbor, watching the boats bobbing against the wooden piers. Corrine sipped on a bottle of Evian and sighed heavily every few minutes, shaking her head in a disgusted fashion, as if she were waiting in line at the DMV rather than sitting in the sun on a tropical isle. Mella, on the other hand, was sunny and fun, joking with the counter boy and spilling splotches of yellow mustard on her shirtfront.

Both of them perked up when I said that Cole was waiting at the hotel for them.

"What's he like now?" Mella asked me. "Still good-looking?"

"Yeah, he's cute, I suppose."

"But is he straight?" Corrine interjected.

"Yep." I thought about Cole's crush on Laney. Once again I wished I could race to the phone and tell her that I was having cheeseburgers in paradise with a couple of supermodels. I could almost hear Laney's wisecracks: *Make sure you cut up their food for them. Don't let them go to the bathroom alone.*

As soon as Mella and Corrine had been taken to their bungalows (the two largest on the property), I headed back to the airport one last time to pick up Sam Carraway, Cole's editor friend. His plane was late, so I sat in the airless waiting room, sipping tepid orange juice from a box and reading *People* magazine. When his plane finally arrived, I stepped forward every time a single guy came through the door. I wasn't sure what Sam looked like. In fact, I wasn't even sure how old he was. Every man I scooted toward smiled and looked at me strangely, probably trying to determine if I was hitting on him. I was just starting to wonder if Sam had missed his plane when I heard my name being called. Loudly.

"Kelly McGraw! Kelly McGraw!"

I turned around to the Customs door and saw a man standing there. He looked about thirty-nine and had dirty-blond hair turning a little gray, a scar running along his left jawline.

"Hey!" he said, when he saw me looking at him. "You must be Kelly. Give me a hand, will you?"

I stepped forward with my hand outstretched, but instead of shaking it, he placed a big Prada shopping bag in my hand. "Presents for the crew," he said.

"Great." I said a silent prayer that I was included on the gift list.

"God, great weather," he said, as we walked across the gravel parking lot to the car, the sun beaming down on us. "How's Cole holding up?"

"Well, I think."

"Not nervous, then?"

"I don't think so." The thought of Cole being nervous struck me as odd, but then this guy had known Cole a lot longer than I had. As we stowed his bags in the tiny trunk I asked him exactly how long they'd been friends.

"Oh, a decade at least. We met when I was just starting in the magazine business and Cole was building up his book."

We got in the car, and I pulled away from the airport, on my now-familiar route back to the hotel.

"Don't get me wrong," I said, "but you don't seem like you'd be friends."

"Why do you say that?"

I sneaked a sidelong look at him while Sam took off his sweater, revealing a navy-blue T-shirt over an obviously in-shape chest. His forearms were tanned, an expensive-looking tank watch on his wrist. He had a rough-and-tumble look about him, and yet the Prada shopping bag, along with the obvious quality of his basic blue T-shirt and the tank watch spoke of money. "You just seem like the East Coast type, and Cole…"

"Cole what?"

"Well, Cole doesn't."

Sam laughed, a big booming laugh that filled the little car. "You can say that again. How's it going for you, working with him? He can be an asshole when he's in a mood."

"I've learned that, but I think we've reached an understanding."

"You must have because he's been raving about you."

I'd slowed for a stop sign, and I turned to look at Sam. "He has?"

Sam nodded. "He said you're the best assistant he's ever had."

"Wow." I stepped on the gas again and drove through the intersection, feeling a distinct pride, but again that burst of guilt hit. No matter how good an assistant I was, I would be quitting soon.

* * *

That night, Sam took the whole crew to dinner on Peter Island, a small private isle about forty minutes across the water from Tortola. As we neared the shore, I could see that the center was forested and mountainous, the perimeter a circle of sandy beach. The elegant restaurant-bar, just a short walk from the dock, was painted a warm ochre hue, with waves crashing just beyond the candlelit stone walls.

The eight of us were seated at a long rectangular table, Chad, the stylist, on my right, Mella on my left. During drinks and appetizers, Chad and I talked about his boyfriend back in Chicago, a "compulsive cheater," as he called him. After listening to Chad's complaints and his self-portrait as a long-suffering companion, I finally asked him why he put up with such crap.

"Oh," he said. "I've got someone on the side as well, so I can't really bitch too much."

I was left pondering a response to that when Mella tapped me on the shoulder. She was wearing a beaded black shell over a teal miniskirt, her hair gorgeously tousled and wavy from the humidity.

"Check it out," she said under her breath. Holding her hand under the table, she jabbed a finger toward Cole, who was seated at the end, Corrine to one side. Corrine was leaning across the corner of the table, practically in his lap; Cole wore the look of a trapped animal.

"She's going to be so mad if she can't score with him," Mella said, a little laugh in her voice. "She's such a starfucker."

"But he's not really a star anymore, is he?"

"Actually, he's got this legendary status now that he's stayed out of New York for so long. Everyone's dying to figure out why, and all these people are forever claiming they just ran into him. You should hear the stories. Some people say he was snared in a porn ring, others swear he was arrested for fraudulent billing."

"Hmm," I said noncommittally, happy to hear that none of the rumors sounded close to the truth. I decided to change the subject. "So, speaking of rumors, are you part Swedish? I could have sworn I heard that."

Mella rolled her eyes and took a sip of her vodka drink. I noticed that she hadn't even nibbled on her food, probably because it was after four. "I have one Swedish ancestor but most of my family is Polish. The whole Swedish thing was made up by my first manager, along with my name."

"Your name isn't Mella?"

She shook her head. "Mandy Schpitske."

"Mandy Schpitske?" I coughed. If she knew what my mother would do with that information, she'd rue the day she'd told me.

"Uh-oh," Mella said, her eyes directed across the table again.

Cole was pushing his chair back and shaking his head in Corrine's direction. He got up from the table, leaving her with an embarrassed, stern expression on her face.

"Rejected, the poor girl," Mella said, and she did sound sorry for Corrine.

"Oh, he rejects everyone," I said, thinking of the other beautiful models I had seen him turn down.

"Ten bucks says Corrine goes for Sam next."

Sure enough, Corrine had her elbows on the table and was eyeing Sam a few chairs down, the way a hit man eyes his mark. I couldn't blame her.

"What's his story?" I asked Mella. My sea bass had just been delivered, and I took a bite of the flaky fish, which had a hint of Caribbean spice to it. I was grateful for the food, since I was feeling the effects of my three piña coladas. It was my last hurrah, after all.

"Cute, isn't he?"

I glanced at Sam again and nodded. He was wearing a tan linen shirt, the cuffs rolled haphazardly up his tanned arms. His blond, wavy hair was rakish and messed, and he was laughing at something Francie had said. I usually didn't go for older guys, but there was no denying his deliciousness. Plus I liked his taste. He'd given everyone, including me, Prada wallets before we left the hotel bar tonight. I had turned mine around and around in my hand like it was the Holy Grail. I'd never thought that my job with Cole would get me Old Navy, much less Prada.

"He's from some wealthy family," Mella said, "and he never takes their money, but from what I hear he may soon have to. He's apparently getting cleaned out by a nasty divorce—custody battle, the works."

"He seems so happy, though." I thought of Sam's cheerful attitude when I'd met him at the airport and the way he'd seemed so pleased to give everyone the Prada wallets tonight.

"He's always like that. He seems to be able to laugh everything off."

My sister, Dee, had been exactly the same way. Even during my mother's divorce from Danny and our subsequent moves from place to place, Dee was never angry or cranky like me, never seemed to mind a bit. The thought of Dee made me feel strangely lonely, especially here in a foreign place with a group of people, most of whom I'd known only a few hours.

I excused myself to go to the bathroom, but instead walked out of the restaurant and up a winding road lit by ankle-high lights, following signs that read Deadman's Beach. I needed a moment's peace, a little respite from group activity.

The road curved at the top and descended to the left until it reached a swath of sand. I stepped out of my sandals and walked into the water, standing in the darkness for a few minutes, letting the cool waves lap against my shins. It should have been serene, yet it wasn't. Or maybe I wasn't. I felt a vague fear somewhere deep inside me.

A particularly large wave rushed onto the beach then, splashing my legs and the hem of my sundress. I backed away from the water and turned toward the restaurant, but I was unable to shake that fear. It felt familiar, and the more I focused on it, the more I retreated inside myself, into the hole of dread in the pit of my stomach. The piña coladas, I thought vaguely. I should get back to the table and drink some water. My feet kept moving, and yet, in my head, I seemed to shrink more and more away from my surroundings, my mind a mass of swirling thoughts I could barely make out. I was mildly aware that I was nearing the restaurant, my feet continuing to trudge as if on a well-known path.

I rounded a corner of the building and, as I did so, stopped and stared through a window at the group of people I was with: Corrine, trying her hand again with Cole; Sam, regaling the rest of the group with some story; Mella, sipping at her vodka. *Go inside,* I told myself, but now my feet wouldn't move at all. There was only a tingling numbness at the bottom of my legs.

After a moment or two, I stopped seeing the group inside, and instead my own reflection in the glass became clearer and clearer. At first I noticed the dangling silver earrings I'd worn tonight and the slash of lipstick I'd applied in the bathroom. Yet the longer I gazed at myself, the more the picture changed. My hair was no longer pulled back, but rather hung lankly around my face, the bangs overgrown and pushed aside. The earrings disappeared, as did the lipstick. In fact, I seemed to be wearing no makeup at all, and my eyes were hollow, empty.

Somewhere in the back of my mind, a logical voice told me to stop, to just ignore that girl in the glass, but I was paralyzed on my numb feet. I stared at myself, at what I was beginning to realize was the person I'd been over the summer. I didn't have an actual memory of a distinct day, but I gradually became aware of a vague recollection that I used to walk the streets at night, peering into restaurant windows, staring at the golden, gleeful patrons inside. I was struck by how sad this was, this feeling of being on the outside looking in, and the longer I stood there, the more frightened I grew. It felt like the old Kelly, the one from this summer, was trying to take over again.

22

A shrill scream sounded in my head. Again and again. I raised my hands to my temples, massaging them, but it wouldn't stop.

Slowly, I opened one eye. The thought of opening both seemed impossible. The one eye searched the hazy room, fixating on the old-fashioned black phone on the nightstand. I concentrated all my efforts on extracting an arm from the sheets. I raised the receiver to my ear and finally, blissfully, ended the screaming.

"Good morning," said a pleasant, singsongy Caribbean voice. "This is your wake-up call."

"Grfff," I mumbled by way of thanks, and hung up.

I staggered to the shower, rubbing my temples. After that run-in with my former self in the window last night, I'd finally wrenched myself away and gone back to the table without a word to anyone. I'd applied myself wholeheartedly to the craft of ordering cocktails, hoping to chase away the old Kelly. For all my talk of embracing the different parts of me, the different women I used to be, I was afraid that I would revert wholly back to the depressed Kelly of the past summer. Cole had come round to my side of the table at one point, gesturing to what was probably my thirty-third drink and saying, "You'll be ready tomorrow morning, yeah?"

I'd given him a haughty look, snapped, "Of course," and kept drinking.

So now I had to make good on that promise. The hard spray of the shower felt like little pellets stinging my back, but I was glad I could feel at all. Not bothering to dry my hair, I threw on my straw hat, a pair of white shorts and a light blue tank top, and headed for the lobby.

Cole was already seated in a wicker chair near the front desk, four black cases at his feet. "You okay?" he said. His face had a slightly sarcastic, questioning look, but his voice was soft.

"Just a headache." *Headache* seemed a particularly mild word for the jackhammering that was going on in my skull. "I'm fine. What do you want me to carry?"

He stood up and put his hands on his hips, studying me. "It's a big day."

"I know. I'm ready, and I'm excited about it."

"Do I need to be worried about you?" Somehow I knew that he meant more than just the hangover.

I looked up at him, the subject of my memory loss hanging between us. I thought about confiding in him about that image I'd seen in the glass last night, how close I'd felt to my old self, but it seemed too amorphous to explain properly. "Nope. No need to be worried."

"Just say something if…you know. If you want to…"

I put a hand on his arm. "I know. Thanks."

Cole stopped at a roadside deli and plied me with eggs, sausage and passion fruit before we drove the rest of the way around the island to the beach where we'd be shooting. The next day we would move to the Baths on Virgin Gorda, and after that there'd be one more day on St. John's.

As soon as we got to the beach, Cole and I began setting up, and the combination of the food, the work and Cole's surprisingly caring and understanding attitude made me feel much better, clearing some of that bullet-to-the-brain sensation. It also pulled me away from the image in the window, allowing me to let her fade away, to decide that I'd imagined it; it was just a figment of Caribbean rum.

Sam arrived in the hotel van with the rest of the crew a few hours later. The first shoot that day involved both Mella and Corrine, one wearing a black bikini, the other white. Chad fussed around them for what seemed like hours, trying on one necklace after another. He and Sam finally agreed on chokers made of rough brown cord, three tiny shells dangling from each.

The shoot went remarkably well right from the start. Cole was more relaxed than I'd ever seen him, immediately developing a joking rapport with the models. If Corrine was still upset after getting shot down by Cole the night before, she didn't show it. Maybe she'd ended up with Sam.

"Mel," Cole called out, "step closer to Corey."

Neither woman seemed annoyed at these nicknames he'd bestowed on them. Mella took a step to her left, her jutting hip nearly touching Corrine's as they stood with the glittery water behind them. Since the sun wasn't that high yet, I was kneeling below them, holding a giant reflector so we could light their faces properly. The alcohol was beginning to flush itself out of my system by way of my sweat glands, causing rivulets to run down my back, and my tank top to cling to me. But I didn't dare complain or move. I knew how important this shoot was to Cole.

"All right, now, Corey," Cole said from behind his camera. "Turn a little toward Mel. A little more. That's it. And

Mel, lift your head toward the sky. Right. Right. Corey, I want you to tilt your head down."

From my vantage point in front of them, I could start to see what Cole was going for: two gorgeous women on a beach standing very close together, yet not touching. Mella's head was thrown back, Corrine bending toward the graceful, angular line of Mella's collarbone. When Cole instructed Corrine to open her mouth ever so slightly, it became perfectly clear, and undoubtedly erotic, for it seemed as if Corrine might kiss the hollow of Mella's neck. The crew was silent and frozen now, even me with my sweaty tank top, my knees crushed into the sand. The only sounds were the *whish, whish* of the lapping water, the quick *tic, tic, tic* of the camera and Cole's now-quiet directions: *more, Corey; lean closer; Mella, eyes closed please; tilt your head to the right; that's it, that's it, that's it.*

After another ten minutes, Cole asked for a wardrobe change. "The bright bikinis, please. Those splashy, trashy ones."

Mella and Corrine went through cosmetic touch-ups and hair changes and returned with minuscule string bikinis in psychedelic sixties prints, their hair in high ponytails.

"Right," Cole said. "Kelly Kelly is going to start off this one."

I was standing over to the side at that point, digging through Cole's bag for a lens, and this was news to me. I stood up abruptly. The crew all looked at me. I noticed Sam with an odd expression I couldn't interpret.

I walked over to where Cole's tripod waited. "What are you talking about?" I whispered to him.

"I want you to take a few shots to start." His voice matched my lowered tone.

"Why?"

"Because I think you can do it, and I want a different perspective. I want to see what you would do here."

"But this is your big break."

"Then don't muck it up for me. Take a few shots."

I glanced around at the crew. Robbie stood with brushes in his hands, waiting to run onto the set if needed, same with Francie with her apron of makeup. Mella and Corrine had their feet in the water, both seeming a bit impatient. Only Sam wore an expression that I could now read as concerned. A panicky feeling clawed inside my chest. What was I supposed to do? I might fail miserably. I might be awful. I was too hungover to do this.

But then I reminded myself that this might be my last chance to do something so extraordinary. I planned to quit when I got back to Chicago. I gave Cole a nod, and he smiled.

"Mella, Corrine," I said, "can you move to your right about ten feet so I can get the palm trees in the background?"

Both of them moved obediently, and I thought, *Well, that's something else I'll never get to do again—order around a pair of supermodels.*

Once they were standing in front of three sky-high palms, I had to decide how to pose them. Cole had already gone for the sexy, these-girls-are-about-to-make-out angle. We needed something completely different.

I looked over and saw a group of six guys, probably fifteen or sixteen, standing on the side of the road, gaping at the girls. They had bare, deeply tanned chests and wore low-slung surfer shorts.

"Can you guys come here?" I called to them.

They glanced behind, thinking I was talking to someone else.

"Yeah, you guys," I yelled.

Laughing and punching each other, they made their way toward us. I stole a glance at Sam, whose expression had darkened, but Cole gave me a thumbs-up.

I introduced myself to the guys and asked if they'd help

me take a picture. They could barely speak because of their proximity to stunning, barely dressed women, but they all nodded, shooting sidelong glances at Mella and Corrine.

"Okay, I want you to make a circle around them."

They did as they were told, but stood a good two feet away from the models.

"Closer, closer," I said.

When they were finally right next to them, I thought for a moment.

"Now, you and you—" I pointed to the two best-looking guys, both of whom had dark hair, smooth brown skin and dimples "—I want you to pick up Mella and Corrine and put them on your shoulder."

Corrine sent me an I'm-gonna-kill-you look at this point, but Mella just gave a laugh and started climbing onto her partner's shoulder.

"It's all right, Corrine," I said in my most authoritative voice.

She sent an imploring glance to Cole, who nodded at her. She huffed and did the same as Mella until they were each perched on the shoulder of one guy, the other boys surrounding them.

"Okay, now I want the rest of you to look up at them and cheer."

The guys stared at me stupidly.

"Pretend you just won a soccer game, okay? You're celebrating."

They nodded at this, apparently understanding perfectly, and started to hoot and holler.

"Mella, Corrine, raise your arms like you just got an award."

The guys yelled louder. The two who were holding the models gazed up at them, bouncing them a little. Mella laughed and laughed, holding up one hand in a peace sign. Cole began yelling, too, and soon I heard Robbie, Francie and Chad join in. As the shouts rang around the beach, I looked in the viewfinder. It was perfect: the blue skies and palm trees behind the tight knot of bodies, the guys all staring adoringly at the models, lifting their arms in victory salutes, their mouths open in mid-yell. As soon as Corrine cracked a smile despite herself, I clicked off a round of shots. And suddenly I felt like cheering, too.

The shoot had drained away my headache and given me reason to celebrate, so I agreed to a drink with Cole when we got back to the hotel.

"You were brilliant," he said, raising his beer to me. "Bloody brilliant."

"Really?" I knew it had gone well, but I wanted him to tell me.

"It was absolutely fantastic! The girls up high and the guys, the way they were all cheering. You put it all together, and that's what a good photographer does."

"I hope they turn out."

"Ah, they will!" He tipped his glass and clinked it against mine.

"Well, the ones you took in the black and white suits, they were stunning."

Cole and I went on like this, wrapped up in our little mutual admiration society, until we were joined by Sam, showered and looking very gorgeous in tan shorts and a thin, light blue sweater, yet wearing a dour expression on his face.

"I'm glad you two are here," he said, slipping onto a bar stool next to us, not bothering with any other greeting. "I need to talk to you."

"Have a beer, mate," Cole said. "Relax."

Sam shook his head. "Look, I think the shoot went great today. All of it." He nodded at me, and I decided to take that as an indirect compliment. "But there are two problems.

One, we hired you, Cole, not Kelly, and for you to just unilaterally ask her to take shots is not acceptable."

"Bugger off," Cole said. "She was brilliant."

Sam held his hand up. "I agree. I think the shots with the guys are going to be great, but you didn't know that, and you could have wasted some very expensive time if your gamble didn't pay off."

"This is bloody bullshit. You never used to put these parameters on me. You never used to give a crap what I did."

"Coley, I don't have to remind you that this is a different time now. This is not five years ago." Sam said these words quietly.

Cole put his glass down and hunched over, his elbows on the bar. The elation from this afternoon ebbed away, and for the first time I noticed the tinkle of glasses from other tables, the recorded steel drum music in the background.

"The other problem," Sam said, turning to me, "is the way you asked those guys to pick up the models."

I opened my mouth to protest, but felt like a schoolkid being reprimanded, so I closed it again, waiting to see what the principal had to say.

"Do you know how much it would have cost us if Mella or Corrine had fallen on her ass and broken an arm or something?"

I shook my head. It had honestly never occurred to me, but now that I thought about it, each of Mella's limbs was probably insured for a bazillion dollars by Lloyd's of London.

"And now, technically, we have to pay those guys. Of course, we don't know who they are, and they probably don't even realize it, but since you didn't have them sign a waiver or anything…" He lifted his hands and shoulders in an elaborate shrug.

I felt even more like a fourth-grader now, one who thinks she can run with the big kids, only to get shoved down on the playground.

"Leave her the hell alone," Cole said in a grumbly voice. I liked him more and more all the time.

"I'm sorry," Sam said. "But you know I'm right."

"Doesn't make you any more interesting. I'm going to use the phone." Cole pushed his glass away and left the bar, leaving me sitting in an awkward silence with Sam.

I wondered for a second if I should run after Cole. I knew that this shoot was instrumental for the resurrection of his career, but our friendship was too new. I didn't truly know what he was like yet, whether he needed space, whether he needed hand-holding.

Sam looked utterly miserable now that he'd effectively chased his friend away.

"I want to apologize," I said. "I really didn't know we'd have to pay the guys, and I guess I just didn't think that they would drop them."

"It all worked out, and I hate to play the heavy like this, but it's my job. I have to represent the magazine, you know?"

"Sure."

I had drained my beer out of nervousness sometime during Sam's slap on the wrist, and now I was left thirsty, with nothing to occupy my hands.

As if he sensed it, Sam signaled the bartender. "What are you drinking?" he said to me.

"Carib," I said, naming the Caribbean beer. It was probably made solely for the tourists, but I liked its light, almost lemony taste. Besides, I'd sworn off piña coladas and vodka forever, and I couldn't bring myself to drink margaritas without Laney.

"So, anyway," Sam said, probably seeing me drifting off, "I really do think you did a great job, overall. Let's just not talk about this anymore, okay?" He took a swig of the Stoli and soda he'd ordered.

"Great." I wondered what we would talk about now that we'd removed the subject of my mess-up. Maybe I should excuse myself, go back to my room and change for the night. There was nothing planned, though. Mella and Corrine had already said they were staying in for the evening, and I didn't even know if Cole would show up again.

"How long have you been doing this?" Sam said, gesturing with an arm. "The whole photography thing."

"Oh, I really don't even... I'm not... I'm actually a financial analyst."

His green eyes went wide. "Really?"

"Yeah, I was at Bartley Brothers for eight years."

"Wow."

I nodded. People were always impressed when they heard that.

"So, how did you switch to photography?"

"I just needed a break." I supposed that was true enough. I hadn't left Bartley Brothers willingly, but I *had* needed a break for a long time. "And I'd always loved photography. I saw Cole's ad at the school where I took photography classes, and the rest is history."

"He was having problems for a long time getting an assistant."

"Imagine that."

We both laughed, like two people talking about a friend they both hold dear, which, I supposed, was the case.

"He's been through a lot," Sam said. "You have to give him slack if he's tough sometimes. A lot of things have happened...." He trailed off, clearly referring to New York.

"I know about it," I said. I felt a vague twinge of pride, as if I was saying the secret password at a clubhouse door.

"Really?" He ran a hand through his damp blond hair, a gesture that seemed sexy to me. I saw those few silvery strands in the blond, giving him an appealing, worldly look, so different from the guys I usually met or hung out with. The pink scar along his jaw was intriguing, too, making me want to run my finger along its slightly jagged line.

I dragged my eyes off him and studied my beer. "He told me the other night."

"Well, that's great. I just hope you understand that for him to tell you is a really big deal. He never tells anyone. Never. And I hope you know that it's got to be kept in complete confidence."

"Give me a little credit." My voice was prickly with indignation, but at the same time I appreciated his loyalty to his friend, his instinct to protect Cole.

"Sorry. If Cole trusts you, then I trust you."

"Thanks."

From there it became easier to chat, and Sam and I ran the gamut of topics from schools we'd attended to books we'd read to funny Cole stories. Sam was great to talk to, that booming laugh of his putting me back in a happy mood, and the minutes slipped by until we'd been talking for at least an hour. By that time, I was in desperate need of a shower and a monumental nap. I wondered how I could excuse myself and yet figure out some way to meet up with him later.

"This has been fun," I said, swinging around on my bar stool so that I was facing him.

"Yeah, I'm glad we got to talk." Sam turned toward me as well, and our knees were almost touching now.

There was a pause, during which something shifted between us. We looked at each other, both of us seeming to try and figure out what was happening. In my mind, I was thinking of Laney's words about one-night stands, how they're designed to be shared with men who are entirely inappropriate but who you're entirely attracted to nonetheless. Sam certainly fit the bill. Nearly a decade older than me, married already, kids already, going through a bitter divorce and living more than a thousand miles away. And yet those green eyes with the faint web of lines at their corners, the tanned, scarred jaw, the blond untamed hair—I wanted it all.

This was my self-proclaimed last hurrah, after all, the time when I should get any such instincts out of my system before I settled back down into a normal routine, a normal life, a quest for a family of my own.

And so I did something I rarely did. I made the first move.

I slid the fingers of my left hand down my leg, jumping the slight distance between us, and placed them lightly on his golden-brown knee. I could feel heat below his skin, the faint, soft tickle of his hair. We were frozen there for a moment, and my mind began to scream at me to pull away, make an excuse, laugh it off, because his complete lack of response made it clear that we weren't on the same wavelength. But then he shifted his glass to the other hand, reached down and placed his hand over mine. His fingers were a little cool from the icy drink, but I could feel a pulse beat in his fingers, sending a warmth through them, through me.

My own pulse ricocheted in my throat, constricting it. Was I supposed to talk now? Say something sexy? I racked the recesses of my brain, but found only a few cheesy phrases—*Interesting development, hmm? So, do you do this often?* I decided to keep my mouth shut.

"Do you miss your job at Bartley?" Sam said, breaking the heavy silence.

I blinked a few times, startled. What was he doing? But then I realized that Sam was just making conversation, that he wanted to flirt, to keep talking, to play with words. He was, most likely, being an utter gentleman. But I wasn't in the mood for a gentleman. I wanted a one-night stand. Suddenly, I knew this with a fierce clarity. I wanted to obliterate everything else. I wanted something so intense and raw and sensory that it would make me forget what I couldn't remember.

Ignoring his question, I gripped his hand tighter. "Any chance you'd want to have a drink on my balcony? We could watch the sunset." My boldness shocked and pleased me. My heart pinged faster inside my chest.

Sam studied my face for a moment. It occurred to me then that I hadn't showered since that morning, that I must look a sweaty mess after working in the sun all day. But then I reminded myself that this, too, was supposed to be the beauty of a one-night stand—the grimy realness of sex instead of the powdered, pretty version I usually put forward for men who might lead to something in my life.

"Yeah," Sam said, his voice low, a little hoarse. "I'll get a few beers for the road."

I shook my head. "Don't."

And then I took his hand and led him out of the bar and down the flagstone path, past the clear, powder-blue water of the pool, past the stone wall that kept the beach at bay and finally up the peach-painted steps to my room. A golden light seeped through the slats in the louvered doors that led onto the deck, but I didn't even bother to open them. The rest of the room was dim now that the sun was setting. The maids had made my bed, leaving the rust-red coverlet smooth.

I sat down on the edge of the bed and waited. Sam stood just inside the door, looking at me. I started to chew the inside of my bottom lip, wondering if I'd gone too far too fast, if maybe he was going to turn me down. But then he walked the few steps toward me, took one of my hands in his again and leaned forward, finally pressing his lips against mine.

23

I woke up, immediately sensing that something was off but unable to detect exactly what. I blinked rapidly, seeing the bright white of the sun trying to push its way through the slats in the deck doors, hearing the slap of waves against the supports below my room. That's what it was—I was in the Caribbean. But no, something else was awry. I heard the low, heavy sound of someone breathing, and I remembered. I rolled over to find Sam on his back, one arm stretched overhead. His tanned chest was bare, the rust-colored sheet pulled up to his hips.

For a moment I considered creeping across the room to get my camera. I could take a picture and bring it home to show Laney, the way men do when they return from a fishing trip. *Here's my first one-night stand,* I would say proudly, *ain't he a beaut?*

With that thought, images of the actual event began to

sting me: Sam pulling me to stand as he kissed me. Me raking my hands through the surprising softness of his silvery-blond hair. The amazing way his skin smelled like sun, making me want to bury myself in the smooth curve of his neck. Him trying to take his time, wanting to kiss and kiss and kiss, while I began pulling at his sweater, needing to get right to it. Him finally understanding, crushing my chest with rougher kisses, lifting me up, my legs around his waist. The both of us crashing back onto the bed, our clothes seeming to disappear, and finally the comforting weight of him on top of me, inside me.

We'd had sex once more before we'd both fallen asleep. In fact, it had still been early evening. I glanced at the bedside clock now. Only six-thirty in the morning. I didn't need to meet Cole in the lobby for an hour and a half. I watched Sam sleeping, his hair even more tousled than usual, lips slightly parted, head lolling to one side. Strangely, he seemed even more attractive to me. Why was that? Was I the typical female who fell for everyone she slept with? Come to think of it, I *had* fallen for everyone I'd slept with— Ted, my high school boyfriend; Remy, the gay guy; Steve, my college boyfriend; Eric, the guy before Ben; and Ben. Those were different, I reminded myself. I'd been dating those men *before* I'd had sex with them. Pleased with this distinction, I closed my eyes again.

The two-freckled man was leaning over me. He was saying something kind and reassuring, but there was a hesitancy to his words, something he was concerned about. Why couldn't I hear them? What was it? He sat back and I focused on those two freckles under his left eye. He tried to smile, tried to make me laugh, but my face felt stiff. His image kept fading in and out in an odd way.

He was surrounded by white—the white of his clothing, the white of his skin, brilliant white walls. He seemed to go fuzzy for a moment, so that all I could make out was the vivid blue of his eyes, the dark of his hair, and then his face would zoom into focus again and I could see the finer de-tails—those two freckles, the thick eyebrows, the way he smiled reassuringly.

Whatever he was saying, I suddenly didn't want to hear it any longer. It was too hard, too depressing. I wanted him to stop talking. Why didn't he stop already? But his lips kept moving and moving. I felt helpless, as if I was sinking away from him, into some dark space. He was still there, though, hovering above me, still saying the words over and over, just in some different form, trying to explain something.

I felt someone rubbing my shoulder from behind. What the hell? Was he here? But then it came to me—Sam. I had only dreamed of the two-freckled man.

I feigned sleep, making my breathing slow and heavy, but Sam kept up the gentle caress of his fingers on my bare shoulder. It was a kind, lulling touch, but why, exactly, was he doing it? Wasn't he supposed to be gone now? Shouldn't I never set eyes on him again? Wasn't that how one-night stands worked?

I tried to think back to the random guys Laney had slept with over the years. There were a few she'd gone to break-fast with, but for the most part she was out the door early, or they took off themselves, never to be seen again, leaving Laney lots of room for embellishment when she gave me the play-by-play later that day.

I lay there, feeling the soft stroke of Sam's touch, and at the same time trying to calculate what I might look like at the moment. I'd never dried my hair yesterday, just put a hat on my wet head, so it was probably misshapen and frayed. Meanwhile, the minimal mascara and lip gloss I'd applied yesterday morning could never have survived. Basically, I figured I looked like a particularly nasty "before" picture from a magazine makeover spread. Maybe if Sam left soon, before I was "awake," I could avoid the embarrassment. Then it struck me—I'd *have* to see him. All day today and all day tomorrow. If Laney and I were still on speaking terms right now, she'd flunk me for my first fling effort. I could just hear her sighing, saying, *Kell, you don't have a one-nighter with someone you work with!*

The room was getting hotter as the sun shone through the louvered doors with growing force. The ceiling fan overhead spun lazily. I wondered how in the hell to get Sam out of my room without having to face him just yet. Meanwhile, his fingers kept up their gentle manipulations, now moving from my shoulder to my arm. I opened my eyes and stretched my eyeballs to their greatest capacity in an effort to see the clock on the nightstand: 7:40 a.m. Shit, shit, shit. Twenty minutes until I had to meet Cole. Sam, of course, wouldn't have to be ready until nine-thirty with the rest of the crew, so no wonder he wasn't up and rushing around as I should have been.

I let another five minutes crawl by before I decided there was no way around it. He'd have to see me now. We'd have to speak.

I pulled the sheet up to my cheekbones before I rolled over, hoping for a casual, veil-made-accidentally-of-bedding look that would hide most of my face.

"Hi." My words were muffled by the cotton.

"Hey."

I hated him for a second, because, if possible, he looked better than the night before. His green eyes were sharp and clear, his white teeth revealed by his pleased grin.

"I have to get going. I need to meet Cole in fifteen minutes."

He made a murmur of disappointment. "I'd try to talk you out of it, but after the lecture I gave you guys last night about losing money, I'd be a hypocrite."

He smiled at me, and I tried to smile back, though of course, he couldn't see it from beneath my sheet. We lay there silently for a second. What was I supposed to say?

Should I acknowledge the fact that this man had contorted me into a human pretzel only hours ago? Or did one simply act as if nothing had happened? I tried to dredge up some of Laney's stories, but I couldn't remember anything about this part. Why hadn't she told me it would be so awkward?

"I really didn't expect that to happen last night," Sam said. Well, that was one way of broaching the subject. He laughed. "I mean, I came down to the bar to bitch at you guys and..." He laughed again.

"Yeah, well, I hadn't exactly planned it, either." It came out snippy, and I tried to add a little giggle at the end, but it sounded like I was choking on my bedsheet. "I really have to go."

"Sure." But he wasn't moving. Why wasn't he moving? Oh Christ, I couldn't get out of bed and walk around naked in front of him. It struck me somewhere in the outer reaches of my mind that I'd done a lot more with him last night than simply trot naked through a hotel room, but I couldn't shake my overwhelming sense of shyness. *Leave, leave, leave.* I lifted his wrist and looked at his watch. Seven forty-five. Shit.

"You probably want me to go," he said. *Finally!*

He rolled off the bed and stepped into his clothes, dragging his hands through his hair a few times. Then he kneeled on the bed, leaning over me, reminding me of the two-freckled guy. For a moment, the images of those two faces—Sam's and then the man from my dream—disoriented me, both of them in front of my eyes, one shifting into the other and back.

"You okay?" Sam said. "I could call Cole and tell him you're running late, say you're not feeling well." His forehead was wrinkled with concern.

Despite myself, I was touched. "No, no. I'm great. Thanks for last night."

Were you supposed to thank your partner for random sex? Was that somehow implying that I thought him a whore? Or was I the whore? This was all so confusing.

Sam leaned closer and kissed my cheek. "You are a wonderful, wonderful woman."

I opened my eyes, and we looked at each other. Why did he have to be so damned cute, so fucking sweet? Why did he have to live in New York and be way too old for me and have kids already and be in the middle of a divorce?

God, maybe I *was* the kind of woman who fell for everyone she slept with.

The next few days were a tangled blur of poignant victories and wistful goodbyes. Over it all hung intermittent layers of confusion and loneliness and, when I let myself see it, a healthy dose of fear.

The victories came into my life via Cole, whom I now viewed as one of the kindest people on the planet, albeit under a tough, spiky exterior. He'd been reprimanded by Sam for letting me take those shots, yet whenever Sam turned his back, usually to make a phone call, Cole handed me the camera and told me to give it a go. To the rest of the crew he would say, "Anyone who tells Sam she's taking these shots will be personally executed by me." They all smirked and kept their mouths closed. They all loved him by now, just as I did. It seemed Cole was back in his element again, back to his place on top of the mountain.

I loved the heavy, sharp-edged feel of the camera in my hand. I loved calling out instructions to the models, the stylist. I loved turning my head, squinting at the sun and asking Cole what he thought about doing it this way or that. We'd begun to get a sense of teamwork, sometimes silently knowing what the other wanted. It was the type of teamwork that many financial analysts had with their colleagues who followed the same stocks—though of course I'd never shared that with Attila—and so the whole exercise was poignant for me, knowing I'd have to quit. I really had to.

During the lunch break, I'd stolen away from the group,

and taken a seat at a picnic table outside a local bar. I'd decided to figure out my finances, instead of skating by, assuming that the chunk of change in my bank account would last forever. Using the back of a postcard, I scribbled down my monthly expenses, the wages that Cole was paying me, the ridiculous amount I'd spent on clothes at Saks, and finally the cash I had left from the severance package and the sale of my house. I did the math over and over, trying to shave off a few pennies here and there, but the conclusion was inevitable. I could last another few months, but after that time, I wouldn't be able to afford rent or utilities. I certainly wouldn't be able to buy any more clothes.

And I had to look at the bigger picture, too. In six short months, I'd be thirty-one, only four years away from my self-imposed married/kids/country house deadline. But at the rate I was going, I was well on my way to a basement apartment and a houseful of cats. So I knew I'd have to say goodbye to my job with Cole and get back on the clear path I'd set for myself. There was simply no other way.

I ordered a beer then and, trying not to cry, toasted the quickly approaching end of my "hobby" of a job.

Meanwhile, I also had to say goodbye to Sam sooner than I thought. I'd assumed he was on location the entire time, but as it turned out he had only one more day with us. That morning after he left my room, I dived in the shower, slapped on as much makeup as possible, threw on a sundress that was, in actuality, way too dressy for work, and ran out to meet Cole.

When Sam arrived an hour later with the rest of the crew, he gave me a secret smile, a quick squeeze of my hand, but nothing else that might embarrass us, something I profoundly appreciated. What would the rest of the crew think if they knew he'd been throwing me around like a sack of potatoes only hours before? Sam looked even more gorgeous in shorts and a baseball cap than he had naked in my bed that morning. Was it me, or did the guy just get better looking?

We were shooting at the Baths on Virgin Gorda that day. At one point, I was making my way over the huge boulders that littered the beach, searching out a site for later in the afternoon. I concentrated on keeping my dress down and my ass covered, on making my sandaled feet grip the slick stone. I climbed over one monstrous rock, slipped down the other side and picked my way through the wet sand, looking for that perfect spot. I had just found someplace interesting and was lifting the light meter to check the reading when someone or something grabbed my arm. I gasped as I was pulled backward into a dark space, one of the caves that lined the beach.

"What?" I said stupidly. I'd had enough flashbacks of the two-freckled guy and the old Kelly to wonder whether it was happening again. I struggled to stay conscious, blinking furiously. And there was Sam, grinning like a little boy.

"I needed to see you," he said.

"Jesus, you scared the shit out of me." My heart drummed against my ribs.

"I'm sorry. I just wanted to get you alone for a second." He grasped my wrist and made small, reassuring circles on my skin with his thumb.

The cave was dank and thick with humidity. Water slapped against the walls somewhere deep inside as Sam's fingers encircled my wrist caressingly. My heart rate slowed, I looked into his eyes and decided then and there to sleep with him again that night. I could hear Laney's voice yelling in my head, *No, no, no, you idiot! A one-nighter means one night. Don't you get it? You don't go back for more! You'll only get hurt!* But since Laney had decided to stay away from me for a while, I ignored her. I whispered in Sam's ear that I'd meet him after dinner.

The heated looks Sam and I exchanged throughout the

rest of the day puffed me up and left me feeling like I was, quite possibly, the sexiest woman on the planet. That night at dinner, I wore a slitted skirt and high-heeled sandals that I'd bought on my shopping spree with Laney. Sam and I sent each other more of those looks, and I could have sworn that the temperature soared after the sun went down.

The whole crew was there, since it was Sam's last night, and we were on post-dinner port and coffee when I started to count the minutes until Sam and I could escape, back to my hotel room, or maybe his. But then Mella, in her sunny way, turned the conversation to Sam, and everything changed.

It started out easy enough. "Why are you running back to chilly Manhattan when you could stay here with us?" she asked. Everyone else joined in, cajoling him to postpone his flight. He and Cole had made up, and Cole called down the table, "Yeah, c'mon, mate. Stick around awhile."

"I wish I could," Sam said, and under the table he gave my leg a light kick. "But I have to get back."

"Back to that boring magazine," Mella said. "Call them and tell them that we're a problem shoot. Tell them you've got to stick around."

"Well, you're all a bunch of deviants so that wouldn't be a lie," Sam said, and everyone laughed. We were all giddy on the wine and the Caribbean breeze.

"Seriously," Sam said, "my son has a soccer game tomorrow night, so I've definitely got to leave."

Someone called to the waiter for more port, and the conversation split up into little, individual ones again. Chad, who was on my right, wearing all white (including a little white beret) began bitching about his errant boyfriend. I nodded and managed to make appropriately outraged responses, but my mind was still on what Sam had said—*my son...my son has a soccer game*. I'd managed to forget that he had the divorce back home and two kids. I had conveniently pushed away the fact that he was singularly wrong for me, for what I wanted to do with my life, and although I shouldn't care less—we were on a Caribbean island, for Christ's sake! It was just sex!—already I couldn't think of it like that. I liked him. Or at least, I thought I could like him if we spent more time together, and so being with him again that night would have been dangerous. I'd had too much heartache this year as it was. I'd lost too many people.

And so, when he knocked on my door an hour later, I stepped outside, kissed him on the cheek and said goodbye.

24

U Chic had booked Cole and me first-class tickets home from Puerto Rico to Chicago. Normally that would have made me very happy, but as I sank into the wide leather seat, it seemed like a metaphor for my life—too big and slightly awkward feeling, with enough room to squeeze in someone else. And yet no one fit the bill.

The saccharine voice of the flight attendant came over the intercom announcing our flight time, and I dutifully fastened my seat belt.

"Christ, I hate flying," Cole said, arranging and rearranging himself next to me—organizing magazines in the seat pocket, fumbling with his seat belt, then unclasping it again to reach down and get something else from his bag.

I picked up the in-flight magazine, trying to figure out what movie we'd get, what kind of music I could listen to on the headphones, anything to keep myself from thinking about landing at O'Hare and taking a cab back to that lonely apartment. I tried to get myself psyched up, telling myself that I was about to turn over another new leaf. I was about to recreate myself again, this time back into someone with definable goals and a plan for getting herself there.

"So, what happened with you and Sam, eh?" Cole said.

I sat motionless for a few seconds, trying to figure out if he really knew something or whether he was just fishing. "What do you mean?"

"What do you think I mean? I'm not a blithering idiot. I know you two were snogging."

I wasn't sure if "snogging" was a British term for kissing or having sex, or whether it was a Coley Beckett word that he'd made up to signify God-knows-what, so I didn't answer him right away.

"Oh, c'mon," Cole said. "I know you fancy him."

"Did he say something to you?"

"God, no. The man's a bloody vault when it comes to that stuff, but I could see something was happening."

I sighed. "Well, you won't see anything more. It was just one of those island romances, you know?"

The plane was accelerating down the runway now, hurtling faster and faster. Cole leaned his head back and closed his eyes, and yet his hands tugged at the collar of the lime-green bowling shirt he wore. "I *hate* flying," he said again. "Especially the takeoff. It's bloody unnatural. Talk to me, Kelly Kelly."

"How about a question?"

"Fine." His eyes were still squeezed shut. The front wheels lifted off the ground, soon followed by that weird moment of suspension when the bulk of the plane became airborne.

"What's going on with Sam's divorce?"

"What's not going on, now that's a better question. Are we in the air?"

"Yeah."

Cole opened his eyes. He slammed down his window blind, then, after a second, raised it again as if to double-check something. "It's quite messy. She wants the kids and is trying to restrict his visitation rights for no good reason except to mess with him. It's killing the poor bastard."

"Why are they getting divorced?"

"Ah, they got married too young. Right out of university. If you met her, you'd never even think they were together. They just don't match. But old Betsy, she was willing to stick it out because of Sam's money."

"So he's wealthy?" I thought of Mella's mention of family dough.

"*He's* not, but his family's filthy rich. Once he got out of school, Sam wouldn't take any of it, and this made Betsy very unhappy. She kept trying to talk Sam into borrowing some family cash so they could buy an apartment or a better car, but he wanted to do it on his own. I think little Betsy got pregnant just to make Sam see that they would need more money, that they would need his family's money, but he's always refused. And he did do it on his own, although, of course, he doesn't make anything like his father. He got into publishing by himself, and he's worked his way up slowly. It's what he wants, but Betsy finally got fed up and filed for divorce."

"It's so sad for the kids." I thought of my mom's two divorces, of Dee and me always wondering about our dads. Sam didn't seem the type to run from his family, however, and I said as much to Cole.

"Oh, he's a dedicated father," Cole said, "unlike me."

I'd been drifting off about Sam and didn't know if I heard him right. "What did you say?"

He tugged at the collar of his shirt again and peered outside at the diaphanous white clouds. "Nothing."

"You said Sam was a dedicated father, unlike you. What did you mean?"

He shook his head.

"Do you…do you have kids?" The thought struck me as inordinately bizarre. Coley Beckett—bristly photographer, previous hard-core partyer…and daddy?

"One," he said.

"Where?"

"Back in England. She's four."

It dawned on me then. "That was the little girl in the photos, the ones you had me develop."

He nodded, and I thought back to that day—Cole sniping at me about the need to get the pictures just right. The way I'd left him sitting in his studio, staring at the little girl. He'd said she was his niece, and I'd never given it a second thought.

A flight attendant came down the aisle with a flimsy smile, asking if we wanted a drink. I waved her away, afraid she might break the spell, afraid Cole might clam up.

"So were you married?" I asked.

"Ha. No."

"Dating someone?"

"No."

"Well, who was she? Some model?" When he didn't say anything, I jumped to conclusions. "Was it Britania?"

"Jesus, no!" He looked at me, annoyed, but then just as quickly the expression disappeared from his face and he only looked sad. He groaned and rubbed the stubble on his jaw. "It was right after the debacle with Britania," he said, looking out the window. "I wasn't sure where else to go. I didn't know if I'd ever work again. So I went back to England with my tail between my legs, and I basically lived with my mum and dad. I didn't tell them anything about New York. They thought I was still on top of the world, and I wanted to believe it, too, so I drank for about three weeks straight. I bought cocktails and dinners for everyone in that little pissant town, trying to show them that I was still the big man…." He drifted off.

"What happened?" I asked softly.

"Well, one night, I was with a lovely girl named Amanda,

although I can barely remember a thing about it. She came to my mum's house a month or so later and told me she was pregnant. I was a stereotypical arsehole. I said it wasn't mine, I said she'd been sleeping with a fleet of blokes. It scared me so much that I took off and moved to Chicago. But she got my address from my mum, and she kept writing me. I went home when she had the baby, took a paternity test and…"

"And she was yours."

He nodded.

"Wow." The concept of Cole as a father was overwhelming, confusing. "What's her name?"

"Josie."

"And so how often do you see her?"

"A few times a year. Amanda married this very nice bloke, and he's basically her dad." Cole bit his bottom lip, a vulnerable action the likes of which I'd never seen.

I reached over and patted his forearm. It was a hopelessly inadequate gesture.

"But you see, Sam's different from me," Cole said. "He'll never leave those kids."

I nodded. Sam had a life he was devoted to a thousand miles away from me. It was just as I had thought.

We arrived back in Chicago on a Monday afternoon, and the first thing I did was call Laney at work. All my selfish hopes that she was missing me, worried about me, pacing her office when she couldn't get hold of me, turned out to be complete fantasy.

"Hey, Kell," she said in a lazy sort of tone.

"Hey," I replied, just as noncommittal.

A pause.

"How've you been?" she said, as if nothing had happened between us, as if I was just going to say "fine" and ask her the same thing.

"Great!" I infused my voice with enthusiasm. "Just got back from the Caribbean."

"What? What were you doing there?" Her voice was excited, and just for a second, it really was like the old days.

"I went for work. With Cole." I filled her in on some of the more glamorous parts—working with the supermodels, how I'd gotten to take some of the shots—and she made the appropriate oohs and ahhs. I was dying to tell her about Cole's crush on her, and about Sam, too. I wanted to give her every detail and hear her usual analysis, but I held back. There was something mildly withdrawn in her voice that told me we weren't exactly fine.

"So what's going on with you?" I said.

She sighed. "I've been doing a lot of thinking. Can you meet me at Uncle Julio's in half an hour?"

"Of course." Maybe it would be okay.

Ten minutes later, I hailed a cab to the restaurant, but when I saw Laney sitting at one of the wooden tables there, I knew the stalemate wasn't over. She was ramrod straight on the stool, arms wrapped tightly around the bag on her lap, her lips pressed together. It was the face she made when she was unhappy, when she was really pondering something that troubled her. And the worst part—symbolically at least—was the lack of margaritas on the table. Whoever arrived first always bought the first round.

I walked slowly toward her, wanting to postpone the conversation. In those few seconds as I approached her, I saw a progression of all the Laneys I'd known—the girl on the yearbook staff with the big bangs, the younger sister in the crazy, loud household, the punk-wannabe college girl, the eager advertising babe, and finally this polished woman with the red coat and the stylish hairdo. I was as proud of her as I had been of Dee. It's cliché, of course, to say that your best friend is like a sister, but the conclusion was true. She was family to me, and yet now I wondered if I was about to lose her.

I slid onto the stool opposite her. The place wasn't crowded yet, and so we had the long table to ourselves.

"You look tan," she said.

"Really? I tried to wear a hat."

She smiled a small, almost wistful grin. "With your complexion you've got to wear at least 30 SPF."

"I know." She was always telling me that when we went on vacation together.

She blew out a puff of air. "So here's the thing."

Oh, God. We were getting right to it, whatever it was.

"I've been doing a lot of thinking," she said.

"Wait. Before you get there, can I just say I'm sorry for not telling you about Ben? I'm really, really sorry."

"Kell, it's okay. Just let me get this out, all right?"

I nodded.

"I've been a bad friend."

"What?" *I* was the bad friend here. *I* was the one who'd relied on her too much, who'd conveniently forgotten to tell her that I was seeing my ex again.

"It's true." She put her bag on the table and crossed her arms. "I've been getting upset at you lately. Annoyed, I guess you could say, and it wasn't really about Ben. It was more to do with your job with Cole, how you were turning your life around."

I opened my mouth to protest, to tell her that I hadn't turned anything around, but rather that I'd just pissed away a chunk of the year.

Laney kept talking, though. "As upsetting as it was this summer to see you so down, I got used to it. I guess what I got used to was taking care of you."

She shot me a look. I shook my head. What was she talking about?

"C'mon, you know how it is at my house. I'm always Laney the crazy one, Laney the fuck-up. And the guys I date, they don't rely on me for anything except to look good. And yet this summer when you were depressed, I was Laney the savior. In a messed-up way, I think I actually liked that you were so out of it."

"No, that's not true," I protested. "And however you felt, it doesn't matter. You helped me when no one else did, and I'll always be grateful for that."

A waitress came by. "Can I get you ladies a swirl?" she said, her voice chipper. "It's margarita and sangria mixed together."

"No, thank you," Laney and I said in unison. The waitress dropped the cheerful face and walked away.

Laney leaned closer to me over the table. "I didn't know it at the time, but I liked being the caretaker. I didn't try very hard to get you to see a doctor. I didn't call your mom, or even tell Ben how bad it had gotten. I didn't do anything because I wanted to be the one who was looking after you. It's sick, but when you came out of it, I started feeling strange. I think I wanted you to go back to being depressed. And that's why I got so clingy, why I kept talking to you about doctors and memory loss research. And that's why, when I realized that you were turning to Ben again and not me, I just sort of lost it."

"Well." I had to pause for several moments after that, still trying to process all she'd said. I tried to be mad at her for it, but how can you be mad at someone who loved you, who took care of you despite everything? "Lane, it's okay. Really. I don't blame you at all. In fact, I'm still grateful."

"Listen, I'm no saint. I've got to be honest with you. I tried to sabotage your job."

"What?"

"I didn't really know I was doing it at the time, but do you remember that night we had drinks with Cole?"

I nodded.

"I asked him why he'd been run out of New York. I made some ridiculous toast about taking it up the ass. I was trying to get you in trouble, Kell. I was jealous, I think, that you had this new job you were so excited about." Her voice nearly broke. "I'm a bitch, and I can barely stand myself."

"Honey, it's okay." I reached across the table and stroked her shoulder, thinking about that night. I'd assumed it was just the vodka that had made her tongue so loose, but ultimately there was no harm done, so I hadn't given it another thought. Besides, I loved her like a sister. Still did.

"It's not okay." She shook off my touch.

"Sure it is. We're always okay. It's me, right?" I leaned forward and peered at her downcast face, but she wouldn't meet my gaze. "Let's just forget it. Call it even."

"No. I need to figure this out. I'm messed up. I think I need to start seeing someone. Do you have Ellen's number handy?"

We both laughed—rough, short laughs that quickly ended. I wasn't sure if she was serious.

"I have to be by myself for a while, all right?" As she said this, Laney looked at me with pleading eyes. "Can you understand that and just give me a little time?"

"Isn't that what this last week was for?"

"Yeah, but I still need time to sort it out on my own."

"How much time?"

"I'll let you know."

"When?" I had to stop her from leaving, had to stop her from doing this, because it felt very much like she was breaking up with me.

"I'll let you know," she repeated.

I felt a surge of anger in my gut then. How dare she just cut herself off from me, from our relationship? You didn't walk away from fifteen years of friendship and say, *I'll let you know,* like they do at the end of a job interview.

I opened my mouth to tell her this, but Laney took a deep breath and said, "Okay, Kell, I'm sorry, but I've got something else to tell you. I can't believe I didn't say this earlier, but Jess called me this morning. She was looking for you."

I gave a curt nod. There'd been a message from Jess on my machine, too.

Laney's eyes took on a pained expression.

"What?" I said. "What is it?"

She reached out and rubbed my leg. "Oh, honey," she said, and she sounded like she used to, when we were friends forever, always.

"What?" I asked, letting myself feel annoyed in order to block out the flutter of panic.

She squeezed my knee. "Ben got engaged to Therese. She's pregnant."

25

I sat on the couch in my apartment, stacks of unopened mail on the coffee table in front of me. In my mind, I kept repeating Laney's last words—*Ben got engaged…. She's pregnant*—in the hopes that the repetition would give them meaning. But instead my brain only answered with a dull pain in my temples. Another one of my goddamn headaches.

Had Therese gotten pregnant on purpose? Was that all it took to make Ben change his mind about marriage and kids? Was that all I would have had to do? Just chuck my little white birth control pills instead of swallowing them dry in the morning? The thought of intentionally getting pregnant made me sick. It seemed so horrifyingly retro, so fifties. And then another thought dawned on me. Wasn't I supposed to get my period today? Because of the pill, I was like clockwork nearly to the minute, so that I could always expect my period by ten in the morning on every fourth Monday—this

Monday to be exact. I looked at my watch. It was 6:30 p.m. I ran to the bathroom and dropped my pants. Nothing.

No, no, no, no, *no,* I thought. There was no way I'd gotten pregnant from my night with Sam. In addition to the pill, we'd used a condom. It would be some kind of freak medical miracle if I'd gotten pregnant. But then what was the explanation? Flying? Wasn't it true that air travel could mess up your cycle? Unfortunately, it sounded to me like an old wives' tale.

I moved back through my darkening living room and sank onto the couch again. I tried to imagine myself pregnant, but nothing came, no images of my bloated abdomen, of the discomfort, the joy—nothing. Shouldn't I be able to picture myself in a filmy romantic daydream with a flowing dress over my ripe belly, traipsing through a flower garden to meet my smiling husband? Maybe it was because I wasn't involved with anyone right now. Maybe that was why it was so hard to envision. Strangely, this was the first time I'd ever actually attempted to imagine myself pregnant. It had always been a goal of mine to have kids, one I'd held since high school at least, but in actuality, I saw now that it was more of an assumption than a goal. I'd always *assumed* I'd have kids. I'd taken for granted that I would get pregnant eventually, after I got to a certain stage, a certain age. And yet now I couldn't even picture it. What was wrong with me?

I thought about Ben then, experiencing a shot of pain with the realization that he was getting married, that *he* was having kids. Ben, the one who wanted to travel, to have fun. Was he happy about it? Was it what he'd wanted all along, just not with me?

I picked up the phone and dialed my mom's work number. She wasn't someone I usually turned to in a time of crisis, but there seemed to be no one else.

"The Biz," she answered in a world-weary voice.

"Hey, Mom, it's Kelly."

"Sweetie!" Finally, someone who *wanted* to talk to me.

"How's work?" I asked. It was a safe question, one I'd gotten used to leading with since Dee died.

"Complete craziness. Madonna's becoming a master yogi, so you can imagine the press."

"Yeah. Wow," I said, although, as usual, I couldn't imagine why anyone cared.

After a few more minutes of celeb gossip (Michael Jackson had bought a gorilla; Nicole Kidman was going brunette) I filled my mom in on everything—my job with Cole, my thoughts that I should find another analyst position, the way Ben and I had been seeing each other again and the fact that he was now a husband-and-daddy-to-be. I skipped the issue of my memory loss, not wanting to dump too much on her. I hadn't confided in her in so long for fear that she couldn't handle it after Dee's death, but it struck me now that maybe I was the one who couldn't handle it. Maybe I didn't want to talk about what was wrong in my life and I'd just used my mother's allegedly fragile mental health as an excuse. Because she responded emphatically, immediately and with definite opinions and advice, just as I'd hoped she would.

"Ben," she said, her tone strong and dramatic, as if she was making an official proclamation, "is a complete schmuck."

I laughed despite myself.

"And as for your photography job, Kelly, I think you're right. It was a diversion, something you could do because you had a little extra money in the bank, but it's not going to last you for the rest of your life. You have to be able to take care of yourself. You can't assume you'll meet someone and get married and that he'll do it for you."

I knew she was speaking from very personal experience, but I also knew there was truth in her words. My mother was the hardest working person I'd ever met. She'd single-handedly raised two kids, with no financial or emotional support from anyone, and although I'd always wanted a different life than the one she'd had, I respected her opinion immensely.

She had confirmed for me the conclusion I'd been drawing all along, and it made the steady thump in my temples hurt all the more. When I hung up, I remembered the pain relievers in the cabinet. Maybe just one wouldn't hurt. In the kitchen, I stared at that cabinet for a few seconds before I finally swung the door open, pushed past the cans of tuna and the bottles of Wellbutrin and found the one with the pain relievers. I didn't recognize the name of the medication. I opened it and peered inside at the long blue pills that looked potent enough to tame a wild boar. Before I could analyze it too much, I shook one out and popped it in my mouth, taking a swallow from my water glass. I put the bottle in my purse.

Next, I picked up the phone and called Cole. Fifteen minutes later, I was on the El, headed for his studio and the conversation I'd been dreading.

"You are not quitting, you silly bitch!" Cole's eyes flashed angrily at me, and he wielded his bulky black address book like a weapon, waving it around my head as I sat—*slumped* is probably a better word—in his beanbag chair.

"I have to," I said. "I've loved working with you. Mostly, anyway." I tried a smile to lighten up the situation, but he only scowled deeper. "I just can't live on this money."

"I'll pay you more!" He said this with a pleased smile, as if he'd just discovered the cure for cancer.

"Do you have any idea what I was making at Bartley Brothers? Do you know what I could probably make right now when I get back into the field?"

He shook his head.

I told him. It was a sum well into the six figures, a sum that was much less, I'm sure, than he'd been making in his heyday, but enough to be impressive just the same.

"Well." He looked troubled at this bit of information. "I could give you a few dollars more an hour," he said pathetically.

I did the math in my head. "That still would give me barely $24,000 a year. It's not enough to buy a house in this city or even get a decent apartment."

"Bollocks!" He slammed the date book down on the butcher-block table.

"It's true. If you figure that a down payment would be at least—"

"That's not what I mean! You've got talent, *real* talent. Surely you know that."

I felt a flicker of pleasure at his compliment, but was immediately struck by the thought that ultimately it didn't matter. Practically speaking, talent didn't pay the bills; it didn't bring you any closer to fulfilling your goals. You could be the best photographer in the world, and it wouldn't mean you could make a living at it.

"Look, Cole, I told you about my memory loss. It's been a whirlwind for me since I realized it, and working with you has been the best part. I'll never regret that, but I have to be realistic. I'm already over thirty, and I want to be married and have kids someday." I thought about the way I'd tried, and was unable, to imagine myself pregnant that afternoon, and added, "I think."

"What does any of that have to do with your being a photographer? You can be a mommy and a photographer, too. If you just keep working at it, you could make a name for yourself."

"But you don't know that I could ever make any money at it. I'd like to pretend that money doesn't matter, but it does. I want other things in my life, too. I've always wanted a house somewhere and a nice car and nice things…." It sounded so lame and shallow to my own ears that I let my words die away.

I brushed my bangs away from my damp forehead. The room was getting warm. Too warm.

I thought about asking Cole to turn the heat down, but he spat out his next words. "Don't you think I want that, too? Do you think I like living in the same place I work? Do you think I like having to struggle now when I used to have anything I wanted? Don't you think I want to send money to Josie?"

"Yes. No. I mean…" Again my voice failed. The strength of his emotions had startled me. Cole had always seemed the type who could live happily in the room over someone's garage. I'd never really thought about what he'd had to give up after Manhattan.

He crouched before me, taking one of my hands in his. Up close, I could see the lines etched around his eyes.

"You've got something," he said. "You've got an eye that takes most photographers years to develop. The way you look at a shot, it's brilliant, totally new, totally you. If you keep working on it—"

"Can you guarantee that I'll make it someday?"

"I think it's a real possibility."

He was making this so much harder than it had to be. I wanted to quit and move on. I wanted to stop thinking about this job, about being a photographer; I wanted to stop thinking altogether. Once I got another analyst position, I could slip back into the comfortable confines of that day-to-day life, the one I knew so well, the one that came with enough money to let me do whatever I wanted. Of course, I would never stop taking pictures. I'd always have photography— it wasn't like I was giving it up. But this job was a hobby, just as Ben had said.

So why was it so hard to leave?

"You don't know that I'd make it on my own, Cole. No one can say if I'd ever make money at this, so don't pretend you can." My voice rose a little. It was too hot in here. It was time to go.

"Kelly Kelly." The way he said my name twice like that, in a tone so tender, made me feel like crying.

This was embarrassing. I pushed myself awkwardly to my feet. "I've got to go."

"Don't do this." He rose so that we were both standing now.

He was too close to me, then he seemed far away. I couldn't get enough air. I was confused for a second. What was I doing here? And then in the next instant, I remembered that I'd quit, that I was leaving. I took a step, but one of my knees gave way and I staggered slightly before I righted myself.

"Are you all right?" Cole dipped his head down, his face near mine, his eyes concerned. Too close again, and yet in the next instant he zoomed away from me, then back again, as if he were a human rubber band.

I couldn't breathe. I took a step back.

What was I supposed to be doing?

The light in the room became blindingly bright, then faded, then burst back to full strength. Something in my head started to pound. I felt a rise of nausea in my stomach.

Finally, I thought faintly. I was getting my period. I wasn't pregnant, after all.

I welcomed a tiny wash of relief before my knees quickly buckled again. I felt the muscles of my face go slack, the tension in my shoulders loosen. I sank to the floor, past Cole's arms, which shot out a second too late. I felt the side of my head strike his hardwood floor.

26

I heard the low murmur of whispered conversation. I tried to blink, but my lids felt glued to my eyes. I kept working on them until at last they opened a crack, revealing hazy light, a dark shape coming clearer.

Laney, I realized. It was Laney. She was sitting next to me, trying to smile, but her eyes were worried and red.

"Did I get my period?" I said. It was the first thing that came to mind.

Laney's eyes went wide. She made a weird-sounding laugh, then looked over her shoulder at someone standing behind her. That person nodded, said, "Yes," and I felt utter joy at the confirmation that I was not having Sam's baby. But then I realized how odd that was. Why was I asking her whether I'd gotten my own period? Why was Laney asking someone else? Who else would know but me?

The questions made me tired, made my head hurt. My

eyelids fell shut again like heavy cellar doors. I let my mind roam vaguely, a hazy search for context, but before I could set anything straight, I focused on the sound I'd just heard— "Yes"—and the figure behind Laney who'd said it. Although it was only one word, I recognized that voice from my dreams.

I forced open my eyes again, forced myself to look at the figure, to focus. It was surprisingly difficult. I felt as if I was looking through binoculars that wouldn't cooperate. I kept staring, willing my eyes and my brain to play nice together, and finally, slowly, the figure came clearer. Tall, male, pale skin, and two freckles under his left eye. I made my own eyes open wider. It was him. I had a momentary fantasy that he was here to save me from something, maybe myself, but then he smiled, and I took in the whole of him—the broad shoulders, his rippled dark hair, his white lab coat. And that's when something crystallized. Actually, that's when many things—details, snapshots, flashes of feeling—rushed into my brain as if the dam that had been holding them back had finally given way, and yet none of them seemed in context or in the right order. I could see my hand shoving the key in my mailbox, the key refusing to budge; I could see Sam in my hotel bed; the image of Ben through my viewfinder; a doctor's office; Ellen Geiger's front room; the feel of me crying, and crying, Laney bringing me Chinese food.

I opened my mouth. "What's going on, Lane?"

"You fell, sweetie."

"Where? Where did I fall?"

"At Cole's," she said.

"Oh." I tried to make the images stop and focus there, on Cole's studio, and I remembered quitting, the room being too hot. Cole's face too close, the dizziness, the floor swooping up toward me. "Am I okay? Did I hurt myself?"

I wriggled my toes under the sheet. They seemed to work

all right, but my back felt creaky, my head ached. And beyond that, I had the feeling that something more was wrong. There was that scared look in Laney's eyes, the look she could never hide from me.

"The fall didn't cause any injuries," Laney said. "But…" She stopped and looked over her shoulder again at the two-freckled guy.

"Can I have a moment alone with Kelly?" he said.

"Oh, sure," Laney said. She leaned toward me, over me, and that's when I realized that I was lying down. "I'll be right outside," she said, brushing her fingers against my forehead.

"Okay."

"I mean it. I won't leave, you know?"

"Sure. Thank you." My voice sounded weird, formal.

Laney stood, and I saw then that Cole was standing on the other side of her. He grinned at me. "Feel better, Kelly Kelly," he said.

They both turned away, and as they left the room, I could have sworn I saw him take her hand.

The two-freckled man sat on the edge of my bed. Up close, he wasn't quite as sexy as I'd made him out to be in my daydreams. The dark hair had shots of gray through it, which made me think of Sam, but his nose was thick and coarse, his ears jutting too far from his head.

I scooted around on the bed, trying to find a comfortable sitting position, but my back still ached and my head hurt like hell. It was strange to be talking to this guy from my dreams while he was fully clothed and I was in a thin cotton gown.

"Do you know your name?" he said.

"Kelly McGraw."

"And do you know mine?"

"Dr. Sinclair. Neurosurgeon." I actually surprised myself with that last bit. The details, images, bits of information kept swirling round and round, waiting for me to catch them, to call upon them.

"Do you know where you are?"

I glanced around, seeing a tiny white TV extended from the ceiling on a steel arm, a pink plastic pitcher on a cart near my bed, a basket of daisies, a half-empty IV bag hanging from a steel stand. "I'd say a hospital."

A debilitating wave of terror rushed in as I spoke the words out loud, the realization hitting me at that instant. It was as if this fear had been waiting for me all along, like the dark form of a man waiting in the shadows.

"And do you know why you're here? Aside from the fall, I mean."

I waited a moment for the particles of information to form into whole concepts. Some were clearer than others, some too far away to reach, and the answer to his question was out of my grasp. I shook my head.

"Kelly, do you remember seeing me in my office back in May?" Dr. Sinclair asked.

May, May, May, I chanted in my head. The month of my birth, the month Ben had broken up with me, the month I'd been fired from Bartley Brothers. I had a flash then of Dr. Sinclair, my two-freckled man, sitting in a lab coat on a little stool, me above him, wearing only a sheet. No, it was a gown, similar to the one I had on now. But when was that?

"I don't know," I said, and I felt tears well in my eyes.

He patted me awkwardly on the arm. "Do you feel up to this conversation? It can wait until tomorrow."

How tempting it was to accept his offer. I could push away his questions, along with the ones of my own that were racing about in my mind, mixing with the jumble of random information. It felt familiar, somehow, the concept of putting off something that was simply too hard to deal with. And yet I sensed that I had already shoved too many matters far away. They wouldn't stay there, obediently, any longer.

I wiped at a tear that had dripped down my nose. "No. Please tell me."

"You were referred to me by Dr. Markup," he said.

"The headaches," I said, suddenly remembering Dr. Markup's office, the pounding pain in my brain that had brought me there. The headaches were intermittent and very brief at first, so that I could chalk them up to stress. Eventually, though, they'd stuck around longer, become nearly unbearable. They made dim light seem searingly bright and painful. They made me nauseous and anxious.

"That's right," Dr. Sinclair said. "Do you remember the tests we did? What we found?"

It was something horrible. I could sense that, and it seemed closer now, refusing to go away this time. "I don't think so," I said.

"We diagnosed you with AVM. Arteriovenous malformation."

"Bleeding in the brain." I spit out the phrase forcefully, like a game show contestant who has finally came up with the winning response.

"You remember this now?"

"A little. Not really." Had I actually known this all along but been ignoring it? No. It was something I'd learned in the weeks after my horrid birthday, and I truly had forgotten it— maybe I wanted to forget it—starting that day at the dry cleaners.

"Well," Dr. Sinclair said, "an AVM is a very tricky condition. We don't know why these bleeds start, nor do we truly know how to treat them."

I looked away from him, toward the tiny white TV on the arm high above my bed. I wished it was on, showing something inane like *The Price Is Right* or an infomercial for knives that cut through beer cans, something mundane and ordinary. But it was just a dusty gray screen, and I couldn't stop the awareness that was growing in my mind, the processing. A few more errant pieces seemed to fall into place—my flashes of the two-freckled man, the whiteness surrounding him. The vision of myself in that bath. The way I'd passed out at Cole's with my legs "flopping," as he'd put it. The headaches, the queasy stomach. They'd all been memories or symptoms of my AVM, ones I'd been able to chalk up to hangovers or ignore altogether.

Dr. Sinclair consulted something in his chart. "We treated you as far as we could back in May and June, and you were told to follow up with us in a few months. When we didn't see you, we called and you said that you might go elsewhere for a second opinion. Did you do that?"

"Not that I know of." I got a vague image of myself in the month after my birthday, moving numbly through my old town house, trying to fathom the massive earthquake-like shift in my life. No job, no Ben, compounding the fact that there was no Dee, and then this hideously surreal news from Dr. Sinclair.

"Your friend informs me that you've had some memory issues for the last month or so."

"Mmm-hmm." I sounded like Ellen Geiger.

"Why didn't you come to me when it happened?" Dr. Sinclair asked.

I turned to him again. "Because I didn't remember you."

"That makes sense." He smiled, his teeth unnaturally white and ruler straight. He seemed to me like the kind of man who works very hard at his looks, who maybe isn't as self-assured as the image he puts out to the world, and that made me like him. He asked me all sorts of questions about the memory loss, rarely responding to my monosyllabic answers, just making notes, nodding encouragingly. I wished Laney was with me. I wished *someone* was here other than the two-freckled man and myself.

There was a quiet moment while Dr. Sinclair flipped

through the chart and wrote something one place, flipped again, wrote more.

A nurse in pink scrubs came into the room. "Oops, sorry, Dr. Sinclair," she said. "We've got lunch when she's ready." She gave me a cheery, condescending smile.

He twisted around in the chair to see her. "Thank you, Shelly. I'll let you know." He twisted back to me. "Well, it seems that some of your memory has returned, and you're very lucky in that respect."

I felt like laughing. *Lucky?* Instead I said, "But why did it leave to begin with?" The words came out loud, strained, and he looked startled. "Is it just the AVM or is it something else, something I did?" I wasn't sure what I meant, but I felt culpable.

He dropped his chart in his lap and leaned forward. "Your bleeding was rather widespread, so it's very likely that the bleed is what caused your memory loss."

"But it could be something else."

"I'm not sure what you mean."

"What else could it have been?"

"In all likelihood, your medical condition is the reason you suffered the memory loss." He pursed his lips. "Your friend Laney also tells me that you've experienced a great deal of emotional loss this year. Is that right?"

"Yes, I lost my job and my boyfriend."

"And your sister some months before, correct?"

I nodded.

"It's possible that stress played a role in your AVM, and your memory loss, as well," he said. "Clinically speaking, stress has biophysical ramifications. It causes narrowing of the blood vessels and therefore can be a triggering event in AVM bleeds. Also, psychologically speaking, sometimes when the mind has too much to deal with, it can shut down or seal off a portion of itself. And yet it's unlikely that anyone will ever be able to tell you for certain what the precise causes were."

I leaned my head back on the pillow and closed my eyes, feeling stupid and yet brilliant at the same time. I might have triggered my AVM with the stress in my life, and at the same time might have caused the memory loss that made me forget the AVM.

I recalled now how I had felt I had something awful in my brain, not just the bleeding but the news of it, the reality, something rotting and stinking that could change me. I'd pushed that reality further and further from the front of my mind, and didn't tell anyone about it, not even Laney or Ellen Geiger, because I didn't want it to be true. I'd simply refused to accept the rumble of another earthquake. It made me feel even more out of control than I already was, made me feel on the brink of pure craziness.

I'd seen Ellen because I knew I needed help, but I could never bring myself to tell her about my diagnosis. She knew something unsaid was bothering me, but all I would tell her was that I was worried about someone's opinion. It was true enough. I was terrified about Dr. Sinclair's opinion, about what horrible news might pour from his mouth to destroy me. I wouldn't go any further with Ellen. I'd wanted her to work her magic on the other parts of my life, to focus on the more banal day-to-day issues I'd always taken for granted, to help me forget about the new, scarier cloud looming over me. And it had worked. Somewhere along the way my mind had finally cooperated, and I'd forgotten it all.

"You should know," Dr. Sinclair said, "that although it's possible that you will continue to remember parts of those months, you may plateau. You may even forget things again. Memory is very spotty and very unpredictable."

I nodded. If there was anything I'd learned since that day at the dry cleaners it was how unpredictable memory was. And life, too.

"Would you like to know what we've learned from your scans?" Dr. Sinclair said.

No, I thought. Don't tell me. I don't want to know. I don't ever want to know. I wondered if I could just will myself away again, back to the state where I didn't know anything for sure, where I couldn't be trusted to remember. And yet it wasn't possible anymore. I'd lost the ability to hide.

"Yes," I said.

He flipped through the chart again, his fingers moving deftly as if he knew exactly what he was looking for. I envied that sure-handed search of his. "As you may remember, the original hemorrhage caused the headaches you had last May. What we've found is that you've had repetitive bleeds, one episode of which occurred roughly a month ago and was located in your frontal and temporal lobes. This hemorrhage could have easily contributed to or caused your short-term memory loss."

So maybe it hadn't been all my own doing. Maybe I hadn't completely willed away my own memory.

"An additional bleed led to your fainting episode yesterday," Dr. Sinclair said.

"That was only yesterday?"

He nodded. I wondered why it seemed so long ago. "We found a prescription bottle in your purse." He held it up to show me. "Had you taken one of these?"

"Yes. I had a headache."

He gave me a patient smile. "You don't remember me telling you not to take these?"

I searched the new store of information in my brain, but nothing came to me on this topic. I shook my head.

"Dr. Markup prescribed these when you were first complaining of headaches, but once I saw you I warned you against them because they contain an agent that can make you bleed more. In fact, I believe they contributed to your fainting episode."

I said nothing. I was furious at myself now. I'd put myself here. If only I hadn't taken that blue pill, I might have gone on, blissfully unaware. But would that have been better or worse?

"It might have happened, anyway," Dr. Sinclair said, seeming to sense my thoughts. "Unfortunately, the treatment options haven't changed radically since I saw you last. I'm very leery of surgically excising the bleed because of the diffuse nature and the danger of causing further harm. The other available treatment is focused radiation, which, as you may remember from our talks, has its own problems. The only real option right now, in my opinion, is to closely monitor you for any other bleeds or functional issues."

"What do you think will happen to me?"

"In terms of what?"

I remembered his office now, the one in the Radisson Hotel building, where Laney's sister had seen me. I could see the rolled-out paper on the examining table, the diplomas scattered over the walls. And I remembered him sitting on a little stool with wheels, giving me his clinical recitation of possible ramifications.

"This thing could kill me," I said. "Isn't that right?"

He dipped his head to one side, as if in reluctant acknowledgment of my statement.

Those next few days in the hospital were like being in the middle of a violent, clanging battle, one within myself, where one side was on the edge of victory, only to be hurled back by the last-ditch efforts of the other troops. A certain feeling tried to be the victor in this battle—a feeling of being on the brink of that madness and depression of the past summer. How easily it would be to fall back into those open, comforting arms and shut myself off from the world again. But my new life kept pulling me away from that ledge, reminding me that I would have to fight for a normal life, but it would be worth it. I had Laney again, and I had Cole.

Even my mom had rushed to Chicago when I'd called her, and she spent her days sweet-talking the nurses and giving me a running commentary on the celebrities we saw on TV. She could handle this, I realized. She could handle more than I'd given her credit for, and somehow that gave me strength to give those brutal armies a final heave-ho.

Once that war in my head slowed, my reaction to my dreary prognosis was a sinking disappointment at the utterly unromantic explanation for my memory loss. All those crazy thoughts—that Beth Maninsky was a covert operative for the CIA, that maybe I was the spy, that maybe I'd witnessed a murder, that the two-freckled man was someone I'd been having illicit sex with—were just that, crazy thoughts. Instead, I was left with my own psychological run for cover and this vague description of bleeding somewhere in my brain, where I couldn't even truly feel it, couldn't see it. I would have to take the word of Dr. Sinclair that it could happen again, that hypothetically it could lead to a quick death tomorrow on the subway, or it could abate, letting me live until the age of one hundred and twenty. More likely, it would be something I'd have to deal with on a regular basis—keeping my stress level down, getting regular blood-work, making visits to Dr. Sinclair's office and possibly going through radiation treatments in the future if it became bad enough.

It helped that my memory hadn't completely returned. In fact, I hoped I never recovered the parts of my life I couldn't remember. It seemed like some merciful god was keeping the more agonizing moments at bay. For example, I could recall now being fired by Bartley Brothers. I could see the self-satisfied smirk on Attila's face and hear the pity in his voice, but I couldn't remember Ben dumping me later that evening. I could remember moving into the Lake Shore Drive apartment, putting up those pictures of Ben and spreading my green duvet over the bed, yet my memories of packing up my town house, of turning that key for the last time, seemed permanently gone, and for that I was grateful. It was enough to know it had happened, without recalling the specifics.

For lack of anything better to do with me, they let me out of the hospital after three days filled with CT scans, blood tests, urinalyses and an angiogram.

Laney and Cole picked me up when I was discharged. They were dating, they told me on the way home. It had all started after I'd passed out in Cole's studio. They'd stayed up all night in the hospital, waiting to learn what was going on with me, and somewhere in the middle of their worry they'd found each other.

Cole was driving Laney's car as they told me this. That hula girl on the dashboard swung her hips to and fro, and Laney kept glancing over her shoulder as if nervous of my reaction.

"We know it's quick," she said, looking to Cole for confirmation.

He nodded, uncharacteristically quiet, and glanced at me in the rearview mirror.

"But we're sure it's right," Laney said. "It just feels so right. And we know this might be weird for you…" She glanced again at Cole.

"You guys, it's fine," I said, and they both seemed surprised. Of course it was fine—what else was I going to say? I was just happy to have Laney back again, although I wondered whether I might lose her once more, this time to Cole.

"You're sure, Kelly Kelly?" Cole said with another look at me in the mirror. "You know how fucked up I am."

"And what an arsehole you are," I said, mimicking his accent.

Laney turned around in her seat and reached over it to grab my hand. "You all right?"

I shrugged.

27

When we got back to my apartment, Laney told Cole she'd call him later, and she stayed with me that night. I loved her for it, but it was strange and horrible at first. The fight we'd had hung there in my apartment, struggling for space with the news of my medical condition. Laney helped me unpack from my Caribbean trip, the two of us moving awkwardly around my bedroom, slipping clothes onto hangers, throwing others in the hamper.

"These are cute," Laney said, holding up a pair of lilac pants that Melanie had talked me into.

"Thanks," I said.

She moved past me toward the closet, our forearms brushing, an odd feel of physical closeness. "Maybe you should clean these first," she said, eyeing them.

"I'll look at them later." I took a T-shirt out of my bag and put it in my dresser drawer.

"I could take your cleaning in tomorrow if you want," Laney said.

"No, I can do it."

"Well, it's no problem, you know? I can get us some coffee and then just swing by there on the way and—"

"Laney," I said, my voice brittle. "I can handle it."

I turned around from the dresser. She was standing by my closet, the lilac pants in her hands, a wooden hanger in the other. After a moment, she finally looked at me. "I guess I fucked this up, too."

"What?"

"Us. I shouldn't have told you about the whole caretaker thing. My issue. I should have just figured it out for myself."

"No, of course you should have told me. But I'm just not sure now what's normal help from you and what's going overboard. I don't want it to get worse. I mean, I'm not sure how this can get worse, but I don't want to lose you, and so I don't want too much help from you…" I trailed off, feeling tears come to my eyes.

I wanted everything back to normal, back to the way things were before my birthday, my diagnosis, my memory loss. But even as I had that thought, I knew it wasn't true. I was glad that I had seen Ben for who he was, who we were together. And I was glad I'd gotten to be a photographer's assistant for a while. There were so many things I was grateful for, so many things I'd learned since that day at the dry cleaners. But I wanted Laney and me back to the way we'd always been. I needed that.

I blinked away the tears and saw that Laney had her head in her hands, her shoulders shuddering. I moved around the bed to her side.

"Okay, well, don't ruin the pants," I said, taking them from her.

She gave a pathetic little laugh and looked at me, her eyes red and runny. "I'm sorry."

"I'm sorry, too." We hugged each other tightly, and both of us cried a little more.

"I'm seeing Ellen, you know," she said, pulling back and wiping her eyes with the back of her hand.

"Really?"

"Yeah, she's pretty good."

"Well, tell her to expect a call from me," I said. "Dr. Sinclair says that I've got to control my stress."

"Want to go together?" Laney said. "We can make it a weekly thing—therapy and margaritas. I'll bring the shaker and the limes, you bring the tequila."

We both laughed. "Sounds good," I said. "But how about a confession right now? It's a good one, and there's no way I'm telling Ellen."

"What is it?"

"It's a pretty hot story. I'm not sure if you can handle it."

"Oh, my God! Did you have sex?"

I grinned and stood up, refolding the shirt in my hands.

"You did!" Laney said. "Get over here." She pulled my arm until I sat back on the bed. "Tell me!"

And so I gave her the whole story of Sam, every tiny detail, with Laney shrieking and clapping. And then she told me how she'd broken up with Gear and how she and Cole had started. They'd stayed up all night talking in the hospital waiting room, and once they'd gotten word that I was all right, they'd gone out for coffee and just kept talking. Cole told her that he'd had a crush on her since that first day they'd met, and Laney admitted she'd been thinking about him, too. She was charmed by how sweet he was and by his randy accent. Cole also spilled the story about Britania and why he'd left New York. She told him about her music and her dream to be in a band.

"It was amazing," Laney said. "It's like he just gets me. He totally understands me, and yet he really likes me."

I watched her as she talked. She seemed head over heels

about him. She seemed truly happy, and that's all I could ever ask for my friend.

"But you know, even if this thing works out with Cole," Laney said, lying back on my pillows. "You and I are the important part. I won't let anything happen to us, okay?"

I felt a surge of relief through my chest, and I flopped back on the pillows with her. "Okay," I said. There was a pause. "So have you kissed him yet?"

She squealed, and I clapped, and then Laney told me the rest of the story. Sometime during the tale, somewhere between Cole kissing the back of her neck outside the coffee shop and creative use of the beanbag chair back at his studio, something settled over Laney and me. We seemed to fall back into the place we'd been before my birthday. We felt like us again.

Laney called in sick for a few days. We saw movies and split bottles of wine and stayed up late talking on the couch.

When Cole came over to pick her up two days later, he brought a large pizza, and the three of us ate it, standing over the box in the kitchen.

"How are you, Kelly Kelly?" he said. He folded a slice of pizza into a roll and ate it with large bites, his other hand reaching for Laney, rubbing her back. It was odd to see them touch like that, and yet they both seemed unaware of it, like two people who'd been together a lifetime.

"I'm good," I said. "I think. I mean, I feel fine."

"Great. So when are you coming back to work?"

He and Laney looked at me, and the kitchen was silent. I could tell that they'd talked about this.

"I'm not, Cole. Nothing's changed."

"Right. You're still a bloody great photographer and a brilliant assistant. Don't be daft, Kelly Kelly."

"I'm actually being quite smart. I'm being logical about this. I need to get a real job."

Cole gave me a cross look.

"Sorry," I said. "I just mean a job that will pay me some solid cash."

"Well, I already told you—"

"Coley," Laney said softly, putting a hand on his forearm. "Leave it alone."

"But—"

"Just leave it be for now," Laney said.

"Hmph," he said, his mouth full of pizza. "Just for now. But you and I will revisit this," he said, waving a paper towel at me.

He turned to Laney then and dabbed a drop of sauce off her chin with the paper towel. She smiled, giving him a look that even I couldn't read.

I called Ben a week after I was discharged. He'd sent flowers and left messages at the hospital a few times, but I hadn't talked to him yet. I needed to speak to him now for a few reasons. For one thing, I wanted to see if it was true— if he was marrying Therese—and how he would explain it to me. For another thing, I now had a reason for my behavior over the summer—the way I'd waited at his house, took those surveillance pictures. At the time I'd done that, I'd had this desperate notion that my relationship with Ben was the one aspect of my life I could control. I couldn't alter Dee's death, I couldn't make Bartley Brothers take me back and I couldn't change my medical diagnosis, but maybe if I could get Ben back, I'd thought, maybe I'd feel in charge of my life again. And so I'd focused solely on Ben, on getting him back. I'd gone overboard, though, way *way* overboard, my sadness pushing me to go to odd, strange lengths.

The last reason I called Ben was to see if he'd heard of any analyst openings. I hadn't changed my mind about getting another job in the financial world. In fact, the medical bills had started trickling in, and I knew then, more than ever, that the job with Cole wasn't going to work.

"Ben Thomas," he answered on the first ring, sounding annoyed and slightly panicked. I'd been watching the business stations that morning, and I knew that a stock he traded was plummeting. I could have waited until the market closed to call him, but he would have to talk to me once he heard my voice, and this call would make his day all the more shitty. I figured he deserved it.

"Hey, it's me," I said when he answered.

A pause, then, "Wow. How are you?"

"Okay."

"Hold on. Let me close my door."

While he put me on hold, I wondered if he'd taken the partner office that I'd had my eye on, the one tucked at the back of the floor, tiny but hidden.

"Kell," he said when he picked up the phone again. "Are you all right? I called the hospital a few times, but you were always sleeping or getting tests done."

"I'm doing pretty well." I coughed to evoke a little sympathy, then got to the point. "I hear congratulations are in order."

He sighed. "It's not what I want. It's what I have to do."

That phrase struck something deep inside me, like the muffled clang of a distant church bell. It reverberated in my head.

It's not what I want. It's what I have to do. It's not what I want. It's what I have to do.

I still asked Ben about analyst jobs, dutifully scribbling down the company names and phone numbers he lauded like consolation prizes. But I never called any of them because I realized right then that life, mine at least, had to be a mixture of *both* elements—what I *wanted* and what I *had* to do.

I called Cole and asked for my job back, the only job I'd ever loved, the thing I wanted most. And after he'd given a whoop of joy that sent a happy tingle of confirmation through me, Cole agreed to give me a raise. Yet it still wasn't enough. So I did what I had to do. I paged through the housing section of the *Reader,* viewed at least thirty of the dumpiest apartments known to man, and finally rented a small studio in Rogers Park that made my old town house look like a palace.

My new place has a fraction of the space I'm used to and none of the creature comforts. My lovely fall wardrobe that I spent so much on at Saks is crammed in a foot-deep closet with most of my other worldly possessions, and that's *after* I gave away at least fifteen pairs of shoes to Goodwill. And there's an artist in the apartment above me who likes to paint at three in the morning, accompanied by Marilyn Manson screeching full-blast on his stereo, no matter how many times I thump on the ceiling with my broom. The water pressure is pathetic, there's no air-conditioning and my kitchen is actually smaller than the closet. Still, I've filled my walls with photos of my friends and family and the shots I've taken around Chicago. I always splurge on fresh flowers, and when I've got a handful of candles going at night, the place feels like my home.

And I did something else I had to do. I took a job at Katie's Coffee. Now, five days a week, I open the store at 5:00 a.m. and work until ten o'clock, when I get on the El and head to Cole's.

This coffee job isn't what I want, certainly. There's nothing more embarrassing than having to serve one of my old business colleagues on their way to his or her six-figure job.

"Do you want your soy topper steamed?" I hear myself asking, trying not to grimace, trying even harder not to notice the quick flash of sympathy that lights their eyes.

At the end of the day, I'm exhausted, but it's a good exhausted, somehow more gratifying than the thumping brain stress I used to have after a day at Bartley Brothers. And there are other upsides. I now know how to make myself a killer white chocolate mocha, even better than the one at Starbucks.

28

It's been six months since I was in the hospital. Some days I love my life, particularly when I'm working well with Cole, when I'm having dinner with Laney and him, when I'm out practicing with my Nikon, when I saw William's sweaty pink face on a billboard. On other days—when I'm sponging down sticky tables at Katie's, when I'm lonelier than hell on a Saturday night, when I feel the scary, familiar tug of those summer months—I'm not always so thrilled. I guess this is because my life truly is a combination of what I want and what I have to do. Luckily, the scale weighs a little heavier toward the what-I-want side, and that helps me get up at four-thirty every morning.

In fact, the scales may be tipping even further in my favor, because last week Sam called while I was working at Cole's. I thought at first that he was calling to ask me out, maybe tell me he was coming to town, and I felt a quickening excitement in my belly. I'd been thinking about Sam a lot, pumping Cole for information about him, getting on the Internet and running Google searches on his name, and debating whether to call him myself. And yet there he was, calling me! But after a few minutes of idle chat he began talking about *U Chic,* and it seemed clear that this was a business call. Probably another assignment for Cole, I figured, since Cole was getting more work than ever, even from the people in New York who'd been avoiding him for years.

"It's a small job," Sam said. "It's for one of our inserts, and it won't pay much."

"Well, let me get Cole," I said, trying not to sound disappointed. "I'm sure he'll want to at least consider it."

"Whoa, Kelly. I thought you understood. I'm calling you."

"What?"

He chuckled, and I remembered hearing that same quiet laugh in my hotel bed as his warm hand trailed over my shoulder.

"I'm calling to offer *you* the job."

I blinked a few times, my mind a whirring fit of starts and stops. I wondered for a moment if it was my AVM, if I should sit down or call Dr. Sinclair, but then it cleared. "Are you kidding?"

"Nope. Have you seen this month's issue of *U Chic?*"

"Not yet."

"Well, we used one of your shots with the models and that group of guys. Everyone over here loved them."

"Really?"

"Absolutely. So we want you on something else. What do you say? Want to hear about it?"

I nodded, and, as if he could see me, he started making plans.

* * *

Now I'm in a hotel room in Manhattan, one paid for by
U Chic, and I've just put on the silver dress that Laney and
I bought during my shopping spree. It slides over my head,
the cool lining stroking my skin. I step up to the mirror on
the back of the door and smile at my reflection. The dress
has been in a garment bag since last October, but it's lived
up to my memories.

Today is my thirty-first birthday, exactly one year after
everything started to crumble. When I'd mentioned to Sam
that the shoot was scheduled for my birthday, he'd told me
we'd celebrate that night, and he'd asked me to bring something extra special to wear. In fact, he'd invited Laney and
Cole, too, and they're in the room next to mine. The thought
of Cole in a tuxedo is one I'm having trouble with, but then
again, Cole has managed to surprise me many times.

I step into the delicate bone-colored sandals, thinking
about my shoot for *U Chic,* which went amazingly, fantastically well today. It was only a few bottles of suntan lotion,
and I'm getting paid next to nothing, but being there in that
rented studio—consulting with the art director, taking my
Polaroid test shots the way I'd learned from Cole, adjusting
the lights, raising the Nikon to my face—made me feel as
if I had arrived on some new and wonderful planet, one that
had been waiting for me all along.

Whether I will ever make a living at this remains to be
seen. Whether I will still be working in a coffee shop when
I'm forty is a real possibility. Whether something romantic
will happen with Sam and me tonight, whether I'll be married by the time I'm thirty-five, whether I'll *ever* get married and have kids—all these things are complete toss-ups.
All I know right now is that my life is a clean slate. And I
can't wait to see what I make of it.

Book Club Questions

1. One of the themes of the novel is the concept that our lives are always ours to remake. Why does it take a memory loss for Kelly to realize that? Where do you see her in five years? Ten years?

2. Do you agree with Kelly's decision to cut off her relationship with Ben? What do you think will happen with Sam and her?

3. Did you fault Laney when she admitted that she had, in a way, enjoyed it when Kelly was depressed? Have you ever experienced a time when you felt needed and important during a crisis experienced by a friend or family member?

4. Were you surprised by Cole's revelation of why he had been blacklisted from the New York fashion world? Do you think he will permanently revive his career? What do you think of Laney and him together?

5. How did the death of Kelly's sister, along with the loss of Ben and her job, combine with her physical condition to cause her memory loss? Do you think the physical was more instrumental in the memory loss than the psychological?

6. What would *you* do if you found yourself in Kelly's situation and your life was suddenly a clean slate?

On sale in December from Red Dress Ink

The Solomon Sisters Wise Up

Melissa Senate

Meet the Solomon sisters:

Sarah—six weeks pregnant by a
guy she's dated for two months.

Ally—recently discovered her
"perfect" husband cheating on her.

Zoe—a dating critic who needs to
listen to her own advice.

Suddenly finding themselves sharing a bedroom in Daddy's
Park Avenue Penthouse, the Solomon sisters are about to wise
up, and find allies in each other, in this heartwarming and
hilarious novel by Melissa Senate, author of *See Jane Date*.

RDI12031-TR

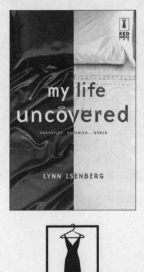

Also available from Laura Caldwell

Burning the Map

Get ready for a journey of life-changing proportions.

Casey Evers was on a path. Career, love—she had it all locked up. Problem was, did Casey truly want to go where she was heading?

Sometimes the only way to figure out where you are and where you want to be is to stop following directions. Join Casey as she burns the map and finds her own way.

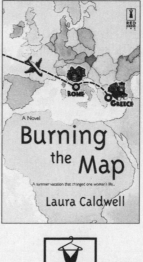

A Novel

Burning the Map

A summer vacation that changed one woman's life...

Laura Caldwell

RED DRESS INK

TM

RDI1102R-TR